Elixirs of Life

The Culpeper House Herbals
by Mrs C. F. Leyel

HERBAL DELIGHTS

ELIXIRS OF LIFE

MRS C. F. LEYEL

Officier de l' Académie Francaise
Fellow of the Royal Institute

with drawings by
MILDRED E. ELDRIDGE

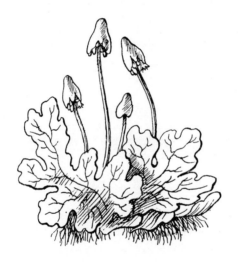

ff

faber and faber
LONDON · BOSTON

First published in 1948 by
Faber and Faber Limited
3 Queen Square London WC1N 3AU
This paperback edition first published in 1987

Printed in Great Britain by
Richard Clay Ltd, Bungay, Suffolk

I dedicate this book to the late Sir Ernest Wallis Budge, M.A. Litt.D. (Cambridge), M.A., D.Lit.(Oxford), sometime keeper of Egyptian and Assyrian antiquities at the British Museum.

Sir Ernest was one of the first Directors of the Society of Herbalists and his active interest in the work and his great knowledge of oriental materia medica contributed very largely to the success of Culpeper House

PUBLISHER'S NOTE

Elixirs of Life was first published in 1948 and was one of a series of Herbals called the Culpeper House Herbals which covered herbs used in medicine and the arts.

July 1987

CONTENTS

ILLUSTRATIONS

INTRODUCTION

U ltimately the food of every living creature depends upon the vegetable kingdom, and although all plant food isn't herbaceous, it is remarkable that so many of the staple foods of both man and his domesticated animals are simply herbs—the grasses, wheat, barley, oats, rice, maize and the pulses, and on these depend not only bread, but milk, butter, cheese and eggs.

The oil-producing olive tree has played such an important part in the history of our early civilization that the food value of another order of trees, the Palms, is sometimes forgotten. Modern transport and commerce has carried the products and by-products of the tropical palm trees—coco-nuts, dates, sago, etc., all over the world, and bananas have within a generation become ubiquitous. Bananas are the fruit of a perennial herbaceous plant, musa, which is cultivated wherever it will grow because it produces more nourishment in a given space than any other crop, more even than wheat and potatoes. Chocolate is the product of a tree—the cocoa tree—Theobroma cocoa, and Kola nuts, come from another tree of the same family. Arrowroot comes from a herb, and so does tapioca.

All nuts are extremely nutritious because they contain a large proportion of oil. Brazil nuts grow on a tree that belongs to the myrtle family. English walnuts and hazel nuts are quite as nourishing as the foreign nuts.

All fruits contain nourishment whether they are the tropical fruits like bael fruit, bread fruit, custard apples, mangoes, prickly pears; the dried figs, dates, raisins, currants, or the familiar fruits of the temperate zones —apples and plums, pears and the various berries—each contain something valuable. For instance there is copper as well as iron in apricots, so they provide a good diet for anaemic people; avocado pears, which before the war were reaching us from America, were a great acquisition because of the large amount of fat and protein they contain.

While all herbs by their very nature provide food as well as other elements that are curative of disease, there are certain herbs which are more nutritious than others.

Fattening herbs like lucerne, fenugreek, gold of pleasure and chickweed, nourish humans as well as cattle and are grown as crops. Lucerne has a very ancient origin. It was found by the Emperor Darius in Medea and carried by him into Greece, and is cultivated to-day in Persia and Peru.

Fenugreek (meaning Greek hay) is one of Egypt's leguminous

13

Introduction

plants and was used by the ancient Greeks and Romans as a condiment. Its popular name in Cairo is helba. It is grown in Italy and parts of Sicily, and in the spring its bright vermilion flowers look very gay.

Gold of pleasure figured in all old herbals and is still said to be found near the burial ground of Hengist and Horsa. The plant contains so much oil that in the days of the Romans it was extracted and used for burning; after the oil had been expressed the cake that remained was used as fodder for cattle.

Saw Palmetto, a native of Florida and Carolina, is another herb that helps the undernourished to put on weight. It is a useful tonic for those suffering from malnutrition. Though one of the palms, it only grows about six feet high.

Among garden plants that we are familiar with, love-lies-bleeding and the star of Bethlehem afford a certain amount of sustenance. Most of the amaranths have been used in the past as pot herbs. Star of Bethlehem was known at one time as Bath asparagus, and the tubers of dahlias and cyclamen contain inulin and starch.

All sugars are natural heart tonics for the aged, and this is why liqueurs were invented to fortify Louis XIV in his old age. The best sugar comes from the maple tree and the sugar cane. This is not the granulated sugar with which we are familiar to-day, which is made from beetroot and which is very inferior, but the brown sugar of Barbados and the loaf sugar from the sugar cane.

The Chinese prescribe ginseng for the infirmities of old age. Rue is the English herb for the old. It improves eyesight and removes the strain of years. Rosemary strengthens the memory, and lavender cures the headaches brought on by fatigue.

But herbs deal not only with the ravages of time, but with the emotions and passions which can destroy the body in youth. St. Ignatius Bean assuages the agony of grief, and eroticism is subdued with infusions of wild thyme—terror is overcome with gelsemiun. Every appetite, mood, fear, aberration and abnormality has its own appropriate restraining herb as Hahnemann has very clearly shown. The art of prescribing becomes a fine art in the herbalist's practice and yet this knowledge of the specific use of herbs was almost general in England throughout the sixteenth and seventeenth centuries.

Aphrodisiac herbs influence the ductless glands through their hormones and nature's hormones are far more lasting in effect than the glands of animals.

Lady's slipper is extolled for its stimulating properties. It is one of the orchids, many of which are regarded as tonic and aphrodisiac.

Introduction

Salep is still prepared from the tubers of some varieties of orchids; but in the days of its vogue it was served regularly in the coffee houses, and even at street corners. Orchids went by the name of Satyrions and were an ingredient of nearly every *poculum amatorium* in the seventeenth and eighteenth centuries. The Epithelial orchids have a similar reputation, and, partly perhaps because they are parasitical like mistletoe, they have been endowed with almost magical virtues—the Vanilla plant belongs to this order. Eryngo roots were also popular for the same reason, and sweetmeats were made from them and sold in the streets in the days of Charles II. There are references to them in the poems of some of the Restoration poets. So great was the demand for eryngo sweets at one time that a whole factory was set up for them at Colchester where their popular name was 'kissing comfits'.

Tropical plants like cotton root, damiana, hygrophila, matico and muirapuama are all prescribed for their stimulating properties, and so is the lady's tresses, a sweetly scented orchidaceous plant found on parts of the Sussex Downs, and other places in England.

Coriander is mentioned in the *Arabian Nights* as an ingredient in love potions. The Greeks venerated the carrot as a love philtre and called it philtron; and the Old Testament recommended Mandragora as a cure for sterility.

Herbs have a very ancient reputation for restoring youth, and in the Lateran Museum in Rome there is a curious bas relief, which dates from the first period of Greek art, in which Medea is seen instructing the Daughters of Pelias how to prepare a bath of herbs in which to boil the limbs of their father in order to restore his youthful vigour. There are constant references in Greek and Roman literature to the use of herbs in rejuvenating baths and potions.

The food of the Lotus Eaters still grows in that tract of Africa which the Libyan Lotophagi occupied when Homer wrote his Odyssey. For a very long time it was confused with the sacred Lotus of China, but there is little doubt that the real food of the lotus eaters was the Jujube tree which is still used in Jereed, where it grows, to make bread, and an intoxicating wine. The plant grows wild in the mountains of China. The gruel which is made from the starch is the common breakfast food in parts of Ludamar.

The lotus of India and China is a different plant altogether—a water lily. It was used as food by the ancient Egyptians and is still the food of Maharajahs. It is given to their honoured guests served with nuts and rice—so is the ancient kiess (*Euryale ferox*) a prickly water plant which has been cultivated as food by the Chinese for thousands of years.

15

Introduction

The plant of forgetfulness, Hsüan'-ts'ao (*Hemerocallis fulva*) is still grown for food. This is the gold needle vegetable known to Europeans in China. It was said to kill grief by producing forgetfulness.

> *How shall I get the plant of forgetfulness?*
> *I would plant it in the north of my house;*
> *Lovingly I think of my husband*
> *And my heart is made to ache.*

It is very similar to another plant called nepenthes, the pitcher plant.

We have grown so accustomed to regard meat as a necessity of life that the full knowledge of the strength to be gained from plants is only to be learnt from the Eastern races. Those who have visited the grave of Confucius at Kuhfeu, will know about the Shih plant which grows there, and which by Chinese tradition is only found 'where neither tigers, wolves, nor poisonous plants exist'. By ancient repute it increases the activity of the brain, and if taken over a long period prevents hunger and tissue waste. It is most prolific in its growth and even very old plants produce a prodigious number of stalks. Some say it is a Yarrow—others an Artemisia.

Dr. Porter Smith, a missionary who made a study of vegetable medicines in China, says the Chinese use it to brighten the eye as they also use the Wild Yam—another of their elixirs.

In China it is quite common for people to live to a great age, and the Chinese subsist almost entirely on Soya beans and other vegetable food and are able to work far harder and longer than Europeans, and to carry incredibly heavy weights for hours at a time.

The young shoots of bamboo are eaten in China and Japan, and the plant is said to contain an element which is as yet unidentified but which is as active as radium.

There are other and much simpler plants which are used to prolong life in China and one of them, the hydrocotyle, grows in England, but it has ceased to interest the country people who once gathered it and made infusions from it.

Sophistication unfortunately has lost us not only our paregorics, but a great deal of our natural food.

HILDA LEYEL

Shripney Manor
8th April 1947

CHAPTER ONE
NUTRITIOUS HERBS

Agar-Agar; Almond; Apricot; Artichoke; Arrow-root; Bamboo; Banana; Barley; Beans; Birds' nests; Bombax; Breadfruit Tree; Broom Corn; Burra Gookeroo; Canadian Bitter Root; Candle-nut tree; Canterbury Bells; Cassava; Ceropegia; Chocolate Tree; Convolvulus; Coreopsis; Cottonroot; Cowhage; Cow-wheat; Crown-Imperial; Cyclamen; Dahlia; Damiana; Dendrobium; Durian-tree; Eryngo; Euryale Ferox; False Acacia or Locust Tree; Fenugreek; Fritillary; Ginseng; Gobernadora; Gold-of-Pleasure; Hazel; Honesty; Hungry grass; Hydrocotyle; Hygrophila; Ice Plant; Kava Kava; Lady's Slipper; Lily of Kamschatka; Lotus; Love-lies-bleeding; Lucerne; Maize; Manna ash; Maple; Mastic; Michaelmas Daisies; Mushrooms; Musk seed; Olive; Orchid; Palms; Potato; Rice; Rocket; Sago (see Palms); Service berry; Spurrey; Star of Bethlehem; Sugar Cane; Sunflower; Sweet Chestnut; Sweet William; Teluga Potato; Tulip; Vanilla; Vegetable Marrows; Vine; Walnut; Wheat

Nutritious Herbs

AGAR-AGAR

*A Japanese Seaweed containing a Carbohydrate called Glose,
which is a powerful gelatinizing agent.*

Botanical names: Plocaria lichenoides, Gelidium amansii (Kutz), Graci-
laria lichenoides. *Natural order:* Algae, Ceramiaceae. *Other names:*
Japanese isinglass, Ceylon moss, Agal Agal. *Chinese name:* Hai-ts'ai.
Part used: Herb. *Natural habitat:* Japan, Ceylon, Macassar, Indian
Ocean, Shores of Malay Peninsula. *Constituents:* A carbohydrate called
glose. Hydrochloric, acetic and oxalic acids prevent agar-agar from
gelatinizing. *Action:* Nutritive.

Agar-agar is a white seaweed collected on the East India coast and sent
to China. It has the property of absorbing and retaining moisture, and
is useful in medicine because of its mechanical action on the intestines,
due to its power of expanding in bulk. It is a nutritive and demulcent
food.

One ounce to twenty ounces of boiling water makes a suitable jelly
for invalids. It can be flavoured with lemon or orange rind. If preferred
the powdered agar can be sprinkled over stewed fruit—a dram being a
sufficient dose. It is capable of taking up two hundred times its volume
of water to make a jelly.

Agar-agar is closely allied to the seaweed which is used by sea
swallows in making the birds' nests used by the Chinese as food, and also
in the making of glue.

The Chinese also use agar-agar as a varnish for the paper they make
into Chinese lanterns.

Nutritious Herbs

ALMOND

Mark well the flowering almond in the wood,
If odorous blooms the heaving branches load,
The glebe will answer to the sylvan reign,
Great heat will follow, and large crops of grain:
But if a wood of leaves o'ershade the tree
Such and so barren will the harvest be.

Botanical names: Amygdalus communis (Linn.), Amygdalus dulcis, Amygdalus amara. *Natural order:* Rosaceae. *Other names:* Almandre, Amyllier. *French name:* Amandier. *German name:* Mandel. *Italian name:* Mandorlo. *Turkish name:* Badem ag. *Indian names:* Bélati-badâm. *Persian name:* Badam. *Arabian names:* Louza, Loaz-el murr-Louz ul nala. *Under the dominion of:* Jupiter. *Symbolical meaning:* Stupidity, indiscretion. *Parts used:* Fruit, flowers, oil. *Natural habitat:* Western Asia and Northern Africa, but cultivated in all the Mediterranean countries in Europe. It grew in the fertile land of Canaan and is seen throughout Palestine. *Constituents: Sweet almonds:* Contain a fixed oil, Oleum Amygdalae B-P 56 p.c.; an albuminous principle or ferment emulsion (which is soluble in water); mucilage 3 p.c.; sugar 6 p.c.; proteids (myrosin, vitellin and conglutin) 25 p.c.; and ash 3 to 5 p.c. containing potassium, calcium, and magnesium phosphates. *Bitter almonds:* Contain a fixed oil 45 p.c.; amygdalin 1 to 3 p.c.; proteids 25 p.c.; emulsion, sugar 3 p.c.; mucilage 3 p.c. and ash 3 to 5 p.c. The ash contains potassium, calcium and magnesium phosphates. *Action: Sweet almonds* demulcent, emollient, nutritive. *Bitter almonds* can be used as a sedative in diseases of the respiratory organs.

The almond tree is a native of Barbary and was cultivated in England before the end of the sixteenth century. It does not always reach fruition in this country, but its blossom is a familiar sight in English gardens in the early spring.

There are many references in the Bible, and in Greek and Hebrew literature to the almond tree, Aaron's rod was formed from a branch of it.

The Romans referred to the almond as a Greek nut, and both Hippocrates and Theophrastus give a description of the tree. Athenaeus says that the almonds found in the island of Naxos were superior to all others, and that those in the island of Cyprus were also excellent.

19

It was the habit of the Greeks to eat almonds before meals to provoke drinking at the end of a meal, and Athenaeus in his *Deipnosophists* quotes Plutarch as having recorded the case of a Greek physician, who was able to drink more than other men because he ate five or six bitter almonds beforehand—the theory being that the drying nature of the almond expels moisture.

Both the sweet and bitter almonds grow on the same tree and differ considerably in their constituents, as the glucoside known as amygdalin, is entirely absent from the sweet almond.

Bitter almonds contain no volatile oil in themselves, but one is formed when water is added, and, after decomposition, dextrose, prussic acid and benzaldehyde are formed—the prussic acid and benzaldehyde together forming the essential oil known as oil of bitter almonds, which is rather poisonous as it contains a large amount of prussic acid. When sweet almonds are mixed with water no prussic acid is formed.

Almonds are imported from Spain and from Sicily, and of the sweet almonds, those known as Jordan almonds, which are long and pointed, are far the best. Green almonds can only be indulged in in the countries where the tree comes to fruition, and those who visit the Temples of Girgenti in the summer can pick them for themselves from the almond trees which surround the temples.

Almond oil has the least acid reaction of any vegetable oil and cold expressed almond oil has always formed the basis of the best cosmetics.

Almond milk is drunk in fevers; and, in cooking, almonds have a very distinctive character. Many good dishes depend on them.

GREEN ALMOND TARTS

Pull the almonds from the trees before they shell, scrape off the down, and put them into a pan with cold spring water, then put them into a skillet with more spring water, set it on a slow fire, and let it remain till it simmers. Change the water twice, and let them remain in the last till tender. Then take them out and dry them well in a cloth. Make a syrup with double refined sugar, put them into it and let them simmer. Do the same the next day, put them into a stone jar and cover them very close; for if the least air comes to them they will turn black. The yellower they are before they are taken out of the water, the greener they will be after they are done. Put them into your crust, cover them with syrup, lay on the lid, and bake them in a moderate oven.

The Hebrew word for almond, Shakad, which means 'awakening', was given to the tree because it grows quickly, and blossoms as early as

January in Palestine, when other trees have made no sign of fruition. The tree is called 'Phylla' by the Greeks in reference to the legend of Phyllis, a Thracian queen, who expired of grief because her husband Demophoon did not return to her from the Trojan war. She was turned into an almond tree when she died.

APRICOT

The apricot shining in sweet brightness of golden velvet.

JOHN RUSKIN

Next him, th' Armenian apricock took place,
Not much unlike, but of a nobler race;
Of richer flavour, and of Taste divine,
Whose golden vestments streak'd with purple shine.

ABRAHAM COWLEY

Botanical name: Prunus armeniaca (Linn.). *Natural order:* Rosaceae. *Country names:* Apricock, abrecock, Abricot. *French name:* Abricot. *German name:* Aprikose. *Italian name:* Mandorio amaro. *Turkish name:* Aci baden ag. *Chinese names:* Hsing, T'ien-mei. *Under the dominion of:* Venus. *Symbolizes:* Doubt. *Parts used:* Kernels, fruit, flowers, oil. *Natural habitat:* Northern China, the Himalayas, Armenia. *Virtues: Kernels:* antispasmodic, demulcent pectoral, sedative, tonic, vulnerary, anthelmintic. *Flowers:* tonic, aphrodisiac.

Galen considered apricots even more wholesome than peaches. The Chinese make a medicine called Apricot Gold which is said to have prolonged age to seven hundred years. The preparation of it is described in the Pent 'Sao. It is made from the kernels of the fruit—double kernels being preferred. The apricots are gathered from trees growing in auspicious places. Modern dietitians advise a diet of apricots for all anaemic people, very largely because they contain a small percentage of copper, which is as necessary in the treatment of anaemia as iron.

In fresh apricots are found such valuable mineral salts as phosphorus and silica. No fruit is more deliciously flavoured, and many favourite liqueurs derive their taste from the kernels of this fruit. In China and indeed throughout Europe, the oil from them is used as a substitute for almond oil.

Nutritious Herbs

The apricot is said to be indigenous to Shansi and there are many legends connected with the tree.

Confucius is said to have chosen a grove of apricots in which to write his commentaries on the Holy books of China.

Apricot flowers are used by the Chinese women in many of their cosmetics. They believe that the apricot tree has a special affinity for women's ailments.

The first apricot trees reached England in the reign of Henry VIII and though they flower so early that the spring frosts often kill the fruit, there are hardy varieties to-day which, if planted on a west wall instead of a south, will thrive and ripen their fruit. From personal experience I have found this good advice. They grow much better in some soil than in others and are seen in their perfection in the apricot village of Aynho, near Banbury, where the Cartwrights, who own the lovely Manorial House, have planted apricots on all the cottage walls.

ARTICHOKE

When first introduced into England the Jerusalem artichoke was peeled, sliced and stewed with butter, wine and spices; or baked in pies with marrow, dates, ginger, raisins, sack, etc. They were called Potatoes of Canada.

Botanical name: Jerusalem: Helianthus tuberosus. *Globe:* Cynara Scolymus. *Cardoon:* Scolymus cardunculus (Linn.). *Chinese:* Stachys sieboldii. *Natural order: Jerusalem:* Compositae. *Globe:* Compositae. *Cardoon:* Compositae. *Chinese:* Labiatae. *French name: Jerusalem:* Topinambour, Hélianthe tubereux. *Globe:* Artichaut. Cardoon: *Cardon*, Artichaut carde. *German name: Jerusalem:* Knollensonnenblume. *Globe:* Echte Artischocke. *Cardoon:* Spanische artischocke, Kardon. *Italian name: Jerusalem:* Tartufo, Pera di terra, Elianto tuberoso. *Globe:* Artichiocco, Carciofo, Cardo senza. *Cardoon,:* Cardo spinoso, Cardone, Cardoncelle. *Turkish name: Jerusalem:* Yildiz koku. *Globe:* Enginar. *Cardoon:* Yabani enginar. *Under the dominion of:* Venus. *Part used:* Tubers. *Natural habitat:* Jerusalem, North American plains. *Action:* Tonic, nutritive, diuretic, astringent.

The Jerusalem artichoke is one of the sunflowers. It was grown by the Indians of North America and brought to Europe by travellers.

Nutritious Herbs

The Globe artichoke is one of the world's oldest cultivated vegetables and was known to the Greeks and Romans. It is cultivated for the succulent part that remains after all the leaves have been pulled out and the seeds removed.

The Chinese artichoke is a comparatively new vegetable and belongs to an altogether different order from the others. The nourishing parts are the tubers. It is called in China Ts'ao-shih-ts'an, Ti-ts'an, and Kan-lu tsu.

The Cardoon, which is regarded by some authorities as a variety of the Globe artichoke, and by others as a distinct species, is also of ancient origin. It grew at Carthage and was described by Pliny and also by Dioscorides.

ARROW-ROOT

The name is derived from the use of the root as an arrow poison.

Botanical name: Maranta arundinacea (Linn.). Maranta ramosissima. *Natural order:* Arundinaceae or Marantaceae. *Other names:* Indian arrowroot, Bermuda arrowroot, Maranta starch, Ara ruta, Maranta ramosissima. *French name:* Arrow-root. *German name:* Arrowroot Pflanze. *Italian names:* Cannacoro, Erba da freccie. *Turkish name:* Ararot ag. *Part used:* The starch of the root. *Natural habitat:* South America, India, the West Indies. *Action:* Demulcent, non-irritant, nutritive.

The arrowroot plant was introduced into England in the early part of the eighteeth century. It is an herbaceous perennial, and has a creeping root with fleshy tubers which are covered with scales. The creamy flowers grow at the end of the long branches, the stem is often covered with the sheaths of the leaves which sometimes measure as much as ten inches in length. The juice, which is the part used medicinally, is usually expressed after the plants are a year old. Sometimes the roots are candied and eaten as a sweetmeat.

Arrowroot is one of the easily digested nutritives and on that account is given to dyspeptics. A well-known digestive food known as Racahout des Arabes, is made from arrowroot and chocolate.

The best arrowroot comes from Bermuda, but it is scarce and very expensive, and the St. Vincent arrowroot usually takes its place. The Brazilian arrowroot is better known as tapioca, and the Oswego arrowroot of America is generally made from maize.

23

Nutritious Herbs

The starch that went by the name of Portland arrowroot was obtained from the roots of one of the arums—the lords and ladies of our hedges, which has poisonous berries. The American *Arum maculatum* also provides a similar starch, and the Chinese make an arrowroot from Nelumbium speciosum, which they call Ou-fên.

BAMBOO

The Palace has arisen firm as the roots of a clump of bamboo.
Chinese saying

Botanical names: Bambusa vulgaris, Bambusa arundinaria, Bambusa aurea, Bambusa puberula. *Natural order:* Graminaceae. *French name:* Bambon. *German name:* Bambus. *Italian name:* Bambi. *Turkish name:* Bambuza. *Spanish name:* Semenedia. *Portuguese name:* Bourra bouga. *Arabian names:* Tabashura, Qasab. *Indian names:* Bansakapura, Báns, Mandgay, Magar. *Chinese names:* Chuk-kwang-chukan, Lu-chu, Chin-chu, Tan-chu, K'u-chu. *Ancient Chinese name:* Chu. *Persian name:* Tabashira-nai, Nai. *Sanskrit name:* Vansa. *Parts used:* Shoots, leaves, seeds. *Natural habitat:* Brazil and Southern Mexico, China and India. *Constituents:* Silica 70·1 p.c., potash, lime, alumina. *Action:* Aphrodisiac, cooling, pectoral, stimulant, tonic.

There are numerous species of bamboo and as the tree only flowers and produces fruit once within a period of from thirty to sixty years, no proper classification exists.

It grows as far north as the Yangtse Valley and the largest trees are found in the provinces of Hupeh, Szechuan and Chekiang.

The sprouts are eaten as food and the wood is used for furniture.

There are only about six species specifically used in medicine, though the substance known as tabashir, which is found in the joints of the large bamboos, and which resides in the interior of the stem, is and has always been regarded as a powerful agent in the treatment of paralysis. This siliceous deposit for which the old Sanskrit name is bansolchana was known to the Indians from the earliest times and gives the tree its importance as a medicine. It is endowed with aphrodisiac and stimulating virtues.

The common bamboo grows to a height of about twelve feet and has

24

dark green leaves lined with orange, with white to pale green edges. A particular beetle is said to live on it and to become radio active through doing so.

Medicinally it is prescribed for consumption, asthma, fevers, dysentery and chronic haemorrhages. The young shoots are eaten as a vegetable and made into a pickle.

The plant is used by the native witch-doctors to produce clairvoyance and a state of ecstasy. It is said to contain noradium, an element at present unknown.

Commercially the bamboo is valuable in the building of huts and in the making of paper.

Riviere in his monograph on bamboos (Paris, 1879) says there are twenty-three species of bamboo known in China, growing chiefly from Canton to Hong Kong. Some of them are said to have solid stems. Ancient Chinese works such as the Pie lu, refer to a drink made from the bamboo.

BANANA

Kind babbling old women called me into their village home-steads, without ceremony, made me sit down and eat large gourds of taro and scented poi-poi which was made of bananas and many indigenous fruits.

A. SAFFRONI-MIDDLETON

Botanical names: Musa paradisiaca, Musa sapientum. *Natural order:* Musaceae. *Country names:* Adam's apple, Plantain banana. *French names:* Bananier, Figuier d'Adam. *German names:* Banane, Adams-apfel. *Italian names:* Banano, Fico d'Adamo, Mela di Paradiso, Pomo d'Adamo. *Turkish name:* Moz ag. *Arabian name:* Maoz. *Sanskrit name:* Kadali, Rambha. *Indian names:* Kachkula, Keta, Kel, Kéla. *Persian name:* Mong, Mouz. *Malayan name:* Pisang. *Part used:* Fruit, leaves, stems. *Natural habitat:* India and tropical regions. *Constituents:* The ash contains potash and soda, salts, phosphoric acid and magnesia. The ripe fruit contains starch, sugar, gum, fat, albuminoids, and non-nitrogenous extractives. *Action:* Astringent, demulcent, nutritious.

The Banana is so sustaining that three dozen are considered sufficient instead of bread, to keep a man for a week. Bananas contain a large amount of carbohydrates, and a good deal of potassium, magnesium and phosphorus. Calcium, iron and sulphur are also present, as well as chlorine and silica. The ripe fruit is rich in vitamins and medicinally has emollient and demulcent properties.

A good flour is produced from the fruit and a syrup is made from it which is used successfully in bronchial affections.

The natives use the leaves of the plant as eye shades and as a dressing for wounds, and a starch prepared from the dried fruit is their cure for dysentery.

There are numerous species of bananas and it is said that in the Molucca islands alone, there are as many as sixteen different varieties.

Lady Callcot, the author of *Little Arthur's History of England*, ate her first banana in 1809 at Funchal and her description is worth quoting:

'Here among other refreshments, we tasted the banana for the first time. It is agreeable, but wants the lightness and spirit one wishes for in a fruit. The plant on which it grows is remarkable for the beauty of the leaves, of which there are about twenty or thirty at the top, of an immense size, being several feet long. At first they open in one piece, but afterwards split and hang down on either side of the foot stalk in fibres; the banana bears fruit but once; when it dies in its second year a sucker always springs at a short distance to supply its place.'

BARLEY

The bristly barley's purple bloom,
Waves in the gale its egret plume,
Waves in the gale as lightly float
The pendants of the bearded oat.

Botanical name: Hordeum distichum (Linn.). *Natural order:* Graminaceae. *Country names:* Pearly barley, perlatum, holiday barley, naked barley, Siberian barley. *French names:* Orge d'Espagne, Grosse orge nue. *German names:* Nackte Saatgerste, Gerste. *Italian names:* Orzo nudo, Orzo do Spagna. *Turkish names:* Memse arpasi, Ciblak arpa. *Under the dominion of:* Saturn. *Parts used:* Decorticated seeds and malt. *Natural habitat:* Britain. *Constituents:* Vegetable albumen, phosphate of lime, diastase, dextrin, sugar, starch, mucilage, gluten, fibrous or ligneous matter. *Action:* Nutritive, demulcent.

Barley is so strengthening and nourishing that the Roman gladiators who depended on it to grow strong, were called Hordearii.

Nutritious Herbs

Barley cakes called amolgaea were the food of the Greek shepherds to whom they gave vigour and strength:

> *The amolgaean cakes of barley made*
> *And milk of goats whose stream is nearly dry.*

Barley was used instead of hops to make malt, and beer was known among the Romans as barley wine.

It is not so nourishing as wheat, but it is more demulcent, and the malt extract contains elements that are to a high degree restorative in wasting diseases, and general debility.

Barley water is one of the best soft drinks. It helps all affections of the bladder and kidneys.

The Indians regard barley as a symbol of wealth and introduce it into many of their religious ceremonies.

BEANS

> *Long let us walk*
> *Where the breeze blows from yon extended field*
> *Of blossomed beans. Arabia cannot boast*
> *A fuller gale of joy than liberal thence*
> *Breathes through the sense and takes the ravished soul.*
>
> JAMES THOMSON

Botanical names: Kidney Bean: Phaseolus vulgaris, *Broad bean:* Vicia faba, *Soya bean:* Glycine soya. *Natural order:* Leguminosae. *French name: Kidney bean:* Haricot, *Broad bean:* Fève de marais, *Soya bean:* Soya, Soja. *German name: Kidney bean:* Gartenbohne, Bohnen, *Broad bean:* Buffbohnen, *Soya bean:* Soja. *Italian name: Kidney bean:* Fagiolo, Faginolo, *Broad bean:* Fava, Soya bean: Fava soja. *Under the dominion of:* Venus. *Part used:* Pods. *Natural habitat:* India, Peru, cultivated all over Europe. *Constituents:* Beans contain a large proportion of protein, starch, fat, phosphorus, calcium, magnesium and sulphur. Soya beans are particularly rich in protein but the fresh kidney bean has four times more phosphorus than the dried, though the dried contains much more starch and more sulphur.

With the exception of broad beans, French beans and scarlet runners, other varieties of beans are usually dried and kept for winter use.

Of the dried varieties the soya bean, cultivated in Manchuria and

27

Japan, is by far the oldest crop grown by man, and it remains the most important food of the masses in Asia to-day. Bean curd and soya sauce are the most important products of the bean.

The method of making both originated during the reign of Huai Nan Wang, A.D. 23, in the Han dynasty, and all sorts of beans—black, yellow, white and green are used. The recipes are laid down in the ancient Pent 'Sao. The sauce is made by boiling the beans with water, wheat, and salt, and then adding yeast to make it ferment.

The proteins in soya beans are about 35 per cent more than in any other known vegetable, they contain as much fat as peanuts, and very little starch; the carbohydrates which average about 30 per cent are made up of galactose, pentosan, sucrose, dextrin and cellulose. Like meat, it is deficient in sodium. In addition to the great protein value of soya beans, the seeds can be produced more cheaply than any other crop of legumes, so crops of soya are now cultivated on a small scale in most European countries, and in America.

The beans cultivated in North China and Manchuria, under the name of Lu Ton, are the P. Mungo variety, from the green seeds of which the Chinese make their vermicelli.

The bean of Pytharogonas is not a bean but a lotus.

A curious bean, Psophocarpus tetragonolobus, with four cornered pods, known as the winged bean, is a native of Malaya, where it is called Rachong bĕlim bing.

The Congo bean is also grown in Malaya, and is used medicinally for the relief of coughs.

Beans, peas, and lentils are grouped under Pulses which are valued for the great nutriment they contain and the cheapness with which they can be provided.

> *'On Sundry sort of pulse we do bestow*
> *That title, though in open field they grow,*
> *As others of 't are in the garden seen,*
> *Witness the everlasting pease and scarlet bean.*
> *The vulgar bean's sweet scent who does not prize,*
> *With ev'ry forehead, and with jet black eyes,*
> *Amongst our garden beauties may appear,*
> *If gardens only their cheap crop did bear.'*

Nutritious Herbs

BIRDS' NESTS

All plants of ev'ry leaf, that can endure
The winter's frown, screen'd from his shrewd bite
Live there and prosper.

COWPER

Botanical name: Plocaria tenax. *Natural order:* Ceramiaceae. *Part used:*
The fronds which the sea swallows make into nests. *Natural habitat:*
Indian and Malayan Seas.

Birds' nests made by the sea swallows from the fronds of this seaweed
are an important food in China.

The birds build their nests on rocks in the Bay of Siam and the task
of collecting them, perilous as it is, is considered worth the lives that are
sometimes lost in the work. The Chinese prepare soups and jellies from
these glutinous nests.

Another species of Plocaria, *P. lichenoides*, is better known as agar-agar.

BOMBAX

A favourite ingredient in many Indian restorative medicines.

Botanical name: Bombax malabaricum, Bombax heptaphyllum. *Natural
order:* Bombacaceae. *English name:* Red silk cotton tree. *French names:*
Bombax, fromager, ouatier. *German names:* Seindenbaum, Affenbro:-
baum. *Italian names:* Bombace, bambagia. *Turkish name:* Bombaks,
Indian names: Rakto-semul, musta-semul, supari-ka-phul, ragat-semul,
mocharas, supari-kaphul. *Mdazan name:* Mulu-elavu. *Sanskrit names:*
Mocha, kanta-kadruma, shemalo. *Parts used:* Gum, root. *Natural
habitat:* Tropical India. *Constituents:* The seeds yield 25 p.c. of a sweet
non-drying oil, which contains insoluble fatty acids 92·8 p.c. The cake of
the seeds contains nitrogenous compounds, fat, extractive matter, woody
fibre and ash. *Action:* Astringent, alterative, demulcent, restorative.

The Bombax tree grows to a great height and is covered with conical
prickles. The flowers are large and decorative; the petals being bright

scarlet inside and greyish white outside. They are followed by green egg-shaped capsules.

Medicinally the bombax tree has valuable mucilaginous and restorative properties, and it is much used in wasting diseases.

The members of the bombax family, which is a small order, are closely allied to the mallows, and abound in mucilage, so their emollient properties are of great importance medicinally.

The order contains the largest tree known, the baobab tree, *Adansonia digitata*, a description of which is in my book, *Compassionate Herbs*. The plants in this family are chiefly shrubs which produce gums valued for their medicinal properties and for their economic use. The woolly cotton in which the seeds of these plants are enveloped is so soft that it makes excellent stuffing for cushions and mattresses, and it has the merit of remaining smooth and not forming into lumps.

The leaves of these plants when dried and powdered are made into a preparation called lalo, which the natives mix with their food to diminish perspiration caused by the hot climate. The wood of these trees is light and soft enough for bees to puncture and they lodge their honey in the holes. In Abyssinia this honey is considered the best.

Most of the plants of this family have fruit of which the pulp is so refreshing that it is made into a drink.

BREAD-FRUIT TREE

'*The bread-tree, which without the ploughshare yields*
The unreap'd harvest of unfurrow'd fields,
And bakes its unadulterated loaves
Without a furnace in unpurchased groves,
And flings oft famine from its fertile breast,
A priceless market for the gathering guest.'

Botanical name: Artocarpus incisa (Linn.). *Natural order:* Moraceae. *Other name:* Bread tree. *French names:* Arto carpe, Arbre à pain, Jaquier. *German names:* Brodbaum, Brodfruchtbaum. *Italian names:* Artocarpo, Frutto di pane, Frutto di rima, Albero del pane, Pianta del pane. *Turkish name:* Etmek ag. *Part used:* Fruit, bark. *Natural habitat:* South Eastern Asia and the islands of the Pacific. Imported into the West Indies at the end of the eighteenth century.

The bread-fruit tree grows to a height of thirty or forty feet and has a trunk as thick as a man's body. It flowers and produces fruit twice a

BREAD FRUIT TREE—ARTOCARPUS INCISA

year and the fruit is often as large as a baby's head. The surface of the fruit is netted. The edible portion lies between the skin and the core and has the whiteness of bread and the consistence of new bread. When roasted it makes a most nutritious food which becomes hard if it is kept. The natives reduce the fruit to a paste called makie, and make use of it all the year round. The bark is made into cloth.

This singular product of nature is as beautiful as it is useful, because the branches of the tree which grow out horizontally have leaves which are nearly two feet in length, and the branches become shorter and shorter as they reach the top of the tree; the flowers are of two kinds, stamen-bearing and pistil-bearing, the latter producing the fruit.

The Jack fruit, another variety, is very similar but it is neither as nourishing nor as delicious.

There are many varieties of bread-fruit but the seedless ones are much the best.

The first description of the tree was given by a navigator, Captain Dampier, in the reign of William and Mary.

BROOM CORN

Grass for the cattle to devour
He made the growth of every field;
Herbs for man's use of various pow'r
That either food or physic yield.

Psalm CIV

Botanical name: Sorghum vulgare. *Natural order:* Graminaceae. *Other names:* Guinea corn, sorghum seeds, sorghum, saccharatum, millet, Egyptian millet. *French names:* Grand millet, Sorgho commun. *German names:* Mohrenbartgras, Agyptische Zeiskorn. *Italian names:* Miglio saggina, Sorga a scopa. *Turkish names:* Dari, Zura. *Indian name:* Jovaree. *Under the dominion of:* Mars. *Part used:* Seeds. *Natural habitat:* Italy, Spain, Southern France, cultivated in U.S.A., China and Cochin China. *Action:* Nutritive.

The broom corn plant yields a flour which is intensely white in colour and is made into bread. The grain is used to fatten cattle and poultry.

The leaves are said to contain hydrocyanic acid and the plant is cultivated on a large scale in America for the manufacture of brushes.

31

This millet was introduced into Switzerland about the end of the eighteenth century, but in England it is rarely hot enough to ripen the seeds; in warm climates it comes to perfection in four months, and is used as food by the African negroes. The flowers when they first come out are very similar to the male spikes of the maize plant, but the seeds which are wrapped round with the chaff are much better protected than other species of millet. This plant was grown in Gerarde's garden in Holborn at the end of the sixteenth century, and has been grown in China from time immemorial. It is one of the three millets the Chinese have always cultivated as food for man and beast. They also distil spirits from it.

BURRA GOOKEROO

The plant has a peculiar, disagreeable musklike odour.
KHORY & KATRAK

Botanical name: Pedalium murex. *Natural order:* Pedaliaceae. *Arabian names:* Khussuke, Khasake-kabir. *Indian names:* Kadava gokharu, Ghati gokharu, Bara gokhru, Farid-buti, Gokru kalán. *Malayan name:* Kathe-nerinnil. *Persian name:* Khasake-kalán. *Part used:* Fruit, leaves. *Natural habitat:* Deccan Peninsula, Madras Peninsula, Ceylon, Coromandel, Cape Comorin. *Constituents:* An alkaloid, fat, resin, gum and ash 5 p.c. *Action:* Aphrodisiac, tonic.

The plants of the Pedalium family are conspicuous for their oily seeds. The sesame is one of the most important members of the family and has been used as food for centuries, the oil being a good substitute for olive oil.

The leaves of the Burra gookeroo are demulcent and mucilaginous, and when dipped in water produce a white emulsion.

An infusion of the leaves is prescribed in rheumatism, and the young shoots and fresh leaves are infused in hot milk and drunk as a strengthening tonic. The mucilaginous properties are released when the leaves are infused.

The plant has a peculiar and rather unpleasant musk-like scent which resides in the yellow flowers. It grows in great profusion on the sea coast of Ceylon and Southern India.

CANADIAN BITTER ROOT

It has received the name of Rediviva because the roots remain alive such a long time.

Botanical name: Lewisia rediviva. *Natural order:* Portulaceae. *French name:* Racine amère. *Indian name:* Spaetlum (name in Oregon). *Parts used:* Root, leaves. *Natural habitat:* North America from Canada to Oregon. *Action:* Nutritious, demulcent.

The Canadian bitter root is one of the most remarkable of all the portulacas. It has fleshy roots which are almost entirely composed of starch, and from the roots rises a rosette of succulent leaves from the middle of which rises a brilliant star-shaped red flower which only opens to greet the sun.

The root is used as food but is expensive because it is difficult to collect in sufficient quantity to make the collection worth while. When boiled it greatly swells and forms an extremely nutritious white jelly which the Indians value.

The botanical name is called after Captain Lewis, who in 1805 made a trail across the mountains where this plant grows, and was introduced to it by the Indians, but found it too bitter for his taste and that of his party. The mountains are called Bitter Root Mountains after the plant. A description of the roots is given by Captain Lewis in his journal.

This is the only species known, and it flowers in July. Captain Lewis found it on the banks of Clarck's river.

Lady Rockley gives a description of it in her *Wild Flowers of the Great Dominions of the British Empire.*

The Californian Bitter Root and the Natal Bitter Root belong to the gourd family, and are quite different.

Nutritious Herbs

CANDLE-NUT TREE

In the Hawaiian islands the entire kernels are strung on a stick, and lighted as a candle.

JOHN SMITH

Botanical names: Aleurites moluccana, Aleurites triloba. *Natural order:* Euphorbiaceae. *English names:* Indian walnut tree, varnish tree. *French names:* Aleurite, Arbre à vernis, Bancoulier. *German names:* Bancoulnuss, Mehlbaum. *Italian name:* Albero della vernice. *Turkish name:* Cila aǧ. *Indian names:* Bangla-akrôt, Hindi-akhrot-higgle-badam. *Malayan names:* Kamari, Kamira, Buah Kĕras. *Persian name:* Girda-gâne-hindi. *Arabian name:* Jouze-barri. *Parts used:* Nuts, oil. *Natural habitat:* India, Pacific islands. *Constituents:* The almond contains cellulose, fat, organic matter, mineral matter and ash containing lime, magnesia, phosphorus, anhydride. The oil contains oleine, myristin, palmitin, stearin, and an acrid resin. *Action:* Aphrodisiac, purgative.

The candle-nut tree which attains a height of about thirty feet, grows throughout India, Malaya, Japan and in the islands of the Pacific Ocean. It is cultivated for its oil which is contained in the hard nut of the fruit.

In Malaya the medicinal use of the candle-nut tree is accompanied by magical ceremonies. For instance, in the treatment of tuberculosis the patient is bathed on three successive mornings with a lotion made by boiling candle-nut in a saucepan to which water and an iron nail has been added.

The nuts are chewed for their aphrodisiac properties and are called by the Chinese, stone chestnuts. The plant is mentioned in the Pêntsao under chestnut.

The Chinese name for it is Shih-li. It is closely related to the Tallow tree of China, Excoecaria sebrifera.

Nutritious Herbs

CANTERBURY BELLS

> *Here are pansies, love lives bleeding,*
> *Wallflowers and sweet Williams bold,*
> *There's a dandelion seeding*
> *In a clump of marigold!*
> *Nay, you might find pimpernels*
> *'Neath those Canterbury bells.*
>
> CHRISTIAN BURKE

Botanical name: Campanula edulis, Campanula rapunculus. *Natural order:* Campanulaceae. *Country names:* Mary bells, Our Lady's gloves, Lady's thimbles, Rampions *French name:* Campanule. *German name:* Glockenblume. *Italian name:* Campanella. *Turkish name:* Can çiç. *Symbolical meaning:* Gratitude, acknowledgement. *Part used:* Root. *Natural habitat:* France, Switzerland, Germany, Flanders and found wild in parts of England. *Action:* Nutritious, galactagogue.

The roots of the Canterbury bells are wholesome in salads, and the *Campanula rapunculus* is cultivated in France as a vegetable, and was grown in former times in England for the same purpose. The root can be boiled like asparagus or eaten raw with oil and vinegar. It has good tonic properties.

Of the alpine varieties of Campanula, one of the most attractive is the *C. Andrewsii* Maud Landal, which comes from Greece, and is a biennial quite easily grown from seed. It flowers in June and July and has pale blue flowers shaped like tubes.

From the Caucasus we have in the last few years the *Campanula collina*, which from stems a foot high produces very brilliant purple bells. This is good in the front of the herbaceous border or at the back of the rock garden.

Campanula poscharskyana is another fairly new arrival and a very attractive one.

Nutritious Herbs

CASSAVA

This is the Tapioca plant.

Botanical name: Jatropha manihot, Jatropha janipha. *Natural order:* Euphorbiaceae. *Country names:* Bitter cassava, manihot, janipha, physic nut, mandioe, tapioca. *French names:* Manioc, manihot. *German names:* Bittere Manioka, Tapioka, Kassavawurzel. *Italian names:* Manioc, Jatrofa officinale, Tapioca. *Turkish names:* Maniok, Tapioka. *Sanskrit names:* Kanan eranda, Paravata-yeranda. *Arabian and Persian name:* Dandenahri. *Indian names:* Bagberenda, Safedind, Bhernda, Mogalieranda, Rattangot, Japhrota. *Part used:* Root. *Natural habitat:* Brazil, South America. *Constituents:* Starch and gluten. *Action:* Nutritious, mucilaginous.

Bread is made from both species of jatropha, and also a soup called casseropo. The *Jatropha manihot*, which is more cultivated than the *Jatropha janipha*, is very poisonous in its natural state until its juice is extracted or the root is dried in the sun, when it is rendered innocuous.

The Indians, however, bake the root without any previous preparation, and make an intoxicating drink from it by squeezing out the juice and mixing it with molasses.

The root yields tapioca and is called the tapioca plant.

The bitter variety contains prussic acid.

The Indians use the juice as an arrow poison. They boil the leaves and eat them as a vegetable.

Medicinally they apply the juice and a decoction of the leaves to cuts and bruises. The jatrophas are common plants in India, and are all poisonous with the exception of a species that grows in tropical America, omphalea triandra, which produces, according to John Lindley, one of the most wholesome and delicious of all nuts.

Nutritious Herbs

CEROPEGIA

In Natal there is a wax-like plant Ceropegia, with greenish flowers shaped like a funnel. Another variety C. Sandersonii, has an umbrella over its tubes. Many of the Ceropegias have green flowers.

LADY ROCKLEY

Botanical names: Ceropegia acuminata, Ceropegia tuberosa, Ceropegia bulbosa. *Natural order:* Asclepiadaceae. *Indian names:* Galôt, Pát á la, tumbadi. *Part used:* The bulbous root. *Natural habitat:* Western India, Punjab, Upper Gangetic plain, Malabar Hill. *Constituents:* A bitter alkaloid ceropegin, fat, sugar, gum, albuminoids, starch. The ash contains manganese. *Action:* Nutritive, mucilaginous.

Ceropegia, unlike many tropical plants of this family, is not poisonous. Every part of this creeping plant with its turnip-like root is soothing and nutritious, and enters into aphrodisiac and tonic preparations. The tubers are nutritious, and have a stimulant effect. When chewed the roots are mucilaginous and somewhat bitter. Many species of this family are used to antidote the stings of poisonous snakes, and most of them have alterative properties.

Caoutchouc and indigo are derived from members of this family. They contain a milky juice which is a notable characteristic of the milkweeds.

Strange-looking varieties of Ceropegia grow in South Africa, and are described by Lady Rockley. 'The flowers are greenish and of a strange funnel or bottle shape. One growing in Natal and the coastal regions has a funnel about three inches long with five points arching over and joined in a flat canopy, which forms a delightful little umbrella over the tube.'

37

CHOCOLATE TREE

Guatemala produc'd a fruit unknown
To Europe, which with pride she call'd her own;
Her cocoa nut, with double use endu'd,
(For chocolate at once is drink and food)
Does strength and vigour to the limbs impart,
Makes fresh the countenance and cheers the heart
In Venus combat strangely does excite
The fainting warrior to renew the fight.

ABRAHAM COWLEY

Botanical name: Theobroma cacao (Linn.). *Natural order:* Sterculiaceae. *French names:* Cacaotier, Cacoyer. *German names:* Kakao baum. *Italian names:* Caccao, Abeno della Cioclolata. *Turkish names:* Kakawag, Hind bademi ag. *Natural habitat:* Tropical America. Cultivated in Ceylon, Java and the West Indies. *Part used:* Seeds. *Constituents:* The seeds contain about 50 per cent of a fixed oil known as butter of cocoa, starch 16 p.c., an alkaloid theobromine, 2 to 4 p.c., caffeine and proteids 18 p.c. sugar, colouring matter and ash 3 p.c. *Action:* Nutritive, emollient and emulcent.

The aroma in chocolate is due to the aromatic principle in the seeds, which develops after they are roasted. Chocolate is usually made by mixing the cocoa seeds when they are ground, with sugar, vanilla, cloves and sassafras nuts. In some countries such perfumes as musk and ambergris are added.

Linnaeus named the plant Theobroma—'food for the Gods'—because it was considered so delicious.

Chocolate is one of the most valuable foods we possess. It has a beneficial action on the heart, and relieves high blood pressure because it dilates the blood vessels. It has a tonic effect on muscle, and also on the kidneys, and the central nervous system. It is nutritious and stimulating at the same time.

Napoleon's habit of combining chocolate and coffee in the same drink is often advocated in France as a strengthening potion.

The method of making chocolate has altered very little since it was first discovered. The seeds are roasted in earthen pots and after they have been bruised, and all the husks removed, they are ground and made into cakes.

The cocoa nibs themselves, which are sometimes obtainable, make a delicious drink and a very nourishing and wholesome one; but they require long and slow boiling. A drink can also be made from the husks.

CONVOLVULUS

The lustre of the long Convolvulus
That coiled around the stately stems, and ran
Ev'n to the limit of the land.

TENNYSON

Botanical name: Convolvulus batata, Ipomoea batatas. *Natural order:* Convolvulaceae. *Country name:* Spanish potato. *French name:* Patate, Batate, Patate douce. *German names:* Batate, Batate prunkwinde. *Italian name:* Batata. *Spanish names:* Tur, Patata. *Part used:* Root. *Natural habitat:* Eastern and Western hemispheres. *Constituents:* Resin, sugar, starch. *Action:* Alterative, demulcent, tonic.

The sweet potato of America, which is a true root and not a tuber, will not, unfortunately, survive an English winter. It is extremely nutritious and has tonic and aphrodisiac properties.

Lady Rockley, in her book *Wild Flowers of the Great Dominions of the British Empire*, says that the sweet potato was imported into New Zealand by the Maoris and was at one time one of their chief foods. It was grown on specially designed terraced gardens, which suggest the terraced gardens of the Incas in Peru.

The carbohydrates contained in the sweet potato include a large amount of cane sugar and glucose, both of which increase after the potatoes are taken from the ground.

The convolvulus family provides many useful products—rhodium oil is collected from the *Convolvulus scoparius*, and prussic acid used in the making of the liqueur noyau, comes from the *Convolvulus domesticus* growing in America. All the family are noted for the beauty of their flower, but particularly the species known as Morning Glory, which has entrancing purple flowers.

The commoner varieties are troublesome weeds in gardens because they are difficult to eradicate, and strangle other plants.

Nutritious Herbs

COREOPSIS

The Coreopsis, cheerful as the smile
That brightens on the cheek of youth
And sheds a gladness o'er the aged.

Botanical names: Coreopsis (Linn.). Calliopsis coronata. *Natural order:* Compositae. *Country names:* Tickseed, calliopsis. *French name:* Coreopsis en Couronne. *German names:* Wanzenblume, Schöngesicht. *Italian names:* Coreopsis, Calliopsis. *Chinese names:* Fang feng, T'un yun, Hui yun. *Under the dominion of:* The sun. *Symbolical meaning:* Always cheerful. *Part used:* Leaves, flowers, seeds. *Natural habitat:* North America, Carolina, Florida. *Action:* Tonic, nutritious.

The Coreopsis is found wild in parts of America and is used medicinally in China. It is non-poisonous. The Chinese eat the young leaves as a nutritious vegetable.

This useful plant flowers right through the summer if the dead heads are cut off, and it keeps a late herbaceous border always gay with its yellow flowers. A particularly good variety is the Calliopsis Golden Crown, which was introduced from America in 1938. The petals are a bright gold and the flower has a deep maroon-coloured centre.

In northern Ohio, when forest land is cleared, a growth of Golden Coreopsis generally appears and this is followed by the Yellow Ragwort.

Nutritious Herbs

COTTON-ROOT

A small shrub with large and beautiful bell-shaped flowers of a deep yellow colour with a purple base; the seed vessels contain the cotton with the seeds among it. It is cultivated for cotton in many countries.

Botanical names: Gossypium herbaceum, Gossypium barbadense, Gossypium arboreum, Gossypium indicum, Gossypium stockaü, Gossypium brasiliense. *Natural order:* Malvaceae. *French name:* Cotonnier en arbre. *German name:* Baumwollenbaum. *Italian names:* Cotone arbusto, Cotone delle Indie. *Turkish name:* Pambuk ag. *Indian names:* Karpas, Kapas, Rui, Shuter-gucht, Binola. *Arabian names:* Kuttun, Nabut-ul-gutu. *Persian name:* Pambah. *Parts used:* Flowers, root bark, cotton seed oil, the hairy covering of the seed. *Natural habitat:* Tropical countries, Asia, Africa, Egypt and America. *Constituents:* The root bark contains starch, chromogene 28 p.c., fixed oil, resin, glucose, tannin, starch and ash 6 p.c. The oil contains oleine and a green colouring matter. The hairs contain cellulose inorganic matter, fixed oil, albuminoids, lignin. *Action:* Aphrodisiac, demulcent, mucilaginous.

Collodium is prepared from the cotton root plant.

A syrup of the flowers is a good cure for hypochondriasis. The seeds are used as an aphrodisiac, the oil as a lubricant and liniment to rheumatic joints.

Malays use the cotton plant in the treatment of fevers. They burn the raw plant for the fumigation of a new-born child, and they prescribe the seeds for illnesses that are attributed to evil spirits.

Gossypium herbaceum is the species that supplies India with its cotton and also England. The seeds are woolly and yield a short stapled cotton. The plant is biennial and has flowers with yellow petals and a purple centre. The capsules when ripe split open and reveal a white tuft round the seeds, which do not ripen in this country. In the Levant the seeds are used as food. On account of their mucilage they are a very useful food and medicine.

In China, because of the unpleasant taste of the seeds, they are roasted before the oil is expressed. The Chinese use the plant as a demulcent application to skin diseases.

Nutritious Herbs

COWHAGE

On the low jungly hills the same plants appear, with a few figs, bamboo in great abundance, several handsome Acanthaceae; a few Asclepiadeae climbing up the bushes; and the cowage plant, now with over ripe pods, by shaking which, in passing them often falls such a shower of its irritating microscopic hairs, as to make the skin tingle for an hour.

Hooker's Himalayan Journals

Botanical name: Mucuna pruriens (Linn.). *Natural order:* Leguminosae. *Country names:* Dolichos pruriens, Stizobolium prurens, prucuna prurita, Setae silique, Hirsutae, cowage, cowitch, kiwach. *French names:* Pois à gratter, Mucune. *German names:* Jackfasel, Stechende Echtefasel. *Italian name:* Fagiolo di Rio Negro. *Part used:* Hair of pods, seeds. *Natural habitat:* The East and West Indies and other tropical places. *Constituents:* Resin, tannin, fat and a trace of manganese. *Action:* Aphrodisiac, nervine.

Cowhage is a leguminous plant with white flowers which have a purple corolla, shaped like a butterfly. The flowers grow in large clusters and are succeeded by thick hairy pods of a brown colour and a leathery substance.

When young the pods are eaten as a vegetable in India, and also in China, where they go by the name of T'ao Hung-King. The seeds are aphrodisiac and anthelmintic.

According to the Pêntsao the chief virtue of the pods of the Dolichos is in controlling the viscera. They are a tonic to the marrow of the bones, and preserve life. The Dolichos lablab, if eaten often enough, is said to prevent the hair from turning grey.

A confection of the seeds boiled in milk, then decorticated, powdered and fried in butter are made into a sweetmeat with twice the weight of sugar, and given to sufferers from paralysis.

An allied species, the pods of which are smooth, is cultivated in the Mauritius as a vegetable and is given as fodder to cattle under the name of Pois noire. In India another variety, *Cajanus indicus*, the Congo pea, is a much valued pulse. These are all annuals or biennials. The most decorative member of the family is the scarlet-flowered *Erythrina indica* which grows almost to the size of a tree.

Another species, the *Dolichos tuberosus*, is an ancient textile plant, and caps, sashes and girdles, used as mourning were made from it.

COTTON ROOT—GOSSYPIUM HERBACEUM

The plant is called Ko in China and grows wild in the mountains of China and Japan on the jujube tree. Its fibres and roots are used as food.

Its English name is Kudya vine; the French name, Puéraire; the German, Knollergrische; and the Italian, Pueraria.

It has the following botanical names: *Dolichos hirsutus, Pachyrhizus thumbergianus, Pueraria thumbergiana.*

COW-WHEAT

The colour of the flower is between the pale yellow of the primrose and the rich brighter yellow of the buttercup.

The flowers are long-tubed and grow in the axils of the upper leaves in pairs, all facing the same way.

Botanical names: Melampyrum pratense (Linn.), Melampyrum arvense. *Natural order:* Scrophulariaceae. *Country names:* Triticum vaccinum, horse flower, poverty weed. *French names:* Mélampyre, Blé de vache, Rugeole, Cornette. *German name:* Kuh Wachtelweizen. *Italian names:* Melampiro, Grand di vacca, Coda di volpe, Coda di lupo, Fiamma, Fromento di vacca. *Turkish names:* Inek bugdayi, Karamuk. *Part used:* Herb. *Natural habitat:* Europe, including Britain. *Action:* Tonic, nutritive.

Cow-wheat, which flowers from June to September, is grown in some countries for fodder, and is said to give a rich golden hue to milk and butter. Cows and sheep both like it. In this country it does not grow in meadows but in the undergrowth of woods where it is common throughout Great Britain. Swine enjoy the seeds which somewhat resemble wheat.

The flowers are long-tubed and yellow, and grow in the axils of the upper leaves in pairs, all turning the same way. There was a prevailing belief at one time that the plant actually became wheat, and it was called mother of wheat. There are three other British specics mentioned by Anne Pratt—the crested cow-wheat M. cristatum, the purple cow-wheat M. arvense, and the lesser-flowered yellow cow-wheat M. sylvaticum.

Nutritious Herbs

CROWN-IMPERIAL

I freely own I have not been
Long of your world a denizen;
But yet I reigned for ages past
In Persia and in Bactria plac'd
The pride and joy of all the gardens of the lost.

ABRAHAM COWLEY

Botanical name: Fritillaria imperialis (Linn.). *Natural order:* Liliaceae. *Country name:* Lily of Persia. *French names:* Fritillaire impériale, Couronne impériale. *German name:* Keizerskrone. *Italian names:* Giglio regio, Corona imperiales, Erbe a companellini. *Turkish name:* Goc buynuza. *Symbolical meaning:* Majesty and power. *Part used:* Bulb. *Natural habitat:* Persia. *Action:* Tonic, febrifuge.

The crown-imperial in no way resembles the other fritillaries. Though as conspicuous, it has none of the delicacy of the snakes-head varieties, but it is a very decorative addition to the spring border and comes out a little later than the daffodils. The flowers are either lemon yellow or orange, mounted by a crown of leaves on a very long stalk.

At the bottom of each flower bell there are drops of sweet water, Gerard says six drops in each flower. Shelley's lines are an allusion to this curious and unexplained peculiarity of the flower:

That tall flower that wets—
Like a child, half in tenderness and mirth—
His mother's face with Heaven-collected tears
When the low wind, its playmate's voice it hears.

These tears in a German legend are worn by the plant in shame and sorrow for not having bowed its head with the other plants on the night of Christ's agony.

The crown-imperial was one of the early plants from Persia which was introduced into English gardens. In Persia the bulbs are cooked and used as food, but in the fresh state they are poisonous. The bulbs are regarded by the Chinese as a valuable tonic to the marrow of the bones, and are prescribed in fevers and for diseases of the eyes.

44

Nutritious Herbs

CYCLAMEN

*I of the gout remove the very seed
And all the humours which that torment breed,
Thorns, splinters, nails I draw, who wondering stand
How they could so come forth without a hand.*

ABRAHAM COWLEY

Botanical name: Cyclamen hederaefolium, Cyclamen europaeum (Linn.). *Natural order:* Primulaceae. *Country names:* Sow-bread, ivy-lea ed cyclamen, bleeding nun. *French names:* Cyclame, cyclamine, Paindef pourceau, Violette des Alpes. *German names:* Europaisches Alpenveilchen. *Italian names:* Ciclamino, Ciclamio, pane terreno, pane porcino, tubero fiorito, rapa di terra. *Indian name:* Hath a gorce. *Indian bazaar name:* Bakhûr-i-Miryam. *Turkish names:* Bakuru marian elmasi, Yer somunu. *Persian name:* Azarbu, Chabok-Punjek-Marium. *Symbolical meaning:* Diffidence. *Part used:* The tuberous root stock used fresh when the plant is in flower. *Natural habitat:* Italy, Southern Europe, Persia. *Constituents:* Starch, gum, pectin. The tubers yield cyclaminin or arthanatin which in action resembles saponin. *Action:* Tonic, stimulant.

The fresh tubers can be made into an ointment and applied externally as a liniment, or poultice.

In the time of Charles II sow-bread was a specific for preventing pitting after smallpox and was used as a complexion wash.

*My virtue dries all ulcerous running sores,
And native softness to the skin restores.
My pow'r hard tumours cannot, if I list
Either by water, or with fire, resist.
Of scars by burning caus'd, I clear the face,
Nor let small pox the countenance disgrace.*

Abraham Cowley endows the plant with innumerable virtues including its usefulness in yellow jaundice.

*In my fire that false gold the jaundice, I
consume (true gold scarce does more injury).*

The tubers are given to swine as food and this is why the European variety is known as sowbread. It is occasionally found wild in Kent and Sussex, but Italy is regarded as its true home.

Nutritious Herbs

The tubers can be baked and made into cakes which are eaten for their tonic and aphrodisiac properties. They are entirely wholesome.

Cyclamens can quite easily be cultivated in England in rock gardens and under pine trees; and in August and September will make a bright rose pink carpet when they are in bloom, and a green carpet when they are in leaf.

The late summer variety is the *Cyclamen hederaefolium* and other varieties are the *C. coum* which flowers in December, and the *C. rapandium* with flowers of a brilliant pink which flowers in May.

The sweet-scented *C. europaeum* is in flower in August.

DAHLIA

Though severed from its native clime,
Whose skies are ever bright and clear
And nature's face is all sublime
And beauty clothes the fragrant air,
The Dahlia will each glory wear,
With tints as bright and leaves as green;
And winter, in his savage mien
May breathe forth storms, yet she will bear
With all: and in the Summer ray
With blossoms deck the brow of day.

MARTIN

Botanical name: Dahlia variabilis. *Natural order:* Compositae. *Country name:* Georgina. *French names:* Dahlia, Georgine. *German names:* Gartendahlie, georgine. *Italian names:* Dalia, Georgina pruinose. *Turkish names:* Yildin çiç, Dalya. *Symbolical meaning:* Instability, pomp. *Part used:* Tubers. *Natural habitat:* Mexico

---

The Dahlia is named after the Swedish botanist Dr. Dahl, and was introduced from Mexico.

The tubers contain inulin as do also elecampane and chicory. There is a considerable demand for inulin in the preparation of laevulose, and as dahlias and chicory contain from 6 to 12 per cent of inulin they may in future be cultivated for this purpose. Laevulose is sometimes called diabetes sugar because it can be digested by sufferers from diabetes. It is also given to children who are consumptive, or who suffer from wasting diseases.

The dahlia is one of the most satisfactory of the late summer flowers because it is not only extremely decorative but if the dead flowers are cut off regularly, it will flower from June till October. The same tubers, if taken up and stored in the autumn, will go on for years. In my own garden I use the semi double-flowering variety called Coltness Gem, for bedding out, and it has proved far more satisfactory than any other bedding-out plant. I have had my tubers about nine years and they are as good now as they ever were.

DAMIANA

A small mint-like plant, bearing yellowish white fragrant flowers, and growing near the Western Coast of Mexico.

Botanical names: Turnera aphrodisiaca, Turnera microphylle. *Natural order:* Turneraceae. *Parts used:* Leaves and tops. *Natural habitat:* California and Mexico. *Constituents:* A volatile oil and a resin. *Action:* Aphrodisiac, diuretic, tonic.

Damiana is a small mint-like plant with yellowish fragrant flowers. It is a nerve tonic to the brain and to the organs of reproduction. It overcomes exhaustion, and is a good remedy for nerves. It is much used as an aphrodisiac, either alone, or combined with other herbs. The plant is said to contain phosphorus. As a general tonic it overcomes cerebral lassitude, loss of nervous energy, and a tendency to loss of power in the limbs.

The plants belonging to this order are natives of hot countries— Brazil, the West Indies, Jamaica, and Guiana. In some species the flowers remain in bloom for the greater part of the year.

Nutritious Herbs

DENDROBIUM

Near the village of Lernai, woods are passed in which Vanda coerulea grows in profusion, waving its panicles of azure flowers in the wind. The dry grassy hills which it inhabits are elevated 3,000 to 4,000 feet; the trees are small, gnarled and very sparingly leafy so that the Vanda which grows on their limbs is fully exposed to sun, rain and wind. It is under these conditions, however, that all the finer Orchideae grow, of which we found Dendrobium Farmerii, Dalhousianum, Devonianum, etc., with Vanda coerulea; whilst the most beautiful species of Coelogyna, Cymbidium, Bolbophyllum and Cypripedium inhabit cool climates at an elevation above 4,000 feet in Khasia, and as high as 6,000 to 7,000 feet in Sikkim.

Large bamboos rather crest the hill than court the deeper shade, and of the latter there is abundance, for the torrents cut a straight deep and steep course down the hill flanks: the gulleys they traverse are clothed with vegetation and bridged by the fallen trees, whose trunks are richly clothed with Dendrobium Pierandi and other Epithelial orchids.

Hooker's Himalayan Journal

Botanical name: Dendrobium ceraea, Dendrobium macraci. *Natural order:* Orchidaceae. *Country name:* Air flower. *French name:* Aeranthe. *Turkish name:* Hava çiç. *Indian names:* Jibanti, Jiba sag. *Chinese names:* Shih kup, Huang-ts'ao. *Parts used:* Plant, root, stems. *Natural habitat:* The Himalayas. *Properties:* Tonic, stomachic, pectoral, antiphlogistic. *Constituents:* Two resinous principles termed alpha and beta, jibantic acids and an alkaloid called jabantine.

The dendrobium is one of the epiphytic orchids which are representative of a very large genus.

The *D. pierandi* is used in Chinese mediciue.

Decoctions are given as a tonic in doses of half to a fluid ounce.

The *D. macraci* is an air plant which grows on the jambul tree. It has large fragrant white flowers with a yellow lip.

The Chinese call the epiphytic orchids lass flowers, which is the ancient name for them. They were used in potions and sacrificial ceremonies to influence the spirit world, and are endowed with almost magical properties.

Lass flowers were planted in the Imperial gardens; added to cosmetics and used to preserve clothes and books from insects.

The Chinese put these orchids in bamboo baskets and hang them from eaves of their houses. They live and bloom on air alone, absorbing much of their food from the atmosphere, and require for a considerable time neither soil nor water. On this account the Chinese and Japanese use them for house decoration, as they go on blossoming for weeks.

The vanilla plant is a climbing epiphyte growing in Mexico and the West Indies. *See* Vanilla.

DURIAN-TREE

It is the general opinion that there is no other fruit either of tropical or temperate climes that combines in itself such a delicious flavour with such an abominably offensive odour.

Dictionary of Popular Names of Economic Plants
by JOHN SMITH

Botanical name: Durio zibenthus. *Natural order:* Bombaceae. *Malayan names:* Pokok durian, Membuang-burok. *Parts used:* Fruit, leaves, root. *Natural habitat:* Indian and Malayan archipelagoes. *Action:* Aphrodisiac, febrifuge.

The Durian-tree is a handsome forest tree which attains a height of seventy or eighty feet and bears leaves somewhat resembling those of the nutmeg tree. The flowers grow in large loose heads from the main stem or the larger branches, and are pale yellow in colour. The fruit is as large as a man's head, round or oblong, and resembles a rolled up hedge-hog because the hard rind is covered with strong prickles. The seeds are the size of a pigeon's egg, and are embedded in white tunics which are soft, tender and edible, and this part of the fruit is so enticing to those who like it that the natives are said to fight each other for its possession. Once the taste for it is acquired no other fruit can compare with it in flavour. It is described by those who like it as having the taste of a rich custard flavoured with almonds—by those who don't, as tasting of bad onions.

It forms an important part of the natives' food and the fruit is valued as a powerful aphrodisiac.

The juice of the flowers causes sore mouth in children. The sores become infected by an animal parasite and leave scars which are never healed.

The Malayans give a decoction of the root in fevers.

The natives also use the soursop, *Anona muricata*, in the same way. This fruit is covered with green prickles.

ERYNGO

the Eryngo here
Sits as a Queen among the scanty tribes
Of vegetable race.
Here the sweet rose would die; but she imbibes
From arid sand and salt sea dewdrops strength:
The native of the beech, by nature formed
To dwell among the ruder elements.

DRUMMOND

Botanical name: Eryngium maritimum, Eryngium campestre. *Natural order:* Umbelliferae. *Country names:* Sea holly, sea hulver, sea holme, ringo roots. *French name:* Panicaut maritime. *German name:* Krausdistel. *Italian name:* Eringio. *Spanish name:* Cando corredor. *Dutch name:* Kruisdistel. *Under the dominion of:* Venus. *Part used:* Flowery shoots and root dug in autumn from plants a year old. *Natural habitat:* On East coast of England and other coasts of England but rare in Scotland. *Action:* Aromatic, aphrodisiac, diaphoretic, diuretic, expectorant, stimulant.

The glaucous sea holly is closely related to the wood sanicle. The flower heads which are tinged with blue grow at the top of the stem. When they first appear they are round in shape and later become egg-shaped. The calyx is thickly covered with bristles and has the appearance of a thistle.

The young flowering tops can be eaten and are slightly aromatic and very nutritious.

The roots which penetrate deeply into the ground are fleshy, and have somewhat the flavour of chestnuts. They can be boiled and roasted. In the sixteenth and seventeenth centuries they were candied and called kissing comforts in allusion to their aphrodisiac properties. An apothecary at Colchester called Robert Buxton made them popular.

The roots are recommended primarily for loss of vital force. They are

ERYNGO—ERYNGIUM MARITIMUM

prescribed for people who are no longer young, and are used for short-ness of breath.

Francis Bacon used to recommend a special drink made of the yolks of eggs beaten up in Madeira to which eryngo roots and ambergris were added, as a tonic for lumbago.

EURYALE FEROX

. . . and we also saw the fruit of the Euryale Ferox, which is round, soft, pulpy and the size of a small orange; it contains from 8 to 15 round black seeds as large as peas, which are full of flour, and are eaten roasted in India and China, in which latter country the plant is said to have been in cultivation for upwards of 3,000 years.

Hooker's Journals

Botanical names: Euryale ferox, Nymphaea stellata. *Natural order:* Nymphaeaceae. *Indian names:* Makana, Mekhana. *Chinese names:* Chien-shih, ki-tu, Chi-t'ou. *Parts used:* The seeds, stems, rhizomes. *Natural habitat:* China, Calcutta, North India. *Action:* Invigorating, nutritive, anti-aphrodisiac, astringent.

Euryale ferox is one of the ancient water plants used as the lotus is, for food, and has been cultivated for thousands of years in China and probably as long in India. The popular Chinese name, Chi-t'ou, refers to the resemblance that the flower bears to a cock's head.

The fruit is large and pear-shaped and the leaves have spiny veins. The whole plant is covered with prickles.

In India this water lily is endowed with tonic, cooling, sedative, and anti-aphrodisiac properties for all of which it is used in medicine.

As a food it is esteemed for its nourishment; and the capsules and seeds are pickled, added to stew and curries, or ground and made into cakes. The seeds, when fried and baked, are known in India as Dhani. All parts of the plant are used medicinally in China, and are con-sidered to be tonic in effect.

Nutritious Herbs

FALSE ACACIA or LOCUST TREE

Along the rail fences the locust trees were in bloom. The breeze caught their perfume and wafted it down the road. Every Virginian remembers those locusts which grow along the highways: their cloud-shaped masses of blue-green foliage and heavy drooping clusters of cream-white flowers like pea blossoms.

WILLA CATHER

Botanical name: Robinia Pseudo-Acacia. *Natural order:* Leguminosae. *Country name:* Locust tree. *French names:* Robinier, Faux acacia. *German names:* Gemeine Scheinakazie, Gewöhnliche akazie. *Italian names:* Falsa acacia, Robinia, Falsa gaggia, Acacia a parasole. *Turkish name:* Salkim çiçegli ag. *Parts used:* Bark, leaves, flowers, root, fruit. *Natural habitat:* America. *Constituents:* The bark contains a poisonous alkaloid called Robinia which coagulates the casein of milk and clots the red corpuscles of certain animals. The leaves do not appear to contain any poisonous principle and have been used as food for cattle. The flowers contain a glucoside, robinia, which when boiled with acids is resolved into sugar and quercetin. *Action:* Tonic, emetic, purgative.

The Robinia must not be confused with the real locust tree. It is constantly called locust tree in America where it grows to perfection. It is one of the most beautiful, though frail, of all trees and has a wood that is extremely hard—in fact, many of the first houses in Boston were built of it. The branches bear strong, crooked thorns, and the flowers come out from the side of the branches and hang in drooping bunches, rather like laburnum, but they are white and heavily scented. The tree in blossom scents the whole air.

Another species that is found at Carthage, *R. violacea*, has flowers which in colour and scent are like violets.

The rose-flowering locust, *Robinia viscosa*, is not as large as other species but the flowers, though unperfumed, are very decorative because of their soft rose colour. A tree grew in the garden of Louis XIV's chief physician, Monsieur Lemmonier, at Petit Montreuil near Versailles, where it was much admired and where it was still growing in 1819.

The sweet locust, *Gleditschia triacenthos*, grows in the greatest abundance west of the Alleghany mountains, often side by side with the red gum and the black walnut. This tree has also been cultivated in Paris and in London. The water locust, *Gleditschia monosperma*, is peculiar to lower Carolina and grows in swampy districts.

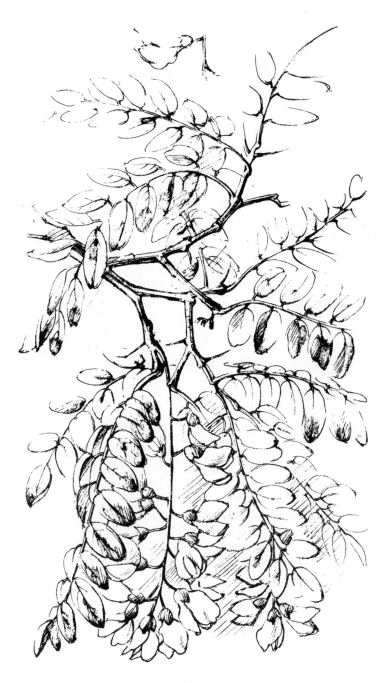

LOCUST TREE—ROBINIA PSEUDACACIA

Nutritious Herbs

A Chinese variety of robinia known in China as Kuang tsing, grows in the mountains, and is common in Northern and Southern China. The leaves are like bamboo leaves and the young plant is eaten as food and made into a dish called pits'ai and into a preserve like ginger. It is said in China to prolong life.

FENUGREEK

In one of the great processions that took place at Daphne under Antiochus Epiphanes, king of Syria, all those who entered the gymnasium to witness the games were annointed with perfumes from golden dishes which contained fenugreek, cinnamon, spikenard, saffron, amaracus and lilies.

Botanical name: Trigonella Foenum-graecum (Linn.). *Natural order:* Leguminosae. *Country names:* Greek hay seed, Bird's food. *French names:* Fenugrec, Sénegrain. *German name:* Griechisches Bockshorn. *Italian names:* Fieno greco, Trigonella. *Turkish names:* Cemen, Hulbe, Boy tohumu. *Arabian names:* Halbah, Shimlet. *Indian name:* Mêthi. *Persian name:* Shembalita. *Malayan name:* Halba. *Part used:* Seeds. *Natural habitat:* Eastern shores of Mediterranean. Cultivated in England, Egypt, India and Africa. *Constituents:* The cells of the testa contain tannin. The cotyledons contain a yellow colouring matter, but no sugar; seeds contain a foetid, bitter fatty oil 6 p.c., also resin and mucilage 28 p.c., albumen 22 p.c., two alkaloids—chlorine (as base found in animal secretions) and trigonellina. The seeds on incineration leave ash 7 p.c. containing phosphoric acid 25 p.c. *Action:* Aphrodisiac, carminative, demulcent, nutritive, tonic.

Fenugreek is eaten fresh in India as a salad. It is cultivated as a fodder plant, and is said to be the Hedysarum of Theophrastus and Dioscorides. It was used to scent poor hay and because of its three-angled corolla is called trigonella. It contains a large amount of mucilage.

The name for the plant in Egypt is helba. It is an annual, rather similar in growth to lucerne and very decorative in a mass because of its brilliant cherry-red colour. It is much grown as a crop in parts of Italy and Sicily and is in bloom there in April. It is an unforgettable sight. I saw it last in the valley looking down from the Temple of Segesta, just before the

53

war started in 1939 and on the road back to Palermo, I met donkeys with panniers strapped to their sides, tumbling over with the rose-coloured flowers, which were destined for neighbouring farms.

FRITILLARY

I know the wood which hides the daffodil,
I know the Fyfield tree;
I know what white, what purple fritillaries
The grassy harvest of the river fields
Above by Ensham, down by Sandford yields,
And what sedged brooks are Thames's tributaries.

MATTHEW ARNOLD

Botanical name: Fritillaria meleagris (Linn.). *Natural order:* Liliaceae.
Country names: Chequered daffodil, turkey hen, ginny flower, Lazarus, bell, pheasant's lily, drooping tulip, dead man's bell, guinea-hen flower, leopard's head, pheasant's head, snake's head, widow veil, snake flower, toad's heads, weeping willow, frits, froccup. *French name:* Fritillaire.
German name: Schachblume. *Italian name:* Frittelaria. *Turkish name:* Mutafan lale. *Chinese name:* Pei mu. *Part used:* Herb. *Natural habitat:* Persia.

The fritillary, an exotic-looking flower in the shape of a snake's head, is found in various colours ranging from white and yellow to the mulberry colour with which we are most familiar in England. It grows wild in parts of Oxfordshire and Hertfordshire. I remember finding it in a field far from habitation near Great Munden in Hertfordshire. At one time it had a great vogue in medicine and Clusius recommended it.

In China two varieties, a yellow fritillary which grows in the mountains of Tibet, *F. rozlii*, and a greyish-white flowered variety, *F. thumbergii*, which is called Pei mu, meaning 'mother-of-pearl', is used to dispel melancholy. A very sweet-scented variety, *F. camchaticensis* is found in the high mountains of British Columbia.

The fritillary, though very unlike in appearance, belongs to the same family as the crown imperial and shares its wholesome properties.

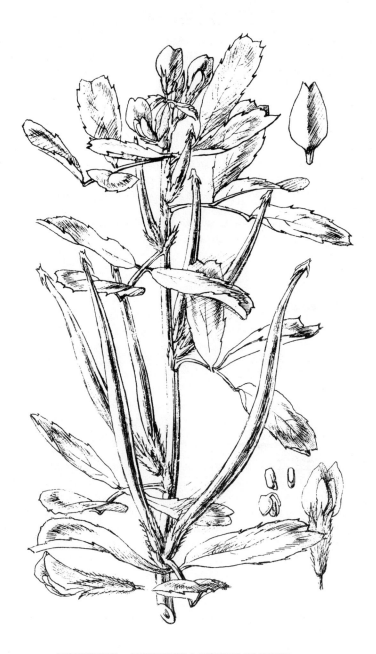

FENUGREEK—TRIGONELLA FŒNUM-GRÆCUM

Nutritious Herbs

GINSENG

The branches which grow from my stalks are
three in number, and the leaves are five by five,
the back part of the leaves is turned to
the sky, the upper side downward.
Whoever would find me must look for the
Kia tree.

A Corean song in praise of Ginseng

Botanical names: Panax quinquefolia (Linn.), Aralia quinquefolia. *Natural order:* Araliaceae. *Country names:* Five fingers, man's health, red berry, tartar root. *French name:* Panax. *German names:* Gensang, Panax Schinseng. *Italian name:* Ginseng. *Turkish name:* Sinseng. *Chinese names:* Jen shên, huang shen, Lu chou. *Part used:* Root. *Natural habitat:* Manchuria, Chinese Tartary. Cultivated in Japan, Korea and U.S.A. *Constituents:* A sweet principle panaquelon, gum, resin, starch, albumen, and a sweet principle. *Action:* Alterative, tonic, stimulant, carminative, demulcent.

So highly is ginseng valued by the Chinese that it is cultivated in other countries in order to be exported to China, because the Emperor had the first claim on all ginseng grown in China and requisitioned most of it. The best variety comes from Manchuria and grows wild, but much of the ordinary ginseng on the market is derived from one of the campanulas and is not the true panax which is an Araliaceous plant.

It is regarded as a powerful restorative and aphrodisiac, and is said to prolong life and benefit the spleen. To the Chinese the spleen is one of the most important organs of the body.

The root of the ginseng resembles that of the mandrake and has a human form. The plant grows up at first with one stem bearing five leaves, and after four or five years a second stem with the same number of leaves is produced, and after another ten years a third, and later a fourth when it begins to grow a stalk from the middle of the heart and this is called by a Chinese word, meaning 'the hundred feet'.

The flowers are pale lilac with filaments looking like untwisted silk.

The best Chinese ginseng grew originally in the mountain valleys of Shang Tang, and was succulent and sweet with a yellow-coloured root. Lu Chou is the modern name for the ancient Shang Tang variety, but the ginseng used to-day comes from Manchuria and is often adulterated with other roots.

The root of the genuine ginseng has a heart, and is juicy and pleasantly sweet, with a touch of bitterness which is very characteristic. The natives chew it or infuse it in wines. The Chinese are very careful not to touch the root with anything made of iron.

Gingseng has a natural affinity for the kia tree which gives it shade. It grows to a great height and has large leaves which grow in the form of a fan. The bark provides fibre for fishing nets.

Ellingwood, speaking of its medicinal properties, says, 'it is a mild sedative to the nerve centres, improving their tone, and, if persisted in, increasing the capillary circulation of the brain'. It helps digestion and cures nervous irritation and nervous prostration.

The Chinese prescribe it for all disorders of the lungs and stomach and as a specific against old age. They extol it as a tonic to the five viscera and as a sedative to animal spirits. It is used to allay fear and to develop character. All forms of debility are benefited by it. The Chinese recognize five varieties of ginseng, the true ginseng which influences the spleen, the *Adenophoria* (sha-shen) which has an action on the lungs, the *Scrophularia* (Hsüan-shên) which treats the kidneys, the *Polygonum bistorta* (mou-mêng) which is for the liver, and the *Salvia multiorrhiza* which is a heart tonic.

It is easy to see therefore that unfavourable European medical reports may not have been based on the true plant, which has always been difficult to obtain and was always very costly.

GOBERNADORA

The whole plant is strongly scented and the flowers are eaten as capers.

Botanical names: Larrea mexicana, Corillea tridentala. *Natural order:* Zygophyllaceae. *Other name:* Gobernadora. *Part used:* Leaves. *Natural habitat:* Mexico. *Constituents:* Tannin, silica, carbonic, anhidrade, phosphoric acids, chloride, potash, lime, magnesia, iron and soda.

Gobernadora is an antiseptic plant containing valuable resins which are used commercially to make soap and varnishes.

The plant is found in the arid regions of the Coahuila Province of Mexico.

It is a small low-growing shrub, with very downy leaves covered with a sort of resin, and has yellow flowers, and very knotty stems.

The flowers are eaten for their wholesome properties, and the leaves are aphrodisiac.

GOLD OF PLEASURE

The leaves are placed with an agreeable regularity from the bottom to the top.

NICHOLAS CULPEPER

Botanical name: Camelina sativa (Crantz), Myagrum sativum (Linn.). *Natural order:* Cruciferae. *Country names:* Myagrum, camelina, camline, cheat, flax, oil seed. *French names:* Caméline, Sésame d'Allemagne. *German names:* Der Leindotter, Echter Dotter. *Italian names:* Miagro falso, Gamelina, Sesameo di Germania, Dradella. *Under the dominion of:* Jupiter. *Part used:* Seeds. *Natural habitat:* Siberia, Turkish Allimany and Sudan. *Time of flowering:* July.

Gold of pleasure was introduced by the Romans for its oil which was used for burning. It is seldom found wild, but is said to grow near Rochester, in the vicinity of the burial place of Hengist and Horsa. It is found on barren sandy soil, and can be planted after a crop without exhausting the ground. It is very nutritious to cattle, and is still cultivated in Germany for its oil.

This cruciferous plant is an annual, growing two or three feet high with long arrow-shaped leaves, and small yellow flowers which are succeeded by egg-shaped ridged pods.

The seeds of the plant contain an oil, which is as wholesome as olive oil.

There are several varieties—a Spanish, an Austrian, an Egyptian, and a cultivated species, *Myagrum sativum*, which is used in cooking as well as in medicine. The origin of its name, gold of pleasure, is a satirical one; it is said to have arisen through the disappointment of the cultivators who were encouraged to grow it as a crop, and who regarded it as a failure and a waste of time.

Nutritious Herbs

HAZEL

The hazel blooms in threads of crimson hue
Peep through the swelling buds and look for Spring.
JOHN CLARE

Botanical name: Corylus Avellana (Linn.). *Natural order:* Amentaceae
Country names: Aglet, beard tree, cats and kittens, cats' tail, chats, cob
nut, crack nut, filbeard, filberd tree, filbert, hole nut, halve, hesill tree,
haselrys, haul, hazel palms, hezzle, lambs' tails, leemens, mit, nuttal tree,
nut tree, nut bush, nut hall, nut palms, nut rag, pussy cats' tails, rag.
French names: Coudrier, Avelinier, Noisetier. *German names:* Hasel-
strauch, Nussbaum. *Italian names:* Avellano, Nocciuolo, Avolano,
Bacuccola. *Turkish name:* Koyun findik ag. *Under the dominion of:*
Mercury. *Symbolical meaning:* Reconciliation. *Part used:* Nuts. *Natural
habitat:* Europe.

Hazel nuts contain such a large percentage of fat and protein that they
can be eaten as a substitute for meat.

The cob and the filbert are the two most cultivated hazels, and, apart
from fat and protein, they contain a good deal of phosphorus, potassium, sodium and calcium.

Nuts are said to prevent hardening of the arteries and to strengthen
the lungs.

The Greeks and Romans ate nuts to provoke them to drink.

The hazel was dedicated to the God Thor, and in classic mythology
the Caduceus of Mercury is symbolized by a rod of hazel. Hazel rods
are used for water divining and for lightning conductors, and in the
time of Agricola were used to discover metals. The hazel is a symbol of
happy marriage and in some parts of Europe was carried at weddings.
To dream of hazels portends riches and content as the reward of hard
work, and to dream of finding hidden hazel nuts forecasts the discovery
of hidden treasure.

GOLD OF PLEASURE—CAMELINA SATIVA

Nutritious Herbs

HONESTY

Enchanting Lunary here lies,
In sorcerie excelling.

MICHAEL DRAYTON

Botanical name: Lunaria annua (Linn.). *Natural order:* Cruciferae.
French name: Lunaire, Monnaie de Pape, Clé de montre, Satin-blanc.
German name: Stumpfes, Silberblatt, Judaspfennig, Zilverbloem.
Italian name: Monete del papa, Ciabatte del papa, Lunaria, Erbe luna.
Danish name: Argentina, Maaneviol. *Turkish name:* Deniz lahanast.
Swedish name: Manefioler. *Under the dominion of:* The moon. *Symbolical
meaning:* Honesty, fascination. *Natural habitat:* Europe. *Action:*
Nutritive.

The honesty plant will grow in any soil, and if it is left to seed makes
attractive winter decoration in the house, because of the silvery leaves
which are left after the seeds have been scattered. The flowers are a
rather hot pink but the white variety is very effective when massed and
will grow under trees where many plants won't.

There is a popular belief that where the pink honesty flourishes the
owner is of an unusually honest disposition.

The flowers have a tonic effect as well as a decorative one. This is a
biennial plant, but seeds so easily that a garden that has once grown it
is never without it. Its old name of 'white satin' refers to the transparent
seed vessels which remain when the seeds are scattered.

Honesty is a wholesome plant and can be used in salads.

HUNGRY GRASS

There's many feet on the moor to-night,
And they fall so light as they turn and pass,
So light and true, that they shake no dew,
From the Featherfew and the Hungry Grass.

The Fairy Music

Botanical name: Alopecurus agrestis (Linn.). *Natural order:* Gramineae.
Country names: Bennet weed, black bent, black couch, black grass,
black quitch, hunger weed, land grass, mousetail, slender foxtail, meadow foxtail. *French names:* Queue de renard des champs, Vulpin des
champs. *German names:* Ackerfuchsschwanz, Kolbengras. *Italian
names:* Alopecoro agreste, Codolino dei campi. *Turkish name:* Sican
kuyruǧu. *Symbolical meaning:* Sporting. *Natural habitat:* Europe.

This is the slender foxtail grass, common on roadsides in England.
The glumes are of a delicate sea green colour tipped with purple and
the leaves have a tendency to curl and often are purplish green in colour.
It comes up much to the farmer's annoyance in early fields of wheat and
clover, and thrives best on dry soil.

The foxtail grasses, for there are three useful varieties—the meadow
foxtail *A. pratensis*, the floating foxtail *A. alpinus* and the tuberous
foxtail *A. bulbosus*—are more important to cattle than almost any other
grasses and they could not thrive well without them or yield so good an
aftermath. So our food deteriorates if they are deprived of them.

The Alpine Foxtail A. alpinus is a mountain grass found in marshy
places in the mountains of Scotland. Anne Pratt says this is of no value
as a pasture grass.

Nutritious Herbs

HYDROCOTYLE

The Chinese call it the Elixir of Life.

Botanical names: Hydrocotyle vulgaris, Hydrocotyle asiatica (Linn.). *Natural order:* Umbelliferae. *Country names:* Farrier's table, farthing rot, flowkwort, penny rot, sheep killing, sheep killing penny, pennywort, sheep rot, sheep bane, water cup, water rot, white rot. *French names:* Hydrocotyle, Ecueille d'eau. *German name:* Wassernabel. *Italian names:* Idrocotile, Scodella d'acque. *Arabian name:* Artániyál-hindi. *Turkish name:* Su Tasi. *Sanskrit name:* Manduka parni. *Hindu name:* Brahmamanduki. *Bengal name:* Thol-kuri. *Bombay name:* Karivana. *Part used:* Leaves. *Natural habitat:* Asia and Africa. *Constituents:* An oleaginous substance vellarine, having the odour and bitter persistent taste of the fresh plant, resin, and some fatty aromatic body, gum, sugar, albuminous matter, salts, mostly alkaline sulphates, and tannin. *Action:* Alterative, diuretic, tonic.

The hydrocotyle plant in large doses is narcotic.

The root given with milk and liquorice is used in dysentery.

The European variety *H. vulgaris*, which is found in Great Britain, is a non-poisonous plant found in bogs and by streams, and is the variety that the famous Chinese herbalist Chang-li-yun, who died in Peking in 1933 at the age of 256 years, is said to have drunk in the form of an infusion to prolong his life. He married twenty-four times and took an infusion every day.

The *Hydrocotyle asiatica* was said by the Indian sage Nanddo Narian, who lived to the age of 107, to contain an ingredient which controls decay and wards off disease. The Chinese name is Chi-hsüeh-ts'tao.

Professor Menier of Paris, who made experiments with it, said that the leaves contain an energizing property which influences the brain. It also contains vitamin G which has a tonic effect on the ductless glands.

The herb has round serrated leaves and is distantly related to the pennyworts.

It has been called in China, snow plant, in reference to its cooling properties. It has leaves resembling the round Chinese copper coins, and is called by the people Ti ts'ien ts'ao (ground coin herb). It is found growing in marshes, and has fragrant round leaves somewhat resembling mint leaves, which are made into an infusion. The leaves only are used

61

by Indian doctors, but the natives recommend the whole plant, root, twigs, leaves and seeds.

The plant known in the vernacular as 'thol-kuri'—*Herpestis monniera* —belonging to the order of Scrophulariae, is frequently mistaken in India for hydrocotyle and both plants are known as 'Brahmi' in parts of India.

HYGROPHILA

When placed in the mouth the seeds become coated with a large quantity of extremely tenacious mucilage which adheres to the tongue and palate.

KHORY & KATRAK

Botanical names: Hygrophila spinosa, Ruelia longifolia, Barberia Longifolia, Asteracantha longifolia. *Natural order:* Acanthaceae. *Country names:* Spirit weed. *French name:* Ruellie. *German name:* Ruellie. *Italian name:* Ruellia. *Turkish name:* Rualia. *Sanskrit name:* Kokli-Laksha. *Arabian name:* Ikshuca-Gokantaka. *Indian names:* Kuliakhara, Goksura, Phulmakhânâ; Ikchura, Kolista, Tálmakhâna. *Parts used:* Whole plant, root, seeds. *Natural habitat:* India, Ceylon, Western coast. *Constituents:* The seeds contain mucilage, albuminoids, traces of an alkaloid and a yellow fixed oil. *Action:* Astringent, mucilaginous, tonic, nutritious.

The hygrophila plant belongs to the acanthus family. It is a spiny annual bush with bright blue or rose-coloured flowers, which are awl-shaped and spreading.

Most of the family have tonic, mucilaginous and astringent properties.

The seeds of this particular species are used for their aphrodisiac properties, as are also the seeds of another member of the family, *Blepharis edulis*, which Malays recommend for toothache.

The plant is used in Ceylon as a remedy for dropsical conditions. The natives infuse two ounces to a pint of water and give the entire quantity within twenty-four hours. It can be bought in nearly all the bazaars in India where it is sold for hepatic diseases as well as for its diuretic properties. All parts of the plant have the same properties though the root and leaves are generally chosen.

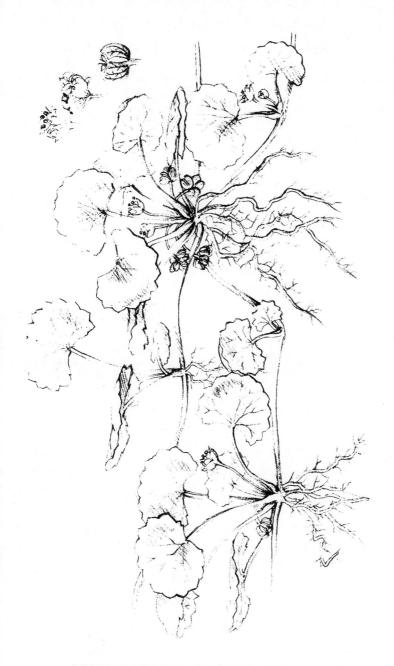

INDIAN PENNYWORT—HYDROCOTYLE ASIATICA

Nutritious Herbs

ICE PLANT

The amomum there with intermingling flowers
And cherries hangs her twigs—Geranium boasts
Her crimson honours, and the spangled bean,
Ficoides glitters bright the winter long.

Botanical name: Mesembryanthemum crystallinum (Linn.). *Natural order:* Ficoidaceae. *Other names:* Diamond, ficoides, fig marigold, hottentot fig, viggie. *French names:* Glaciale, Ficoide cristalline. *German names:* Eiskraut-mittagsblume. *Italian names:* Cristalloide, Diacciola, Erba cristallina, Erba del ghiaccio. *Turkish name:* Buz otu. *Symbolical meaning:* Your looks freeze me. Idleness. *Part used:* Herb and fruit. *Natural habitat:* Africa, Canary Islands, Cape of Good Hope. *Action:* Nutritious.

There are several varieties of mesembryanthemum which grow successfully in the southern parts of England near the sea. Their cochineal pink or yellow flowers make them very conspicuous. Many of them are edible.

The ice plant has always intrigued me since I first saw it in Sicily, and later in the much colder climate of Scotland. I have managed to keep plants alive for several years in my own rockery.

In South Africa, where they are seen at their best, they colour whole tracts of land as the heather does in Scotland. Between Cape Town and Pretoria, as the ridge of the Hex river mountains is approached, the ground is covered in the spring with purple mesembryanthemum. Only such succulent plants could live in such arid ground.

Lady Rockley gives a most vivid description of these curious and exotic-looking flowers which are at their best at midday. Many of them only open then, so accounting for their long name which is derived from Greek words signifying 'middle of the day flower'.

The ice plant was known to botanists of the seventeenth century but so many more varieties have been produced since then, that they include numerous species that open their flowers at all hours. They vary in size from the giant *Cryophytum barklyi* which grows in Namaqualand and attains a height of six feet to such minute specimens as the Conophytums which are hardly visible to the naked eye when not in flower because they grow so close to the earth, and the stones are so much like them in colour.

The South Africans bottle the fruit of such varieties as *M. acinaci-forme* and use it in the treatment of pulmonary tuberculosis, and they make the juice into a mouth-wash and gargle—another variety, *M. mahoni*, is made into an intoxicating beer and into a yeast for bread. The *M. stellatum* serves the same purposes.

In Morocco and in Abyssinia the *M. crystallinum* is used for soap making, and the ashes of other varieties are employed in the manufacture of glass.

M. tortuosum has been administered by natives in the Queenstown district as a narcotic to relieve pain, and a narcotic alkaloid has been isolated from it.

KAVA KAVA

The greedy merchants, led by lucre, run
To the parched Indies, and the rising sun;
From thence hot pepper and rich drugs they bear,
Bartering for spices their Italian ware.

DRYDEN

Botanical name: Piper methysticum (Forst). *Natural order:* Piperaceae. *Country names:* Ava pepper, intoxicating pepper, kava pepper. *French names:* Kawa, Kava, Poivrier Kawa. *German name:* Kawa Pfeffer. *Italian name:* Pepe kava. *Spanish name:* Kava Kava. *Turkish name:* Kava biberi. *Part used:* Peeled, dried and divided rhizome. *Natural habitat:* Polynesia, Sandwich Island, South Sea Islands. *Constituents:* An essential oil, two resins (which are believed to be the active principle), a neutral crystalline 1 p.c. named kavein, or lewinin or methysticin, an alkaloid, and an oleo-resin of a semi-solid consistency. Tastes aromatic and hot like pepper. *Action:* Anaesthetic, aphrodisiac, sudorific.

From the root of kava-kava, a national beverage is prepared by the natives of the South Sea Islands. The root is triturated and then chewed —the chewing being done by the young boys and girls. It is then mixed in a mortar and made into a drink which produces a pleasant form of intoxication, followed by a tranquil condition resulting in incoherent dreams.

Medicinally, the root has a direct influence on the spinal cord. It slows but increases the strength of the heart and is a local anaesthetic of some strength.

It improves the appetite, and stimulates the glands, reduces fatigue, sharpens the mental faculties, and produces pleasant dreams and a sense of peace and comfort.

Taken too long and in too large doses it finally paralyses the respiration. It is not a plant for the amateur to experiment with.

The shrub itself is not unlike the bamboo, it grows to a height of about three to six feet, the stems vary from one to one and a half inches in thickness, the leaves are large varying in size from six to eight inches long, and are nearly as broad as long.

LADY'S SLIPPER

"The Cypripedium with her changeful hues
As she were doubtful which array to choose."

Botanical names: Cypripedium pubescens (Willd.), Cypripedium Calceolus (Linn.), Cypripedium parri florum. *Natural order:* Orchidaceae. *Country names:* Noah's ark, nerve root, valerian, Our Lady's shoe, the sleeve of the Virgin. *French names:* Soulier de la vierge, Cypripède, Sabot de Venus, Soulier de Notre-Dame, Pantoufle de Dame. *German names:* Venus-schuh, Frauenschuh. *Italian names:* Calceolo, Fior farfallone, Pianella della Madonna, Scarpa di venere. *Spanish name:* Zapatito de la virgen. *Turkish name:* Hanim pabuc otu. *Symbolical meaning:* Capricious beauty. Win me and wear me. *Part used:* Root. *Natural habitat:* Armenia, a native of Great Britain. *Constituents:* Volatile oil, resin, fixed oil, volatile acid, tannin, starch, sugar, ash 6 p.c. *Action:* antispasmodic, aphrodisiac, diaphoretic, nervine, nutritious, stimulant, tonic.

Lady's slipper takes its name from the shape of the flowers.

It is the most beautiful of all the wild orchids, and, though rare, is found in woods in Yorkshire and Durham. It is brown and yellow in colour and, unlike other orchids, has two anthers which almost fill the lip. The plant is perennial. The large yellow lady's slipper is indigenous to the lower parts of Canada and the northern and western United States of America. It is found growing in bogs and damp shady woods, where it blossoms from May to June. According to some authorities the orchidaceous plants which have long roots like the cypripedium have different properties from those that have round or oval roots. In medicine it is nutritious and has a special influence on the nervous system. It is a good remedy in insomnia and nervousness when the mind has been overtaxed and there is a sinking of vital powers. It helps to strengthen the eyes, and is a cure for hysteria and melancholia depending on cerebral excitement, and induced by uterine or ovarian disorders. It only relieves the nervous conditions due to functional disorders.

LILY OF KAMSCHATKA

I call her the Red Lily, lo she stands
From all the milder sister flowers apart;
A conscious grace in those fair folded hands
Pressed on the guileless throbbing of her heart.

P. H. WAYNE

Botanical name: Lilium camschatcanve, Lilium avenaceum. *Natural order:* Liliaceae. *Part used:* Root. *Natural habitat:* Kamschatka

---

The root of the scarlet lily of Kamschatka is the source of the food the natives call savanne, which they make into bread. They also boil the roots and eat them for their nutriment as they do other martagon lilies.

The work of collecting the roots is conveniently carried out by the field mouse who arranges them in hoards which are collected by the natives of Kamschatka. This lily has been used medicinally by the natives as a cooling tonic and a healing agent.

In China and Japan the tiger lily takes its place and is used as extensively for food and medicine.

Nutritious Herbs

LOTUS

Bitter as a plumule of the Lotus seed.
A Chinese proverb.

Botanical name: Egyptian: Nelumbium speciosum, *Indian:* Nymphae edulis,Nymphae esculanto. *Natural order:* Nymphaeaceae. *English names: Egyptian:* Sacred bean, Egyptian lotus, Pythagorean bean, *Indian:* Indian lotus, edible lotus. *French names: Egyptian:* Lotus sacré, Lotus du Nile, Nélombo. *German names: Egyptian:* Lotusblume, Agyptische bohne, Nillilie. *Italian names: Egyptian:* Loto, Fava d'Egitto, Loto sacro, Giglio del Nilo, Ninfea d'Egitto. *Arabian names: Egyptian:* Nilufar, *Indian:* Nilufar. *Indian names: Egyptian:* Burrshaluk, Komol, Lamala, Loi-podoma, Kanbal-kukri, *Indian:* Choto-sundhi, Kanval, Chhota-kanval. *Malayan names: Egyptian:* Tělipok, Těnataì. *Chinese names:* Ho Lien-hua (unopened flower Kan Tan), Fukii. *Persian names: Egyptian:* Nilofer, *Indian:* Nilufar. *Turkish names: Egyptian:* Fuli masri. *Under the dominion of:* the Moon. *Symbolical meaning:* Estranged love. *Part used: Egyptian:* Flowers, filaments, anthers, seeds, root and embryo, *Indian:* Roots and flowers. *Natural habitat:* Egyptian: India, Persia, China, Thibet, Japan, Ceylon; Indian: India. *Constituents:* Egyptian: The rhizome and seeds contain resins, glucose, metarabin, tannin, fat and an alkaloid similar to nupharine; Indian: The root contains gallic and tannic acid, starch and gum. *Virtues:* Refrigerant, diuretic, nutritious, sedative.

The classical name for the Egyptian lotus is Kien. In China it is called Ho Hua and the unopened flowers are referred to as Kan tan. The modern Chinese call the opened flowers fukii.

The unripe seeds are eaten, and the ripe seeds are ground into flour and sold in China as bhasabola. This must not be confused with bhosabole which comes from quite a different plant.

In the centre of the seed there is a small green hook which is very bitter and this is called the plumule. 'Bitter as a plumule of the Lotus seed' is a Chinese proverb. This bitter embryo extracted from the ripe lotus seeds is used in medicine by the Chinese and also by Malays in the treatment of 'unlucky' fever. They use the stems in intermittent fevers. The flour from the rhizome of the lotus is called by the Chinese, ghaenfeen. It is not unlike arrowroot and is easily digested.

The Chinese cultivate the lotus on a large scale for food and also the

Euryale ferox. They give a distinct name to every part of the lotus. The stem is called Ch'ieh, the rootlet Mi, the leaf Hsia, the flower Han-t'ao, the fruit Lien, the root proper Ou, the seed Ti, and the caulicle I.

The Indian lotus is also used for food, and the seeds and slices of the root are served fresh with nuts and ice, or are preserved in salt and vinegar for the winter.

The fruit resembles an old French musical instrument, the lotos, which takes its name from the flower.

The water lily lotus in no way resembles the lotus of Africa, (Zizyphus) on which the lotus eaters lived. This is the jujube tree and a wild variety called by the Chinese, Suan ts'ao, a thorny shrub closely resembling the African jujube, grows wild in the plains and mountains of Peking, and is used for fences.

The English variety of lotus, known commonly as bird's foot trefoil or lady's slipper, *Lotus corniculatus*; and the great bird's foot trefoil, *Lotus major*, belong to the leguminous order of plants.

In agriculture they provide a useful crop if sown with white clover. The leaves make a good indigo dye.

LOVE-LIES-BLEEDING

True love lies bleeding, with the hearts at ease;
And golden rods, and tansy running high
That o'er the pale top, smiled on passers by.

JOHN CLARE

Botanical names: Amaranthus spinosa (Linn.), Amaranthus hypochondriacus, Amaranthus caudatus. *Natural order:* Amaranthaceae. *Country names:* Velvet flower, red cockscomb, prince's feather, balder herb, floramor, flower gentle. *French names:* Queue de renard, Discipline de religieuse. *German names:* Fuchsschwanz, Floramour. *Italian names:* Amaranto codato. Disciplina religiosa, Blito maggiore. *Turkish name:* Horoz ibigi. *Indian name:* Chaya. *Indian bazaar names:* Bhui, Ballan. *Under the dominion of:* Saturn. *Symbolical meaning:* Hopeless and heartless. *Part used:* Herb. *Natural habitat:* Southern India, Burma.

In medicine the amaranths have nutritive, tonic, stimulating, demulcent, astringent and diuretic properties.

68

Many of the species, especially the blites, are used as pot herbs and are eaten in the same way as spinach. The small red flowers of the amaranths have been used by cooks to colour food.

In China the amaranths are also used as vegetables and as medicine for their cooling properties. Dr. Porter Smith states that the Chinese believe that the *Amaranthus spinosa* brightens the intellect. The same variety is used in India as well as several others to antidote the stings of reptiles.

LUCERNE

Lucerne is derived from the name by which it is known in Languedoc —Lauserda.

Botanical name: Medicago sativa. *Natural order:* Papilionaceae. *Country names:* Purple medicle, alfalfa, Burgundy hay, lucifer, medick, sanfoin, snail clover, great trefoil. *French names:* Luzerne, Trèfle de Bourgogne. *German names:* Schneckenklee, Luzerne. *Italian names:* Medica, Lupinella, Luzerna. *Chinese name:* Mu-su. *Turkish name:* Kaba yonca. *Symbolical meaning:* Life. *Part used:* Whole herb. *Natural habitat,* Medea, cultivated in Spain, Italy, France, Persia and Peru. *Action:* Fattening, nutritive.

Lucerne is one of the medicks and has from the time of early Rome been cultivated as a crop. In China, under the name of Mu su, it has been grown since the second century B.C. The tradition is that it was brought to China by General Chang Chien of the Han dynasty. It is also found in Persia and Peru.

It is a perennial plant with violet, spike-like flowers not unlike clover, but it is not much grown in England to-day (though it was introduced by the Romans) because it takes several years to reach fruition, though it produces three crops a year and grows again from the same roots. In China the flowers are yellow.

Lucerne is one of the best foods for cattle and is equally nourishing for human beings. It is a valuable food for those suffering from loss of weight, though it reduces weight in those who are too heavy. It is a tonic to the brain and the spinal cord.

Another variety, the spotted medick with small yellow flowers and a heart-shaped purple spot in the centre of each leaf, grows wild in

Cornwall and other parts of England. It is called by country people,
St. Maw's clover, or spotted clover, and sometimes purple grass.
The roots of the black medick make good tooth powder.

MAIZE

Back'd by the pines, a plank built cottage stood
Bright in the sun; the climbing gourd plant's leaves
Muffled its walls, and on the stone strewn roof
Lay the warm golden gourds; golden within;
Under the eaves, pear'd rows of Indian Corn.

MATTHEW ARNOLD

Botanical name: Zea Mays (Linn.). *Natural order:* Graminaceae. *Country
names:* Indian wheat, Indian corn, Turkey wheat. *French names:* Mais,
Blé de Turquie. *German names:* Mais, Turkisches korn. *Italian names:*
Mais, Gran-Turco, Formentone, Grano di Turchia. *Spanish name:*
maiz. *Turkish name:* Misir bugdayi. *Indian names:* Bhuth tha Mokka,
Makka, Buttah. *Arabian name:* Durak shami. *Persian name:* Kho-
shahe-makki. *Symbolical meaning:* Plenty. *Part used:* Seeds. *Natural
habitat:* Peru, Mexico, Central America, cultivated now all over America,
in West Indies, Australia, Africa, India, Europe. *Constituents:* The
stigma or corn silk contains maizenic acid 2 p.c., fixed oil, resin, sugar,
mucilage and salts. Maizenic acid is soluble in water, alcohol or ether.
Action: antiseptic, alterative, anodyne, diuretic, demulcent, lithon-
triptic

Maize has been cultivated by the American Indians for thousands of
years, and as it cannot propagate itself as other cereals do, it is dependent
upon man for its existence, but unlike other cultivated plants it never
reverts to a wild state. It is highly nutritious and will ripen in a hot
summer out of doors in England.

The plant produces ears of corn called cobs which are enclosed in a
sheath of leaves. From the germs of the seeds grow silky filaments which
receive the substance from the flowers and enable the plant to form
grain.

Maize is less subject to disease than any other cereal and much more

LUCERNE—MEDICAGO SATIVA

productive proportionately. The grains vary in colour from a pale gold to chocolate brown and black, but the only variety that grows in England is that with white or yellow seeds. The plant is the staple food of the Mexicans and is now largely used in America as well.

It contains no gluten.

A fermented liquor, called Pulqua de Mahis, is made from the juice of the stalks; a form of cider, which is a popular drink in Mexico.

In Peru, the native home of the maize plant, the corn was called 'Sara', and Mr. Hyatt Verrill tells us that every variety went by a different name. The big kernelled corn was called 'Sara-Moté', the black corn 'Kollo-Sara', the popping corn 'Sara-Cancha', the ground corn used for meal 'Sara-Sancu' and the sweet corn 'Chocli'.

Medicinally maize is a tonic to the organs of secretion and has a nutritive and demulcent effect when absorbed into the system, being converted into soluble dextrine and grape sugar.

The American Indians venerate the maize plant and in *Evangeline* Longfellow describes the ceremony that accompanied the husking of the maize:

> *In the golden weather the maize was husked, and the maidens*
> *Blushed at each blood-red ear, for that betokened a lover,*
> *But at the crooked laughed, and called it a thief in the corn field.*
> *Even the blood-red ear to Evangeline brought not her lover.*

Nutritious Herbs

MANNA ASH

Its buds on either side opposed
Its couples each to each enclosed
In casket black and hard as jet,
The ash tree's graceful branch beset;
The branch, which clothed in modest grey
Sweeps gracefully with easy sway;
And still in after life preserves
The bending of its infant curves.

BISHOP MANT

Botanical name: Fraxinus Ornus. *Natural order:* Oleaceae. *Country names:* Flake manna, manna ash, flowering ash. *French names:* Frêne à fleurs, Frêne à manna, Orne. *German names:* Blumenesche, Mannaesche. *Italian names:* Frassino fiorito, Frassino avoriello, Orno. *Turkish names:* Muzahar dis budagi. *Persian name:* Shirkhisht. *Under the dominion of:* The Sun. *Symbolical meaning:* Grandeur. *Part used:* The concrete saccharine exudation. *Natural habitat:* Southern Europe, cultivated in Sicily and Calabria. *Constituents:* Mannit 69 to 90 p.c., mucilage which does not undergo vinous fermentation, glucose 15 p.c., fraxin, and an acrid resin. *Action:* Laxative, tonic.

This flowering ash tree is a native of Southern Europe and Asia Minor. It yields a sugary sap, which the puncture of an insect of the cochineal family causes to exude. It is collected almost exclusively to-day from Sicily and is used as a mild laxative and tonic for infants. It can be used to sweeten food, and is nourishing and wholesome.

Whether this is the manna of the Israelites remains unsettled. The manna of Mount Sinai is collected from tamarisk trees after they have been punctured by the coccus. The thick syrup that exudes during the day congeals at night and is collected in the cool of the early morning, but other trees and even some herbs are found covered with a sugary sap in some countries.

The manna ash tree attains a height of thirty to forty feet, and is the chief source of the manna sold by chemists and druggists.

Nutritious Herbs

MAPLE

Arrayed in its robes of russet and scarlet and yellow,
Bright with the sheen of the dew, each glittering tree of the forest
Flashed like the plane tree the Persian adorned with mantles and jewels.

LONGFELLOW

Botanical names: Acer campestre, Acer saccharinum, Acer Pseudo-platanus, Acer platanoides, Acer rubrum. *Natural order:* Aceraceae, *Country names:* (For *common maple*): Common bird's tongue, chats. dog oak, Kitty keys, keys, kite keys, masertree, shacklens, whistle wood. (For *great maple*): cats and dogs, chats, cockie-bendie, cocks and hens, hens, keys, knives and forks, locks and keys, mock plane, plane, seggy, shaves, succamon, sycamore, whistlewood.
Common, Acer campestris. French names: Erable champêtre, Petit Erable. *German names:* Feldshorn, Angerbinbaum. *Italian names:* Acero commune, Piccolo acero dei boschi. *Turkish name:* Sendeban ag.
Birds eye, *A. saccharinum. French name:* Erable à sucre. *German name:* Zuckerahorn. *Italian name:* Acero Zuccherino. *Turkish name:* Tath isfendan ag.
Great, A. pseudo-platanus. French names: Erable faux platane, Grand Erable. *German names:* Bergahorn, Falscher platanus. *Italian names:* Acero fico, Acerco liscio, Falso platano. *Turkish name:* Yalan ak ag.
Norway, A. platanoides. French names: Erable plane, Erable platane. *German names:* Spitzahorn, Norwegischerahorn. *Italian names:* Acero platano. *Turkish name:* Ak ag.
Red, A. rubrum. French names: Erable femelle, Erable rouge. *German names:* Roterahorn, Virginischerahorn. *Italian name:* Acero Rosso. *Turkish name:* Kirmizi isfendan ag.
Under the dominion of: Jupiter. *Symbolical meaning:* Reserve. *Parts used:* Sap, bark. *Natural habitat:* North America, Northern India, Japan, Norway. *Action:* Astringent, nutritious.

The sap from the maple is a most nutritious article of food, and the maple sugar of the bird's eye maple is more wholesome even than the West Indian cane sugar and deposits less sediment when dissolved. The wood of this maple is particularly attractive for cabinet making and medical instruments, because of its grey colour and satin-like polish, and the red maple makes a good black dye.

Maples often have a red appearance owing to the puncture of an insect which produces red beads all over the tree. Also in the autumn the leaves turn to an orange-red. The maple, as far as is known, has always been a native of Britain and is said to be one of the few trees that survived the glacial age, but it is in Canada that maples are seen at their best. The scarlet maple, *Acer rubrum*, has inspired the national song of Canada, by its blaze of colour. The bird's eye maple which is found in the northern parts of the United States of America provides for a great industry. Each tree yields from two to six pounds of sugar each season, and the tapping of the trees takes place in the months of February, March and April. The favourite molasses, which in America is an accompaniment of buckwheat cakes, is derived from the sugar maple, and vinegar is another product of the tree.

MASTIC

It seems a romantic isle to me as I stroll along. The very trees bend over me like wise old friends, wailing the lore of ages as the winds creep in from the enpurpled sea. The exotic odours of the fresh flowers intoxicate my senses; though they seem bright living eyes of woods as they dance to the zephyrs.

A. SAFFRONI-MIDDLETON

Botanical name: Pistacia lentiscus (Linn.). *Natural order:* Anacardiaceae. *French names:* Lentisque, Pistachierlentisque. *German name:* Mastixstrauch. *Italian names:* Lentisco, Pistacchio sondro, Cornocapro, Manna del Libano. *Turkish name:* Damia sakiz ağ. *Arabian name:* Uluk-bagh-dame, Kinuak, Rumi-mastaka. *Indian names:* Rumi-mastaki, Rumimostika, Kundar-rumi. *Persian names:* Kinnah, Kinnoli. *Malayan name:* Mastaki. *Parts used:* Bark, leaves, buds, fruit, resin. *Natural habitat:* Asia minor, Calcutta, Levant, Island of Scio, Southern Europe. *Constituents:* A trace of volatile oil, two resins, alpha resin or mastichic acid 90 p.c., and beta resin or mastichine 10 p.c., also an ethereal oil. *Action:* Aphrodisiac, diuretic, stimulant.

In India mastic is used as an aphrodisiac combined with salap. In Malaya it is used for the same purpose combined with opium, honey and aromatic herbs.

The best mastic came from the island of Scio where the inhabitants who grew it and collected it held special privileges from their Turkish masters, who limited its cultivation to chosen people and areas. The lentish trees require very little attention and are very profitable, because the gum which is collected in the form of tears is used not only as a masticatory by all the people of the East, but in the making of varnishes for pictures, and as an ingredient in fumigations. Evelyn says that the tree was introduced into England in the year 1664.

MICHAELMAS DAISIES

The michaelmas daisies among dede weedes,
Blooms for St. Michael's valorous deedes,
And seem the last of flowers that sode
Till the feast of St. Simon and St. Jude.
An early calendar of English flowers

Botanical name: Aster Tripolium. *Natural order:* Compositae. *Country names:* Blue daisy, blue chamomile, sharewort, harwort, starwort, *French names:* Astère, Astère attique. *German names:* Sternblume. Strandaster. *Dutch name:* Sterribloem. *Danish name:* Stiernblomst. *Italian names:* Astero, Astro. *Turkish name:* Yildiz çiç. *Symbolical meaning:* Afterthought. *Part used:* Herb. *Natural habitat:* North America. *Action:* Tonic, nutritive.

The michaelmas daisy has been identified with the anellus plant with which the ancient Greeks decorated the altars of their gods.

The plant is found wild in parts of England, and the lilac flowers with their golden centres make them a conspicuous object on the sea cliffs where they grow.

The michaelmas daisy was introduced into English gardens from America by Sir John Tradescant in 1633. The Tradescants were famous gardeners and one of the family was gardener to Charles I. When he visited America Sir Charles Lyell noticed the michaelmas daisies growing wild on either side of the White Mountains side by side with golden rods. They grow wild in England and have been found on the banks of the Thames.

Two of the most useful varieties for garden decoration are the *Aster frikartii*, which has purplish-blue flowers and is in bloom practically all through the late summer, and the *Chrysanthemum erubescens* which, though a Korean chrysanthemum, is very similar in appearance to the *Aster frikartii*, except that its flowers are pink. They are both about two feet high and look well growing together. The new, very dwarf asters Marjorie, Victor and Nancy grow very compactly and keep the rock garden gay through September.

The succulent leaves and stems can be boiled and eaten in the same way as samphire and are nutritious.

The name starwort is sometimes applied to this plant but the real starwort is the *Pallensis spinosa*.

MUSHROOMS

'At midnight a small people danced the dales,
So thin that they might dwindle through a sieve
Ringed mushrooms told of them, and in their throats
Old wives that gathered herbs and knew too much.
The pensioned forester beside his crutch
Struck showers from embers at those bodeful notes.'

Botanical name: Agaricus campestris. *Natural order:* Agaricaceae. *French names:* Agaric champêtre, Champignon de couche. *German names:* Blatterling, Blatter-pilz, Schwamm. *Italian names:* Agarico esculente, Fungo ordinario, Fungo comestibile. *Turkish names:* Agaric Mantani, Garikun, Katran Ropugu.

The eating of mushrooms is as old as history, and volumes have been written on the cooking of fungi—the various species employed, and the description of the vessels in which they should be cooked.

The common mushroom, which is the one most cultivated, is widely distributed over the world and is grown on a large scale in cellars and caves, in boxes, on the shelves of greenhouses and wherever the temperature and humidity is suitable for its growth.

Mushrooms are quick to grow and as quickly decompose, so they should be eaten the same day that they are picked.

The meadow mushroom *Agaricus arvensis*, sometimes called the horse mushroom, is next in importance to the common mushroom. This is the kind usually used in the making of ketchup.

Nutritious Herbs

The large variety of the meadow mushroom, known as St. George's mushroom, is seldom found in England, but a much smaller mushroom also known by that name makes its appearance about St. George's Day and is quite common in England in the spring.

Several fungi grow in rings and the legend that these rings were formed by the feet of dancing fairies on the grass is a very old one.

Many of the rarer mushrooms, such as the brown mushroom *Agaricus elvensis*, the bleeding brown mushroom *Agaricus haemorrhoidarius*, the wood mushroom *Agaricus silvaticus*, the inky mushroom *Coprinus altramentarius*, the Polish mushroom *Boletus edulis*, the orange mushroom *Agaricus aurantiacus* and the milk mushroom *Lactarius deliciosus* are much more commonly met with on the Continent though they all grow in England.

One of the favourites among mushroom gourmets is the parasol mushroom *Agaricus procerus*. It has a most delicate flavour which is appreciated all over Europe, and has the advantage of not resembling a poisonous toad stool.

Perhaps the most appreciated of all fungi in France are the chanterelles because of their golden yellow colour and their odour of ripe apricots; but in France the use and understanding of mushrooms is part of their fine culinary art.

It is difficult to exaggerate the importance of mushrooms as food, for they contain ergosterol in large quantities—this is the raw material as it were of Vitamin D. Mushrooms also contain a large proportion of sulphur and calcium and they are the nearest approach to meat in the vegetable kingdom.

Perry is the right beverage to drink with them and has an ancient reputation of antidoting poisonous mushrooms.

Though the mushroom is not strictly speaking a herb it is a vegetable food, and so I have included it in this chapter.

Nutritious Herbs

MUSK SEED

'As if nature's incense Pan had spilt
And shed their dews i' the air.'

Botanical name: Hibiscus abelmoschus (Linn.). *Natural order:* Malvaceae. *Country names:* Ambretta, Ab-el-mosch, Egyptian target-leaved hibiscus. *French names:* Ambrette, Graine de musc. *German name:* Abelmosch, Bisam-eibisch. *Italian names:* Ambretta, Abelmosco. *Turkish name:* Auber çiç. *Sanskrit names:* Zatákasturiká, Lata-kasturikam. *Arabian names:* Hub-ul-mishk. Habbul-mislek *Indian names:* Mushak-danak, mishka-dana, mushak-dânak, mishk-dana. *Persian name:* Mushk-danah. *Symbolical meaning:* Weakness. *Part used:* Seeds. *Natural habitat:* The East and West Indies, Egypt and tropical countries. *Constituents:* Gum, albumen, fixed oil, and solid crystalline matter, odorous principle and resin. *Action:* Aphrodisiac, carminative, cooling, demulcent, stimulant.

The *Hibiscus abelmoschus* is an evergreen shrub with very large sulphur-yellow flowers based with purple. It grows to about four feet in height. After it has risen above the ground, it bends and creeps as it were upon itself. The seeds are enclosed in pyramid-shaped capsules and are aromatic and sweet scented when well bruised. The Arabians add them to coffee and flavour soups with them, and cook the capsules as a vegetable. Medicinally the seeds are given to cure a hoarse voice.

They are said to have aphrodisiac properties. In India, where the musk plant is common, a tincture prepared from the seeds is much valued as an antispasmodic medicine, and is extensively prescribed for hysteria and nervous disorders.

A remarkable characteristic of this species is that the flowers spring from the petiole of the leaf as in Turnera ulmifolia.

It is a difficult plant to grow in this country because it must be kept under a frame in the winter and the seeds don't ripen easily.

Nutritious Herbs

OLIVE

. . . Let gallic vineyards burst
With floods of joy; with wild balsamic juice
The Tuscan olives.

JAMES THOMSON

Botanical name: Olea europaea (Linn.). *Natural order:* Oleaceae. *French names:* Olivier, Arbre éternel. *German name:* Echter olbaum. *Italian names:* Olivo, Ulivo, Oleastro. *Spanish name:* Olivo. *Turkish name:* Zeytun ag. *Symbolical meaning:* Peace. *Parts used:* Trunk, leaves, bark, oil. *Natural habitat:* Asia Minor, Syria, cultivated in Italy, France and Spain, Chile, Peru and South Australia. *Constituents:* A fluid oil as olein 72 p.c., palmetin 28 p.c. (a solid oil). It also contains arachin, stearin and cholesterin. *Action:* Antiseptic, astringent, febrifruge, nutritious.

Olive oil is nutritive and soothing. If rubbed into the skin it is absorbed by the lymphatics and protects the mucous membranes against poisonous substances. It increases fat, supplies heat, loosens waste material, and dissolves some forms of calculus.

In the making of cold sauces and in cooking generally it is almost indispensable.

The flowers of the fragrant olive lanhoe are used in China to scent schoulang tea.

The olive tree has a very ancient history in commerce and a very romantic one.

Athene owned the olive tree, and when she and Neptune fought for supremacy over the Athenians, the other gods decided in favour of Athene, because at her command the olive tree had been born, and was more important to mankind than the salt spring which Neptune's trident had opened in the rock of the Acropolis.

Athens, of course, takes its name from the goddess.

ORCHID

'The Orchis race with varied beauty charm.
And mock the exploring fly or bee's aerial form.'

Botanical names: Orchis bifolia, Orchis maculata, Orchis mascula, Orchis latifolia, Orchis morio, Orchis militaris, Orchis saccifero, Orchis pyramidalis, Orchis coriphora, Orchis conopsea. *Natural order:* Orchidaceae. *Country names:* Salep, saloop, purple orchis, spotted orchis, Levant salep, satyrion, long purples. *French names:* Orchis masculé, Orchis mâle, Orchis taché. *German names:* Kuckucksaffenkraut. *Italian names:* Orchide maschia, Concordia, Testicolo. *Turkish name:* Hasieti sahleb. *Arabian name:* Salab-misri. *Indian name:* Salob-misri. *Persian name:* Saalab misri. *Under the dominion of:* Venus. *Symbolical meaning:* A belle. *Part used:* The tubers. *Natural habitat:* Europe including England. Persia, Afghanistan, Nepal, Cashmere. *Constituents:* Starch 27 p.c., mucilage 48 p.c., sugar, albumen, a trace of volatile oil, and ash consisting chiefly of phosphates and chlorides of potassium and lime. *Action:* Aphrodisiac, astringent, demulcent, nervine, tonic.

Many of the orchids found in England make nutritious food, and in the eighteenth century were universally gathered and made into what was then known as salop. This food was served in the principal coffee-houses. There was even a salop house at one time in Fleet Street.

The *Orchis maculata*, *Orchis latifolia*, *Orchis bifolia* and *Orchis Morio* which are said to be the source of the oriental salop, all grow in parts of England.

Surrey, Kent, Oxfordshire, Gloucestershire, Cambridgeshire, and Staffordshire are good hunting grounds for them.

The orchid is said to contain more nourishment for its bulk than any other vegetable matter. In Turkey and Syria the *Orchis mascula* and the *Orchis latifolia* are cultivated on a large scale for their nutriment.

SALOP TO BOIL

Take a large teaspoonful of the powder and put into a pint of boiling water, keep stirring it till it is like a pure jelly; then put in wine and sugar to your taste, and lemon if it will agree.

TO PREPARE THE ROOTS FOR SALOP

Mr. Mault of Rochdale's recipe: Wash the fresh roots in water and separate with a small brush the outer brown skin or dip them into hot water and rub the skin off with a cloth.

Spread the blanched roots on a tin plate and bake them in the oven for from six to ten minutes during which time they will lose their milky whiteness and acquire the transparency of bones. Remove them from the oven and leave them in the air for several days to harden or they can be left to harden for a few hours in the oven. Powder as required.

In mythology the orchis was born from the blood of the wanton son of the satyr Patellanus, who was killed by the Bacchanals at a feast of Bacchus, because he violated one of the priestesses. To propitiate his father the gods turned him into an orchid. The name satyrion, which is used for the orchid, is derived from the belief that the flower was the food of the satyrs, and induced the excesses to which they were prone.

PALMS

I wish I had the power to give a picture of that spot as night crept over the mountains, bringing its mystery. We would sit beneath the feathery palms and watch the snow white tropic bird wave its crimson tail as it swooped shorewards. The chanting chorus of locusts would commence tuning up in the bread fruits as the twilight nightingale and one or two of its feathered brethren sought the heights of the giant palms to warble thanksgiving to the great god of Polotu, the heathen God of Elysium.

A. Saffroni-Middleton
Wine Dark Seas

Palm trees are so amazing growing in their own tropical climate, that it is difficult to believe that the palms used to decorate ballrooms in England are related to them. Tropical palm trees have tremendously tall and elegant stems, and are usually crowned with feathery green plumes.

One of the most interesting of the palm trees is the talifot palm, which is so slow in growth that it takes over thirty years to reach maturity and only blooms before it dies. The sight of the tree in full bloom is lovely beyond imagination. The entire tree is overhung with great silky yellow tassels of blossom, which permeate the air with their scent and attract not only butterflies but humming birds.

The coco-nut palm, the date palm, the elaeis palm, and the sago palm are perhaps the most useful to man, but many of them yield sugar, oil, wine, starch, wax and resin as well as edible fruits and seeds. A small plant belonging to the same order, the saw palmetto herb, provides one of the most nourishing medicines we have, and, the juice of the jagani palm, sometimes called the bastard sago tree (*Caryota urens*), is made into a wine, and the flour from the trunk into a sort of sago. The elaeis palm provides oil.

Not nearly so well known are the delicious edible fruits which some palms, especially the peach palm of Mexico and Central America, produce. These fruits are even more nutritious than bananas, and though they are often eaten raw they are more often made into exotic conserves or rich wines.

More closely related to the bananas than the palms is the traveller's palm which holds in its leaves as much as a quart of water with which to quench the thirst of tired travellers in tropical countries.

ARECA PALM

The views are beautiful, of the blue mountains forty to fifty miles distant, and the many armed river, covered with sails, winding amongst groves of cocoa nuts, Areca palm and yellow rice fields.

Hooker's Himalayan Journal

Botanical name: Areca catechu (Linn.). *Natural order:* Palmaceae. *Country names:* Betel nut, pinang, areca palm. *French names:* Aréquier, Noisette d'Inde, Arec. *German names:* Pinang Palme, Areka Palme. *Italian names:* Palma arec, Arec. *Turkish name:* Fufal ag. *Arabian name:* Fulfil. *Indian names:* Shupari, Kunthi, Sopari, Hopari. *Chinese name:* Ping-Lang. *Persian names:* Girda choba, Papal. *Malayan name:* Pinang. *Symbolical meaning:* All palms symbolize victory. *Part used:* Seed. *Natural habitat:* East Indies, cultivated in India and Ceylon. *Virtues:* Astringent, antiperiodic, anthelmintic, stomachic, tonic. *Constituents:* The kernels contain catechu, tannic and gallic acids, oily matter, gum, arecoline, arecaine and guracine.

The areca palm-tree has very sweet-scented flowers, and fruits the size of an egg, containing the seeds which are chewed for their intoxicating effect. After they are dried they are prescribed to increase the flow of saliva, to lessen perspiration, and to sweeten the breath, and strengthen the gums.

As a masticatory the nuts have a very ancient reputation and they form the basis of many tooth powders.

One of the Chinese names for this nut is Hai-chang-tan, which means 'anti-malarious panacea', and shows the use to which it has been put by the Chinese, who also prescribe it as an infallible tape worm remedy. Its use as an anthelmintic is historic both in China and India, where it has proved equally satisfactory as an astringent in tropical dysentery.

The areca palm is one of the most elegant of the palm trees, because of its graceful stem, which is crowned by a tuft of leaves. The fruit is orange colour and about the size of an egg.

It is indigenous to Sunda islands but is cultivated all over the Eastern Archipelago.

CABBAGE PALM

For a fine and tasty salad there is nothing to equal the crisp white heart of a cabbage-palm.

H. HYATT VERRILL

Botanical names: Oreodoxa oleracea, Areca oleracea. *Natural order:* Palmaceae. *French name:* Palmiste franc. *German name:* Kohlpalme. *Italian names:* Palmisto, Palma cavolo. *Turkish name:* Lahana yaprakh hurma ag. *Natural habitat:* West Indies.

The cabbage palm is one of the gigantic palms. It is of great elegance and beauty. The stem which is often seven feet in circumference tapers to a great height and just below the summit the leaves form themselves into a crown. The seeds are enclosed in sheaths which grow from the centre of the branches and hang down in bunches. The cabbage grows in the centre of the leaves which surround the trunk. This is white, about two feet long, and cylindrical in form. Eaten raw it has something of the taste of an almond but is even more delicious. It can be sliced, boiled and eaten as a vegetable. After the cabbage is cut a species of black beetle lays its spawn in the empty cavity, and the worms which the spawn produces are regarded as a great luxury, and are fried in fat and eaten. They have an aromatic flavour which recalls all the spices of the East.

Nutritious Herbs

COCO-NUT PALM

Give me to drain the cocoa's milky bowl,
And from the palms to draw its freshing wine:
More beauteous far than all the frantic juice
Which Bacchus pours.

JAMES THOMSON

Botanical names: Cocos nucifera (Linn.), Palma indica major. *Natural order:* Palmaceae. *French name:* Cocotier. *German name:* Kokospalme. *Italian name:* Albero del cocco. *Turkish names:* Hindistan cevizi ag, Narcil ag. *Arabian names:* Touz-i-hindi shagratun, nar jiil. *Indian names:* Narikal, Koperu, Nariel. *Persian name:* Drakhte-bading. *Chinese name:* Ye-taze, Yue-wang-t'ou. *Parts used:* Flowers, root, oil and ash. *Natural habitat:* The tropics, Indian Archipelago, Coasts of India. *Constituents:* The fresh kernel contains nitrogenous substance, fat, lignin, ash, palm sugar and inorganic substances. *Action:* aperient, diuretic, anthelmintic, refrigerant.

The milk of the coco-nut has the same properties as the kernel. The root is diuretic, and the old and dried kernels are cut into slices, and used in aphrodisiac preparations. The terminal buds make a nourishing, pleasant and easily digested vegetable, and their oil is used as a substitute for cod liver oil.

The Indian nut alone
Is clothing, meat and trencher, drink and can,
Boat, cable, sail, mast, needle, all in one.

GEORGE HERBERT

The coco-nut palm is a feature of all tropical villages. It grows without effort on sandy shores, and even if it is uprooted by violent storms and hurricanes, roots itself again in the sand. It often lives for a hundred years, providing the inhabitants with milk, nuts, molasses and oil. There is an old Hindu saying: 'He who sees a straight coco-nut palm will go direct to Heaven.' Such a thing hardly ever exists for the climate exposes it to the wind and the storms from the time it takes root.

Nutritious Herbs

DATE PALM

Alleys of blossomed fruit trees girt a cool
White marble screen about a bathing pool,
The Palace rose beyond among its trees
Splay fronded fig and dates and cypresses.

MASEFIELD

Botanical name: Phoenix dactylifera (Linn.). *Natural order:* Palmaceae. *French name:* Dattier. *German name:* Dattelpalme. *Italian name:* Dattero. *Turkish name:* Hurma ag. *Arabian names:* Khurmae-yabis, Tamr-ha-khal. *Indian names:* Khur-ma, Khagur, Chukara. *Persian names:* Khur-mâ, Kunyan. *Parts used:* Fruit, juice from the trunk. *Natural habitat:* Africa, Arabia. *Constituents:* Tannin, extractive, mucilage, insoluble matters and lime. *Virtues:* aphrodisiac, diuretic, nutritive, tonic.

Dates are nourishing and sustaining. The toddy obtained from the stem is diuretic, and by distillation of the fruits, a spirit called lagbi, or rajura-no-darn, is obtained.

A single date palm will bear sometimes between two and three hundredweights of dates in a season. The trees begin to bear when they are from six to ten years old, and continue to bear often for two hundred years. It is the earliest known of the palms, and though it grows in tropical countries, it only attains perfection in comparatively high latitudes. In Egypt, Arabia and Persia it forms the chief article of sustenance.

Three or four quarts of sap can be obtained every day from a single tree for a few weeks. This spirit is left to ferment and forms Arrak.

The fruit was known in England from a very early date and was called by the Anglo-Saxons, finger apples—a name derived from the Greek word for date.

The stones of the fruit are ground and sold as food for camels and other domestic animals, and are also roasted and made into date coffee, which is said to be a good substitute for ordinary coffee.

Nutritious Herbs

GREAT FAN PALM

The Fan Palm, grows on the cliffs near Mamloo: it may be seen on looking over the edge of the plateau, its long curved trunk rising out of the naked rocks, but its site is generally inaccessible; while near it grows the Saxifrage ciliaris *of our English gardens, a common plant in the North-West Himalaya, but extremely scarce in Sikkim and the Khais mountains.*

Hooker's Himalayan Journal

Botanical name: Borassus flabelliformis. *Natural order:* Palmaceae. *Country names:* Tal palm, great fan palm. *French names:* Rondier, Palmier de Palmyre, Bérasse. *German names:* Palmyrapalme, Weinpalme. *Italian names:* Palma di Palmira, Palma del ferro. *Turkish name:* Palmira hurma ag. *Arabian name:* Tafi. *Indian names:* Talgachh, Galati, Taragola, Taltar, Talgahâ, Tál. *Persian name:* Dar-akhte-tar. *Sanskrit name:* Tála. *Malayan name:* Paná. *Parts used:* Root, fruit, juice. *Natural habitat:* India. *Constituents:* Gum, like tragacanth, fat, albuminoid. *Virtues:* demulcent, refrigerant, restorative, nutritive.

This palm tree often reaches a height of a hundred feet, and bears a crown of large fan-shaped leaves. The fruit grows in bunches, each fruit measuring about three inches in diameter, and is covered with a pulp-like substance which is made into jelly by the natives.

The root, fruit and juice of the great fan palm have restorative and nutritive properties. The terminal buds make a good and wholesome vegetable—the juice is converted into arrak, and the unripe fruit is soothing and nutritious.

This palm tree grows in sandy districts on the banks of rivers and provides the natives with their popular drink.

The juice of the buds and the root are used medicinally as a cure for gastritis and local inflammations.

Nutritious Herbs

SAGO PALM

Over my head the beautiful bread fruit trees and plumed palms waved their richly adorned branches. The deep primeval silence, only disturbed by the cry of the solitary Mamoa uli bird, seems to steal into my very being. I can smell the wild sweet odour of the forest, as the night's faint breath steals from the hollows, laden with scented whiffs from the decayed tropical flowers and the damp undergrowth, that a few hours before was pierced by glorious sunlight and musical with bees.

A. SAFFRONI-MIDDLETON

Botanical names: Sagus farinifera, Metroxylon sagu, Sagus spinosus, Sagus rumphii. *Natural order:* Palmaceae. *Country name:* Pearl sago. *French names:* Sagonier, Sagoulier. *German name:* Sago palme. *Italian names:* Sago, Sagu, Palma da stoffe. *Turkish name:* Sago ag. *Indian name:* Sagu chaval. *Chinese name:* So-muk-mien. *Part used:* Prepared fecula. *Natural habitat:* East India islands, Moluccas, Borneo and Eastern Archipelago.

The sago palm is one of the small palms from the pith of which sago is obtained. Sago is one of the most nourishing foods. It has demulcent properties and is very easily digested, so it is particularly useful in digestive complaints, and in fevers.

The sago tree grows very slowly and the trunk which is covered with thorns is formed of the bases of the leaves.

When the stem appears the tree rapidly grows to a height of thirty feet and a girth of five or more feet. The trunk becomes filled with a farinaceous pith and when fully matured a white dust appears on the leaves which shows that the sago is ready to be extracted. The tree is then felled and afterwards grows again in the same way. In Malaya, sago broth or gruel is regarded as an aphrodisiac tonic.

This palm grows on the ridges of mountains.

Sago is also obtained from plants of the Cycad family which are found in the Bahamas. They are only dwarf shrubs.

Nutritious Herbs

SAW PALMETTO (PALM)

Broad o'er my head the verdant cedar wave
And high Palmettos lift their graceful shade!

JAMES THOMSON

Botanical name: Serenoa serrulata. *Natural order:* Palmaceae. *Country names:* Sabal, sabal serrulata. *Parts used:* Partially dried ripe fruit and herb. *Natural habitat:* Atlantic from Florida to South Carolina, Southern California. *Constituents:* A volatile oil, soluble in alcohol; a fixed oil, both obtained from the expressed juice. *Action:* Nutritive, aphrodisiac, tonic and stimulant.

Saw palmetto grows best along the south-eastern coast of the United States of America. It is a decumbent-stemmed palm forming a palmetto scrub for hundreds of miles along the coastline from Georgia to Florida. The fan-shaped glaucous leaves are so dense that it is impossible for human beings to pass through it. The plant grows about a foot high and the leaves form a large crown. The panicles containing the fruit often weigh as much as nine pounds.

The berry is of special value in wasting diseases, and acts as a tonic to the tissues, and the mucous membranes. Its direct influence is on the organs of reproduction, nourishing, soothing, stimulating and reducing or enlarging the glands as the case requires.

Attention was first called to it by Goss and others, because animals who fed on it became so sleek and fat.

It stimulates digestion, greatly improves appetite, and produces proper assimilation. By its use congestion of the nose and ear passages is relieved and it acts as a tonic to the nerve centres and to all the mucous surfaces.

The natives use the leaves for thatching, and for manufacturing paper, and the roots for scrubbing brushes. The Palmetto Royal, an allied species, is used for the same purposes.

Nutritious Herbs

POTATO

Two large potatoes passed through a kitchen sieve
Unwonted softness to a salad give.

SIDNEY SMITH

Botanical name: Solanum tuberosum (Linn.). *Natural order:* Solanaceae.
French names: Pomme de terre, Parmentière. *German names:* Kartoffel,
Potaten. *Dutch name:* Ardappel. *Italian names:* Patata, Pomo di terra.
Turkish name: Patates. *Indian names:* Puttata, ala. *Mdazyan name:* Ubi
Kantang. *Persian name:* Seb-zamini. *Parts used:* Tubers, stems, leaves.
Natural habitat: Virginia and Peru, and cultivated in temperate climates.
Constituents: The tuber contains a large amount of starch, also citric
and phosphoric acid. *Actions:* Alterative, nutritious.

The potato, though allied to such poisonous plants as the deadly
nightshade, provides, through its tubers, wholesome and nutritious
food on which life can be sustained.

The plant was introduced into England from North America by Sir
Walter Raleigh's colonists in 1586, and it first reached Europe from
Peru by way of Spain in the early part of the sixteenth century.

It was called by Gerarde 'the potato of Virginia', and in his portrait
on the frontispiece of his herbal he is holding a spray of the plant in his
hand. Sir Walter Raleigh first planted it in his own garden in Cork, but
finding the berries noxious, and suspicious of their poisonous properties,
he had the plants dug up again and it was left to his gardener to discover
the value of the tubers.

There was great opposition to their cultivation at first from the
Puritans, who rejected them because they could find no mention of them
in the Bible, and for a whole century they were only grown in the gardens
of the rich. In 1760, however, the Scots cultivated them as a crop, having
grown them previously in gardens, and found them a success.

To obtain all the nutriment in the potato they should be baked in
their skins, because much of their value lies close to the surface.

Potatoes contain a large proportion of phosphorus and potassium, in
addition to sulphur, magnesium, chlorine, calcium, sodium, silica and
iron.

Potatoes used raw, provide an excellent outward application for
rheumatic pains and burns.

89

Nutritious Herbs

RICE

Fields of rice occupy the bottom of these valleys, in which were placed gigantic images of men, dressed in rags, and armed with bows and arrows, to scare away the wild elephants!

Hooker's Himalayan Journal

Botanical name: Oryza sativa (Linn.). *Natural order:* Graminaceae. *French name:* Riz. *German name:* Reis. *Italian name:* Riso. *Turkish name:* Pirinc. *Indian names:* Dhan, Pushnee (milled) Chokha, Tandul, Bhat, Chawal. *Persian name:* Birinjishali. *Chinese names:* (ancient) Tao, (modern) Keng, Tao, Mi (when milled). *Part used:* Seeds. *Natural habitat:* East Indies, China, India, East Africa, Syria and cultivated in most sub-tropical countries. *Constituents:* Nitrogenous matter 7·5, carbohydrates 9·75, fat 8, mineral matter 9. Rice contains no fat, more starch than any other grain and a very small percentage of proteins. It is very easily digested. *Action:* Nutritive, demulcent.

Rice more nearly approximates to wheat than any other cereal, in the sense that it contains all the elements necessary to sustain life, and it is the common food of the Chinese and the Hindus. As with other important plants the Chinese have a distinctive name for every stage in the growth of the rice plant as well as for each species—the glutinous, the non-glutinous, the water grown and the upland varieties are all specifically named.

In the East rice symbolizes life and abundance, and is not only showered as it is in England on newly married couples, but is scattered on the head of the bride during the marriage service. The Arabs regard it as a sacred food.

There are two kinds of rice in general use in Europe. Carolina rice, which is particularly suitable for sweet puddings, and Patna rice, which is preferred for curries and savouries.

Rice is very easily digested. It should, however, be used in its unpolished form because the polishing destroys the outer covering which contains the important mineral salts and vitamins. In China the grain, the culm, the awn and the flower of the rice plant are all used as medicine.

It is nourishing, very easily digested, and is particularly helpful in gastric and intestinal complaints.

Rice is cultivated on a large scale in Egypt, but is of comparatively late introduction to America.

Nutritious Herbs

ROCKET

You! who in sacred wedlock coupled are
(Where all joys lawful, all joys seemly are)
Ben't shy to eat of my leaves heartily,
They do not hunger only satisfie,
They'll be a banquet to you all the night
On them the body cheers with fresh delight.

ABRAHAM COWLEY

Botanical name: Hesperis matronalis. *Natural order:* Cruciferae. *French names:* Julienne Cassolette, Girade. *German names:* Frauennachtriole, Matrouenviole, Nachtviole. *Italian names:* Viola delle Dame, Giuliana, Esperide del Giardini, Antoniana, Giranda. *Turkish names:* Buyuk frenk benefsesi, Mensur. *Part used:* Whole plant. *Natural habitat:* Central Europe.

The rockets are all members of the cruciferous order and are therefore edible and non-poisonous. They are eaten in salads, and have been recommended for their antiscorbutic properties. For salads the leaves should be picked before the plant comes into flower.

Medicinally the plant is used while in flower, and many virtues have been attributed to the garden rocket. It is a gland stimulant and aphrodisiac.

The rockets are biennial plants. The stems are very erect and grow from two to three feet in height. The flowers purple, white or variegated, grow in a simple thyrsus at the top of the stalk. There is a double white variety, and the flowers of the sweet rocket give out their scent at night only.

The yellow rocket, Brassica vulgaris, flowers in April in America, from Virginia far northward; in the interior, and on the Pacific coast. It is like the yellow alyssum but is scented.

Nutritious Herbs

SERVICE BERRY

Budding, the service tree, white
Almost as white beam, threw
From the under of leaf upright
Flecks like a showering show
On the flame shaped Junipers green,
On the sombre mounds of the yew,
Like silvery tapers bright
By a solemn cathedral screen,
They glistened to closer view.

GEORGE MEREDITH

Botanical names: Amelanchier canadensis, Amelanchier rotundifolia.
Other names: Sorb tree. *Natural order:* Rosaceae. *Country name:* Savoy medlar. *French name:* Amélanchière. *German names:* Felsenbirne, Felsenbeer. *Italian name:* Aronia. *Turkish name:* Musmula ağ. *Part used:* Fruit.
Natural habitat: Northern United States of America, Canada.

This small tree belonging to the apple family is an unusual sight when in flower, because it is completely covered with white and is called for that reason, showy mespilus. The black fruit which follows is edible, sweet and very pleasant in flavour. It is a wholesome and nutritious fruit and has been used from ancient times to make wine and a drink not unlike cider.

In Finland the tree has a special significance because in Scandinavian sagas the nymph of the sorb tree is the protectress of cattle, and the Finnish shepherds pray to her for the safety of their flock.

The following description of the tree in March is taken from Neltje Bianchan's book *Nature's Garden*. 'Silvery white chandeliers hanging from the edges of the woods light Flora's path in earliest spring, before the trees and shrubbery about them have begun to put forth foliage, much less flowers. . . . Little female bees of the Andrena type, already at work collecting pollen and nectar for generations yet unborn, buzz their gratitude about the beautiful feathery clusters, that lean away from the crowded thicket with a wild irregular grace.'

SWEET ROCKET—HESPERIS MATRONALIS

Nutritious Herbs

SPURREY

*Arenaria balearica forms a dense, strangling mat, on which before long,
everything else, however vigorous, gives up the ghost and expires. But oh!
it is a joy when the whole emerald sheet of it is covered with its wee
brilliant white stars.*

REGINALD FARRER

Botanical names: Arenaria rubra, Spergula diandra (Murb.), Spergula
arvensis (Linn.). *Natural order:* Caryophyllaceae. *Country names:*
Beggar weed, bottle brush, cow quake, dodder, dother, farmer's ruin,
Frank, granyagh, lousy grass, make-beggar, pickpocket, pick-purse,
poverty weed, sand weed, yarr, yarrel, yawn, yur. *French names:* Sper-
gule, Morgeline. *German names:* Der Ackerspargel, Spark, Spergel.
Italian name: Spergola. *Dutch name:* Akher-spurri. *Danish name:* Knae-
graes. *Turkish name:* Cayir otu. *Part used:* Herb, seed. *Natural habitat:*
Europe including Britain, Quebec, North America.

Spurrey is a troublesome weed to farmers because it grows amongst
the corn. It is said to be one of the most nourishing of all plants in proportion to its bulk, and it gives the best flavour to milk and butter.

It is not unlike the chickweed, and has white flowers with reddish cups.
The seeds make good bread and are used by the Finlanders for this
purpose, and the plant is cultivated in Germany and Holland for fodder,
as it suits both sheep and cows. It grows quickly, and the seeds contain
a large percentage of oil.

The sandworts, which are closely related, are also nourishing, and the
sea sandwort is boiled and eaten like samphire or made into a sort of
sauerkraut. It is usually called sea purslane. The French call it
sabloumière, the Germans sandkraut and the Italians arenaria, which is
its botanical name.

The knotted spurrey, spergula nodosa, and the pearlwort spurrey,
S. saginoides, are often referred to as pearl worts, and are placed by
some botanists under a different order.

The Arenarias produce one or two very valuable species for the rock
garden, as for instance Arenaria balearica, A. montana, A. gothica,
A. verna, etc.

Nutritious Herbs

STAR OF BETHLEHEM

The next akin, a flower which Greeks of old,
From excrements of birds, descended, hold,
Which Britain, nurse of plants, a milder clime,
Gentilely calls 'The Star of Bethlehem'.

ABRAHAM COWLEY

Botanical name: Ornithogalum umbellatum (Linn.). *Natural order:*
Liliaceae. *Country names:* Eleven-o'clock-lady, Jack-go-to-bed-at-noon,
John-go-in-bed-at-noon, nap-at-noon, peep o'day, six o'clock flowers,
sleepy Dick, snowflake, twelve o'clock, wake-at-noon. *French names:*
Dame d'onze heures, Ornithogale en jombelle, Belle d'onze heures.
German names: Doldiger milchstern, Vogelmilch. *Italian names:* Bella
di undici ore, Dama d'undici ore, Latte d'uccello. *Turkish name:* Sasal.
Symbolical meaning: Purity. *Part used:* Bulb. *Natural habitat:* Europe,
Palestine. *Action:* Edivle, nutritious.

It has been suggested that the bulbs of the star of Bethlehem are 'the
dove's dung' of the Bible, because the plant grows in great profusion in
Syria and Palestine particularly in the neighbourhood of Samaria
where they are known by that name.

The only species that is found wild in England is the *Ornithogalum
pyrenaicum*, which grows in woods outside Bath and is sold as Bath
asparagus.

The bulbs are nutritious and are roasted like chestnuts.

They were eaten by the ancient Eastern races either raw or cooked.

In gastritis the bulbs are a useful medicine and will often relieve the
pain of gastric ulceration. It has a specific action on the pylorus.

The drooping star of Bethlehem, O. nutans, has loose clusters of
nodding flowers which are larger than the common variety. It is sometimes found wild in England, but must be regarded as an escape.

Nutritious Herbs

SUGAR CANE

O, some are for the lily, and some are for the rose,
But I am for the sugar cane that in Jamaica grows;
For its that that makes the bonny drink to warm my copper nose
Says the old bold mate of Henry Morgan.

MASEFIELD

Botanical name: Saccharum officinarum. *Natural order:* Graminaceae.
French names: Canne a sucre, Cannamelle. *German name:* Zuckerrohr.
Italian name: Canna da zucchero, Cannamelle. *Turkish name:* Seker
kamisi. *Arabian name:* Kufsch-us. *Indian names:* Uk, Ik, Abàh, Ukyo,
Uch Ghanna, Khulea, Kaguli. *Chinese name:* Canchi. *Persian name:*
Nai-sukr. *Part used:* Juice. *Natural habitat:* Tropics, India, Southern
Asia. *Constituents:* Saccharine matter, water, mucilage, resin, fat, albu-
men. *Action:* The juice of the sugar cane is antiseptic, cooling, demul-
cent, nutritive, preservative.

The sugar cane has been cultivated in China since the second century
before Christ, but many of the old plantations have been interfered with
by the cultivation of the opium poppy. Chinese supplies to-day come
largely from Canton, and Hong Kong, though the old sugar provinces
of Hunan, Kiangsi, and Kueichou still produce sugar, much of which is
used for chewing.

Though the plant is indigenous to the Indian islands, it is generally
supposed that the art of making sugar was introduced there by the
Chinese. The sugar cane was not grown by the Greeks or Romans. It
was taken by the Saracens to Sicily, Crete, Rhodes, and Cyprus, and
was grown in abundance in these islands before the discovery of the
East and West Indies. The Moors introduced it into Spain, and it was
grown first in Valencia. There are numerous legends and ceremonies in
the sugar plantations, which are still believed and practised—for instance, it is regarded as a misfortune if a sugar cane flowers twice in one
season.

The old Brazilian sugar canes, which were cultivated before the
eighteenth century, have been replaced by the Bourbon and Java
varieties, which mature more quickly and are much more productive.

Medicinally, sugar is a heart tonic of great value and is of such importance in the diet of the young and the aged that it cannot well be over-

rated. It strengthens the muscles, stokes the engine of the body, burns up acid, and makes food palatable.

The juice of the sugar cane is used in the West Indies to dissolve cataract.

SUNFLOWER

Ah! Sun-flower! weary of time,
Who countest the steps of the sun;
Seeking after that sweet golden clime,
Where the traveller's journey is done;

Where the youth pined away with desire,
And the pale virgin shrouded in snow,
Arise from their graves, and aspire
Where my sun-flower wishes to go!

WILLIAM BLAKE

Botaniçal name: Helianthus annuus (Linn.). *Natural order:* Compositae. *Other names:* Golden flower of Peru. *French names:* Hélianthe, grand soleil, Tourne sol. *German name:* Sonnenblume. *Italian names:* Mirasole, Elianto, Sole, Girasole, Tazza regia, Coppadisole, Corona del Sole. *Turkish names:* Aycic, Gunebakan. *Part used:* Seeds. *Natural habitat:* Mexico and Peru. *Constituents:* About 16 p.c. albumen, 21 p.c. fat. *Properties:* Diuretic, expectorant, anti-malarial.

Every part of the sunflower is so useful economically and medicinally, that it is one of the regular crops in Russia, Roumania, Spain, Germany, Denmark, France, Italy, Egypt, Japan, India, Manchuria, and the Argentine.

The calcium of sunflower seeds has such a healthy action on the teeth and the gums, that in districts where the seeds are chewed teeth do not decay. Unfortunately, sunflower seeds are encased in such a hard shell that it is only those who are accustomed to manipulate the removal of the shell with their teeth, or with their fingers, as the Chinese do, who can enjoy them. The oil expressed from the seeds is an excellent substitute for olive oil and can be used for salads, for cooking and even for burning in lamps. It has even an advantage over olive oil in that it remains liquid at a lower temperature, and it is one of the best oils for the making of margarine.

Nutritious Herbs

In Spain and Portugal the seeds are made into a nutritious bread, or roasted like coffee and made into a drink.

The flowers contain a yellow dye, and the stems a fibre which can be used in making paper; the pith of the sunflower stalk is the lightest substance known and for this reason can be made into life-belts.

The yield in potash from the sunflower's ash is considerable. An acre of sunflowers produces from two thousand five hundred to four thousand sunflower heads, roughly about one hundred and sixty pounds of potash per acre. The tall heads of the flower, measuring about fifteen inches across, produce about fifty gallons of oil to the acre and about one hundred and fifty pounds of oil cake.

The oil is expressed from the seeds, after which the remains make excellent cattle food; the leaves make good food for poultry and stock, and the ash is excellent for potato and other root crops.

Commercially it is better than linseed oil for paint because it dries much more rapidly.

The only difficulty about oil obtained from sunflowers is that it is very difficult to extract from the seeds, and of course there are the usual difficulties over pests and diseases which have to be overcome.

The leaves of the sunflower, when carefully dried, can be used in the making of cigars in place of tobacco. They have very much the flavour of mild Spanish tobacco.

It has been thought that large plantations of sunflowers in certain areas protect the inhabitants from malaria. As an infusion of the stems is a remedy for malaria this may well be true.

SWEET CHESTNUT

Spring in the Apennines now holds her court
Within an amphitheatre of hills
Clothed with the blooming chestnuts, musical
With murmuring pines, waving their light green cones
Like youthful Bacchants; while the dewy grass
The myrtle and the mountain violet
Blend their rich odour with the fragrant trees
And sweeten the soft air.

LORD BEACONSFIELD

Botanical names: Castanea vesca (Gaertn.), Castanea sativa (Mill.).
Natural order: Fagaceae. *Country names:* Sardinian nut, Spanish chestnut, sardian nut, euboean nut, chastey, stoves nut, chesteine, French nut, meat nut. *French name:* Châtaignier. *German names:* Kastanienbaum, Echte Kastanie. *Italian names:* Castagno, Castagno domestico. *Turkish name:* Kestane ag. *Indian name:* Ni-keri. *Russian name:* Keschtan. *Dutch name:* Kastangeboorn. *Parts used:* Leaves, fruit. *Natural habitat:* Italy, Greece. *Constituents:* Gallic acid, tannic acid 9 p.c., resin, fat, gum, albumen, ash 6 p.c. mainly salts of magnesium, potassium, lime, iron, carbonates, chlorides and phosphates. The fruit contains starch 35 p.c., fat 2 p.c., proteids 4 p.c. and sugar 2 p.c. *Action:* Astringent, sedative, tonic.

Though the sweet chestnut is not nearly so common in England as the horse chestnut there are magnificent examples of it in some English parks—Kensington Gardens for instance, and Greenwich Park.

The great chestnut of Tortworth was known by that description in the reign of King John.

The leaves are often very long, glossy on the top, and bordered underneath with sharp spines; the flowers are green and grow in graceful spikes, and the fertile flowers lengthen as the fruit appears. The barren flowers wither early. The fruit does not mature everywhere in this country, and the nuts of commerce come from Italy and Spain.

For chestnuts roasted by a gentle heat
No city can the learned Naples beat.

There are great avenues of these trees in Vallombrosa outside Florence. The fruit is extremely nutritious, and in the Latin countries is used as a stuffing for turkey and also as a vegetable.

The troublesome preparing of chestnuts for food prevents them being as much used in this country where less time is devoted to cooking. The leaves are used medicinally in fevers.

SWEET WILLIAM

And the borders filled with daisies and pied sweet Williams
And busy pansies; and there as we gazed and dreamed
And breathed the swooning smell of the packed carnations
The present was always the crown of all it seemed.

ROBERT BRIDGES

Botanical name: Dianthus barbatus (Linn.). *Natural order:* Caryophyllaceae. *Country names:* Sweet John, williams, tolmeiner, London tuft, bloomy-down, pride of London. *French names:* Jalousie, Oeillet de poète, Bouquet parfait. *German names:* Bartnelke, Samtnelke. *Italian names:* Garofano barbuto, Garofano poeta, Armaria, Mazzetto perfetto. *Turkish name:* Kir karanfil. *Symbolical meaning:* Gallantry, dexterity, diplomacy. *Part used:* Herb. *Natural habitat:* Germany, Carniola. *Constituents:* Many of the species contain saponin. *Action:* Stomachic, tonic.

The sweet william belongs to the same family as the clove carnation. Parkinson refers to the use of nineteen varieties in medicine. The double rose sweet william, an old variety, is fragrant and can be used in the same way as the gilliflower. It has stomachic and tonic properties.

The *Dianthus amatolicus*, an Indian variety, is used internally and externally to allay the bites and stings of poisonous insects and reptiles.

The wild sweet william, phlox maculata, grows in damp woods and beside streams in the east of America.

To-day sweet williams are scented, and this new hybrid is called sweet wivelsfield.

Nutritious Herbs

TELUGA POTATO

The tubers of the Indian potato was the first food of the Mormons when they reached Salt Lake City.

A. HYATT-VERRILL

Botanical name: Amorphophallus campanulatus, Amorphophallus sylvaticus, Arum campanulatus. *Natural order:* Araceae. *Indian names:* Ol, Mar, Jangli suran, ol, Madana masta, Jamkund. *Malayan names:* Kizhanna, Lèkir, likir. *Sanskrit name:* Arsaghna. *Part used:* The tubers or corm. *Natural habitat:* India.

The teluga potato is one of the wild aroid plants. The leaf stalk is white with brown streaks. In Malaya the sliced tubers are cooked and eaten as food but in their fresh state they are poisonous and the fresh juice is used by the natives as an arrow poison.

The dried root can be bought from native herbalists. It is given medicinally as a digestive tonic and restorative.

This is rather similar to an English plant, the common arum, which is known to rustics as lords and ladies. The roots when cooked become non-poisonous, and formerly were made into a powder called Portland sago. The roots were also used as starch.

Mr. Hyatt-Verrill in his book called *Wonder Plants* says that the flower of this potato, which resembles a lily, is known as the mariposa tulip, and although a weed in many places is gathered for its beauty.

TULIP

The tulips that have pushed a pointed tusk
In steady inches, suddenly resolve
Upon their gesture, earliest the royal
Princes of Orange and of Austria,
Their Courtier the little Duc de Thol,
And, since the State must travel with the Church,
In plum, shot crimson, couleur, Cardinal.

But grander than these dwarf diminutives,
Comes the tall Darwin with the waxing May,
Can stem so slender bear such sovereign head
Nor stoop with weight of beauty? See her pride
Equals her beauty, never grew so straight
A spire of faith, nor flew so bright a flag
Lacquered by brush stroke of the painting sun.

V. SACKVILLE-WEST

Botanical names: Tulipa gesneriana, T. Sylvestris. *Natural order:* Liliaceae. *Country name:* Culip. *French names:* Tulipe, Tulipe des fleuristes. *German names:* Gartentulpe, Tulpe. *Italian names:* Tulipano, Lancettoni. *Turkish name:* Lale çiç. *Symbolical meaning:* Consuming love. *Part used:* Roots. *Natural habitat:* The Levant, Macedonia, Thrace, the Crimea, Persia. *Action:* Edible, nutritive.

The tulip was introduced into Holland from Persia. According to Clusius the early flowering tulips were brought to Constantinople from Cavala, a town on the coast of Eastern Macedonia, and the later flowers came from Caffa in the Crimea.

The flower takes its name from its resemblance to the eastern head-dress, and the botanical name is derived from Gesner who first described it.

The wild tulip is yellow and fragrant, and does not open till 10 a.m., whereas the garden tulip opens at 8. It also differs from the garden tulip in the narrowness of its leaves, the simple form of the stigma, the length of its anthers, and the colour of the pollen which is yellow instead of black. Wild tulips have been found in chalk pits in Norfolk, Suffolk, Somersetshire and Yorkshire.

Abraham Cowley recommends the flowers to cure jaundice:

101

Nutritious Herbs

I am a flow'r for sight, a drug for use,
By secret virtue and resistless power
Those whom the jaundice siezes I restore;
The dropsie headlong makes away
As soon as I my arms display.

Dioscorides attributed aphrodisiac properties to the seeds. Both Gerarde and Parkinson recommended the roots preserved in sugar as a good and wholesome sweet with tonic properties. Parkinson says: 'I have preserved the roots of these tulips in sugar, as I have done the roots of eryngoes and have found them to be almost as pleasant. That the roots of tulips are nourishing there is no doubt, for divers have had them sent by their friends from beyond seas and mistaking them to be onions have used them as such in their pottage or broth.'

In Constantinople, the Sultan held a yearly banquet in his seraglio, called the Feast of the Tulips. The gardens were illuminated to shew tulips of every shade of colour.

VANILLA

A climbing epiphyte growing in the West Indies.

Botanical names: Vanilla planifolia, Vanilla aromatica. *Natural order:* Orchidaceae. *Country name:* Epidendrum vanilla. *French name:* Vanillier. *German name:* Vanille. *Italian name:* Vaniglia, Vanigliero. *Turkish name:* Vanilya fidant. *Spanish name:* Vanilla. *Part used:* The fruit. *Natural habitat:* Tropical countries, Mexico, West Indies, cultivated in Java. *Constituents:* Vanillin or vanillic acid 2 p.c., fixed oil 11 p.c., resin, sugar, mucilage, and ash 5 p.c. *Action:* Aphrodisiac, carminative, antispasmodic, tonic and stimulant.

Vanilla is prescribed in hysteria and low fevers and is much used in the flavouring of food.

It is one of the climbing epiphyte orchids which can be planted in sand and leaf mould and trained to grow over stone pillars and trellises.

This orchidaceous plant, in common with other epiphytes, has invigorating properties, and French cooking, which is founded on making food nourishing as well as appetizing, discards all synthetic essences of vanilla and only uses the vanilla bean, which is added to chocolate, ices, and many sweet dishes in France.

The Bourbon pod is considered the best.

VEGETABLE MARROWS

Then said Judes triumphantly: I would suggest lamb, roast chicken, and pimented rice; I would suggest sausages, stuffed vegetable marrow, stuffed mutton, stuffed ribs, a kenafa with almonds, bees' honey mixed with sugar, pitachio fritters perfumed with amber, and almond cakes.

From the Tale of Judes or the Enchanted.
Translated by E. Powys Mathers from the Book of the Thousand Nights and one Night of Dr. J. C. Mardus.

The order cucurbitacae includes marrows, pumpkins, melons, cucumbers and gourds, many of which are of great economic importance. Under cucumis we have the melons and cucumbers—under cucurbita, pumpkins and marrows, and the gourds come under lagenaria.

Citrullus vulgaris is the botanical name of the great water melon which the Egyptians use as food and drink.

Pumpkins and marrows are much more cultivated in America than in England, not only for pumpkin pie which is one of the favourite American dishes, but because many varieties are so decorative in the garden and so quickly grown as a covering to fences. Two beautiful varieties which I have grown in my own garden from seed, given me by that gifted gardener, Mrs. Christmas Humphreys and which I think she obtained from Clarence Elliot, are the avocadella and the zucchini. The former does not spread, but grows in the form of a bush—has very large yellow flowers and tall pale green leaves with long stalks. The marrows which form all round the centre are flat and wheel-shaped with a dark bottle-green skin which is corrugated like a canteloup melon. The pale green leaves against the dark green fruit are very effective. The marrows will keep after they are ripe and can be stored for some time. They are usually eaten cold, sliced and covered with a cream sauce, in the same way as avocado pears, which they resemble in flavour.

The zucchini marrow is an Italian variety; it spreads slightly but does not romp as other marrows do. The marrows are long in shape and striped—the leaves are like an acanthus leaf and are very decorative. This marrow is cooked and can be eaten when quite young and small, or when it has reached maturity.

103

Nutritious Herbs

The following are three American recipes:

PUMPKIN PIE

Line an eight-inch pie dish with rich pastry. Soften a tablespoonful of gelatine in cold water, mix together 1½ cups of cooked pumpkin, with ¼ cup of sugar, ¾ teaspoon of salt and a teaspoonful of cinnamon and half a teaspoonful of ginger and the slightly beaten yolks of 2 eggs and a cup of milk, and cook over boiling water for 5 minutes, stirring all the time. Then add the softened gelatine and stir till it is dissolved. Cool until slightly thickened. Then gradually beat ¼ cup of sugar into the stiffly beaten whites of the eggs and fold into the thickened pumpkin gelatine mixture. Put into a dish and cover with shredded nuts and chill till firm.

FRIED ZUCCHINI MARROW

Wash 2 zucchinis and cut in ¼-inch slices. Sauté slowly in a ¼ cup of butter in a heavy frying-pan for 10 minutes, stirring constantly. Cover and let them simmer for 5 minutes, stirring fairly often. Cook with one clove of garlic finely sliced or one teaspoon finely chopped onion.

FLORENTINE ZUCCHINI MARROW

Wash 2 lbs. of zucchinis and cut without peeling into ¼-inch slices, sauté 2 medium sized onions in 2 tablespoons butter till golden, add the sliced zucchinis and cook over low heat for 5 minutes, stirring constantly, add 2 cups of tinned or fresh tomatoes, salt and pepper, and simmer covered for another 5 minutes. Place in a greased casserole and cover with grated cheese and bake in a moderately hot oven, 375° F., about 20 minutes till brown.

Line 9-inch pie plate with pastry and make fluted rim. Combine 3 well-beaten eggs with a cup of sugar, a teaspoonful of salt, ½ a teaspoon of cinnamon, ½ teaspoon of nutmeg, ½ teaspoon ginger and ½ teaspoon cloves—gradually stir in 2 cups of scalded milk, then 2 cups strained cooked pumpkin. Turn into the pastry-lined plate and bake in a hot oven 10 minutes at 450° F. Then reduce heat to 350° F. and bake 20 to 25 minutes longer until a knife comes out clean when inserted into the custard.

Pumpkin seeds contain 30 per cent fixed oil, traces of a volatile oil, proteids, sugar, starch and an acid resin to which the anthelmintic properties of the seeds are attributed.

Marrows have good digestive properties and are cooling to the blood.

Nutritious Herbs

VINE

Hail Bacchus! hail thou peaceful God of Wine,
Hail Bacchus Hail! here comes thy darling vine,
Drunk with her own rich juice, she cannot stand,
But comes supported by her husband's hand;
The lusty elm supports her stagg'ring tree,
My best belov'd plant, how I am charm'd with thee!

ABRAHAM COWLEY

Botanical name: Vitis vinifera (Linn.). *Natural order:* Vitaceae. *French name:* Vigne. *German name:* Weinrebe. *Italian name:* Vite. *Turkish name:* Asma. *Indian names:* Angur, Drakhya, Drakhsha, Kishamisha. *Malayan names:* Sebĕn gkak, chawat udi, Gundak api, Lakom. *Arabian name:* Kerm. *Persian names:* Angura, Gureb. *Under the Dominion of:* The Sun. *Symbolical meaning:* Drunkenness. *Part used:* Fruit, leaves, juice. *Natural habitat:* Southern Europe, Asia, California, Greece, Australia and Africa. *Constituents:* The pulp contains grape sugar, cream of tartar, gum and malic acid. The seeds contain a bland fixed oil and tannic acid; skin of the fruit contains tannic acid. *Action:* Restorative, astringent.

Grapes contain dextrose, a different sort of sugar from that in other fruits and it is of great nutritive value.

They have refrigerant and demulcent properties and give quick warmth to repair tissue and to stimulate the action of the lungs. Baths made from vine leaves have been used in Eastern countries for centuries.

Though Bacchus is the god of the vine it was Saturn who gave it to Crete. In Egyptian mythology Osiris was the first instructor in the culture of vines; in other countries the tradition is that Bacchus taught men how to grow them and turn the grapes into wine. There are constant references to the vine throughout the Scriptures. From the Bible we know that Noah planted a vineyard.

The vine tree has a very long life in warm climates. Pliny speaks of one that was six hundred years old and some of the Burgundian vines are known to be several hundreds of years old.

The grape has been cultivated from the earliest times and is said to grow wild on the coasts of the Caspian Sea, but the country of its origin is not really known.

Nutritious Herbs

VINE LEAF FRITTERS

Take some of the smallest vine leaves you can get, and having cut off the great stalks, put them in a dish with some French brandy, green lemon rasped, and some sugar; take a good handful of fine flour, mixed with white wine or ale. Let your fritter be hot, and with a spoon drop it in your batter, take great care they do not stick one to the other; on each fritter lay a leaf; fry them quick, and strew sugar over them, and glaze them with a red-hot shovel.

With all fritters made with milk and eggs you should have beaten cinnamon and sugar in a saucer, and either squeeze an orange over it, or pour over a glass of white wine, and so throw sugar all over the dish, and they should be fried in a good deal of fat; therefore they are best fried in beef dripping, or hog's lard, when it can be done.

Nutritious Herbs

WALNUT

The walnut then approach'd, more large and tall,
His fruit, which we a nut, the Gods an acorn call;
Jove's acorn, which does no small praise confess,
T'have call'd it Mans ambrosia had been less
Nor can this head like nut, shap'd like the brain
Within, be said that form by chance to gain,
Or Crayon called by learned Greeks in vain.
For membranes, soft as silk, her kernel bind,
Whereof the inmost is of tend'rest kind,
Like those which on the brain of man we find;
All which are in a seam joined shell enclos'd,
Which of this brain the skull may be suppos'd.
This very skull envelop' is again
In a green coat, his pericranium.
Lastly, that no objection may remain,
To thwart her near alliance to the brain;
She nourishes the hair, rememb'ring how does
Her self deform'd, without her leaves show
On barren scalps she makes fresh honours grow.

ABRAHAM COWLEY

Botanical name: Juglans regia (Linn.). *Natural order:* Juglandaceae.
Country names: Jupiter's nuts, cazya, French nut, Welsh nut, tentes.
French name: Noyer. *German name:* Walnuss. *Italian name:* Noce
comune. *Turkish name:* Ceviz ag. *Under the dominion of:* The Sun.
Symbolical meaning: Intellect, stratagem. *Part used:* Leaves, bark, nuts.
Natural habitat: From Greece to Himalayas, Kashmir. *Constituents:*
Nucin or juglandic acid, resembling chrysophanic acid. Fixed oil 14 p.c.,
volatile oil, resin, no tannin. *Action:* Alterative, astringent, laxative,
detergent.

The walnut tree was introduced into Italy from Persia and has been
cultivated in England for centuries. Almost every farmhouse in this
country has a walnut tree in the garden. The wood is valuable for furniture and the fruit makes a good pickle. The juice, taken after fish, is
said to promote digestion.

The rind and the leaves make a good dye, and the oil is liked by
painters for mixing their colours.

107

Nutritious Herbs

On the analogy of the resemblance between the brain and the nut of the tree, the walnut has been regarded as a tonic for the brain and is used as a hair tonic.

Walnuts have tonic and fattening properties and contain a very large proportion of fat and a considerable amount of phosphorus and magnesium. All nuts have an ancient reputation for keeping arteries soft.

Walnut trees must be grown in pairs or they will yield no nuts, unless there is a tree in a neighbouring garden.

GREEN WALNUTS IN SYRUP

Take as many green walnuts as you please about the middle of July. Try them all with a pin, if it goes easily through they are fit for your purpose; lay them in water for nine days, washing and shifting them morning and night, then boil them in water till they be soft, lay them to drain; then pierce them through with a wooden skewer; and in the hole put a clove, and in some a bit of cinnamon and in some the rind of a candied citron, then take the weight of your nuts in sugar, or a little more; make it into a syrup in which boil your nuts (and simmering them) till they be tender; then put them up in gallipots, and cover them close. They are cordial and stomachic. When you lay them to drain, wipe them with a coarse cloth, to take off a thin green skin.

Nutritious Herbs

WHEAT

Now came fulfilment of the year's desire
The tall wheat coloured by the August fire.
WILLIAM MORRIS

For the few hours of life allotted me
Give me Great God but Bread and Libertie.
ABRAHAM COWLEY

Botanical name: Triticum vulgare, Triticum sativum. *Natural order:* Graminaceae. *Country names:* Amel corn, bloody mars, cone wheat, duck wheat, durgan wheat, rivet wheat, dog wheat, red wheat, white wheat. *French names:* Blé, Froment. *German name:* Weizen. *Italian names:* Biada, Grano, Formento comune. *Turkish name:* Bugday. *Arabian name:* Hintah-burr. *Indian name:* Ghaun, Godhama. *Chinese name:* Sian-mek. *Persian name:* Gandam. *Under the dominion of:* Venus. *Symbolical meaning:* Riches. *Part used:* The grains and fecula. *Natural habitat:* The Euphrates region, N.W. India, Central Provinces, Bombay, Europe. *Constituents:* Wheaten flour contains everything in wheat except the cellulose; a part of starch sugar, and a large proportion of gluten. It contains albuminoids 13·5 p.c., starch 68·4, oil 1·2, fibre 2·7, ash 1·7, free extractive 6·7, and saccharine matter. The ash contains phosphorous.

Action: Demulcent, emollient, nutritive, restorative.

The kind of wheat grown varies with the climate and soil.

In England we grow two kinds, spring wheat *T. aestivum*, and winter wheat, *T. hybernum*.

In the seventeenth century we grew Polish wheat, *T. polonicum*, but the fashion has not been revived since Hungarian wheat has been recognized as the best of all.

The wheat or zea of the ancient Greeks, and the Triticum of the Romans, is still grown in Southern Europe, but it requires a coarse soil.

Wheat is still sometimes sown by hand in different parts of the world, but until the end of the seventeenth century this method of sowing was general.

The number of stalks that a single grain of wheat will throw up is a constant source of wonder. A bushel of wheat will yield as much as forty-seven pounds of flour apart from the bran and other parts, which make a further thirteen pounds.

This phenomenon of the wheat plant has naturally called forth legends in the countries of the East and one of the oldest is that quoted from an ancient coptic manuscript by Sir Ernest Wallis Budge in his *Divine Origin of the Craft of the Herbalist.*

'Adam and Eve being expelled from Paradise where they had lived upon choice food, were unable to eat the coarser foods and were nigh to die of starvation. Our Lord who was Adam's sponsor went to the Father and asked Him if He wished Adam, whom he had created in His own image, to die of starvation. In answer the Father told our Lord that He had better give His own flesh to Adam to eat, and He did so. Our Lord took flesh from his right side and rubbed it down into grains and took it to the Father, who on seeing that our Lord had obeyed His command, took some of His own flesh, which was invisible, and formed it into a grain of wheat, and placed it with the flesh of His Son. He then sealed the grain of wheat in the middle with "The seal of Light" and told our Lord to take the grain and give it to Michael the Archangel, who was to take it to Adam, on Earth, and teach him how to sow and reap it, and how to make bread.'

Unfortunately most of the bread made to-day from wheat contains practically no nutriment because the wheat, instead of being stone ground as it used to be, is ground in steam rollers and deprived of the wheat germ, and other nutritious parts of the wheat. There are still a few millers in England who retain the process of stone grinding and wise people obtain the wholemeal flour from them and bake their own bread.

For those who wish to do this the following recipe which has been worked out carefully by Mrs. Gordon Grant and Commander Geoffrey Bowles will be found most satisfactory and will save a great deal of disappointment if it is carefully followed.

I have used the recipe myself and can testify to its excellence and to its simplicity. The right flour can be obtained from Mr. Maurice Woods of Huby, near Leeds.

THE GRANT LOAF

Materials for three loaves. 3½ lbs. English stone ground wholemeal flour; 2 pints of warm water at blood heat (100°F.) 1 ounce of salt or Maldon salt; 1 ounce of sugar, preferably Barbadoes sugar; 1 ounce of yeast.

The important points are (1) to warm the flour and the baking tins, (2) to froth up the yeast separately, (3) to make the dough wet enough to be slippery and (4) that wholemeal dough must not be kneaded and only requires a few minutes to mix.

Nutritious Herbs

Mix the salt with the flour in a large basin and warm it on the oven top or above a low gas flame so that the yeast will work quicker: crumble the yeast into a pudding basin, add the sugar and ¼ pint of the warm water, leave for 10 minutes to froth up. When frothed up, stir to dissolve the sugar and pour this yeasty liquid into the basin of warm flour, add the rest of the warm water and stir the whole with a wooden spoon until the flour is evenly welled.

The resulting dough should be wet enough to be slippery. Most bread is too dry. Wholemeal flours differ in moisture content and in fineness. Dry and finely ground flour needs more than 2 pints of water to make the dough slippery.

Grease three 4-pint tins inside and warm them well. Spoon the dough into the warmed tins, put them about two feet above the low gas flame or over the oven, cover with a cloth and leave for about 20 minutes to rise about a half. When risen bake in a moderate oven (400°F.) for 45 minutes to 1 hour. An oven thermometer is useful. Tapping the top crust with the knuckles will tell by the sound when a loaf is properly baked. The right sound is soon found. When using a gas oven, put the dough-filled tins straight into the cold oven uncovered to rise while warming up to 400°F. Keep at this temperature until properly baked. When baked, turn out the loaves to cool upside down on a wire grid. If the loaves do not come out of the tins easily leave them to cool in the tins for 10 minutes.

The wheat plant contains the anti-sterile Vitamin E and one of the causes of sterility in women to-day is attributed to the loss of the wheat germ in white bread that is so generally eaten. The separation of this from wheat flour raises a very important national question which will have to be faced sooner or later, as will also the need for composting the soil on which the wheat is grown, and rejecting the use of chemical fertilizers. Sir Albert Howard is conducting this crusade with great success.

Before the war which has led to the present state of famine throughout the world the Germans made a health bread which they called 'Sanitasbrod' and as the question of nourishment is such an important one to-day I think it may be of interest to add a report on this bread by Mr. Edward Osborn of Kimberley Road, Cardiff.

SANITASBROD

'It has occurred to me that you and some of your friends who are interested in 'better food for the people' might like to experiment with bread-making on the lines adopted by a large wholesale bakery in, I think it was, Bennweier near Colmar before 1914, which was the extent of my experience of it. The bread, several kinds, was widely distributed through Health stores in Germany.

The chief point about it was that the grain, after being, I believe, dry cleaned, was soaked in water, malted, otherwise just sprouted, then crushed in the mill (I do not know whether stone or steel rollers), the water in which it had been soaked was returned to the mash, this was then leavened with just air being beaten into it in the mass, then baked at a very mild heat—I've no idea at what temperature—for about ten to twelve hours for wheat loaves, fifteen to sixteen for rye, and the same, if I remember rightly, for a delicious wheaten fruit loaf with raisins or chopped dates. Despite the long baking time, loaves and crust were nice and moist. This description had come from a traveller for the firm, which, I think, styled itself *Sanitas Brod Werke.*

I spent some years in Dresden prior to 1914 and this was by far my favourite—rye or wheat—but especially the one with dried fruit, and I seem to remember something like cinnamon or spice flavour of some kind. It was immensely satisfying: with a loaf, nuts (pine kernels for instance), and fresh fruit in one's knapsack as emergency rations, I have wandered many a mile through the beautiful country over there and felt as fit as the proverbial fiddle.

I feel quite sure that if our miners and others at so-called heavy jobs could have this bread and, N.B., masticate it thoroughly, they would not be reminded of the well-known Bovril advertisement, 'That sinking feeling'.

The loaves were of a dark brown colour, the rye in particular being very dark, more or less chocolate colour, AND, there was something to taste in it, too, not the insipid non-committal touch on the tongue that one gets with our white loaf.

I remember, too, hearing from a German officer that recruits from the country districts where whole corn bread was usually eaten, were more sturdy and had better teeth than those from, say, the French border where the emasculated white loaf had invaded the countryside and the towns. German army authorities were thoroughly alive to this: the German army bread was whole corn rye—milled corn of course, not a kind of baked frumenty! It had to be chewed.'

CHAPTER TWO

BITTER HERBS

Angostura; Balmony; Barberry; Bayberry; Bogbean; Boldo; Calumba; Camomile; Centaury; Chiretta; Dandelion; Fringe tree; Gentian; Gold Thread; Liverwort; Oak; Quassia; Rauwolfia; Simaruba; Tulip Tree; Wormwood; Yellow-wort

Bitters is a popular name for alcoholic drinks which combine the properties of an appetiser and a tonic. They are generally combined with gin or vermouth, or they are ingredients of cocktails. Bitters are tinctures or extracts of bitter aromatic herbs, like angostura or bitter orange. These are the two most popular bitter herbs.

Much less well known, and equally good as tonics, are stomachics like centaury, gentian, condurango, chiretta and camomile. They assist digestion and give a zest to the appetite.

The word 'zest' was invented for lemon peel, because it was so generally used in hot and cold punches as a bitter tonic. Stomachic roots like calamus, canella, cinnamon, nutmeg, allspice and cascarilla are generally reserved for punches.

Calumba—an African herb—is a typical stomach bitter. It improves the assimilation of food and gives tone to the organs of digestion. Yellow gentian is another excellent and dependable bitter tonic. It is a rapid restorative in cases of general debility and combines well with another bitter herb called centaury, which has anti-malarial and antiseptic properties.

Quassia is a good remedy for inactive digestive organs. It has been known to influence some forms of catarrh, but it is exceedingly bitter. Condurango is a good bitter herb, which relieves the burning pains of gastritis. Peppermint controls other acute pains of indigestion. Dandelion is a mild liver tonic and stimulates the flow of bile into the duodenum. It combines well with buckbean, another splendid bitter tonic.

Simaruba is a useful tonic when the digestion has become enfeebled after attacks of fevers.

Chiretta is so safe that it can be given to children, so can gold thread,
113

a plant allied to the hellebores and found in extreme northerly countries like Iceland and Greenland.

Yellow-wort is one of the gentians and shares their bitter tonic properties. The ancients had such a belief in the tonic properties of the wormwoods that they christened them artemesia after the goddess Diana, who is said to have discovered them and revealed their virtues to Chiron, the centaur. Wormwood is an antidote to mushroom poisoning. Absinthe is made from the common wormwood which contains an alkaloid called absinthol, but the wormwoods are an ingredient of other liqueurs besides absinthe.

Culpeper was enthusiastic about the properties of the Roman wormwood, *Artemisia pontica*, and he also praised the sea wormwood, which he considered less powerful in its action. It was common in his days to infuse the flowers in brandy for five or six weeks and to take a teaspoonful before meals as an appetiser.

The Germans used to make an excellent wormwood wine, with the *Artemisia pontica* which they drank to increase their appetite. The whole family of wormwoods are extremely bitter, and 'bitter as wormwood' is a very old proverb.

The camomiles, like the wormwoods, are composite plants. They have a pleasant bitterness and are aromatic. The Spanish manzanilla, a sherry more drunk in Spain than in England, is flavoured with one of the camomiles; and the *Anthemis nobilis* was known to the Greeks who called it 'Easter Apple' because of its flavour; this particular camomile still goes by the name of Roman camomile and makes a very pleasant tea, the bitterness is not too pronounced and it soothes the nerves and greatly assists digestion. Gerarde recommended it as a cure for weariness.

The German chamomile, *Chamomilla matricaria*, is particularly adapted to children's complaints and is the cure *par excellence* for the nightmare that they often suffer from.

All the camomiles are bitter tonics, though some of the species, such as the wild mayweed, are unpleasantly strong.

Nearly all bitter tonic herbs allay fevers and restore elasticity to relaxed tissues. They can be taken in small doses over a long period with great benefit, especially after prostrating illnesses and prolonged nervous strain.

Infusions can be made from any of the herbs I have mentioned, and they do not need the addition of alcohol to make them effective, though if added to alcoholic drinks they make the alcohol less intoxicating.

114

Bitter Herbs

ANGOSTURA

Its principal action medicinally is on the spinal motor nerves and the mucous membranes. It is a cure for paralytic complaints.

Botanical names: Cusparia febrifuga (D.C.), Galipea officinalis. *Natural order:* Rutaceae. *Country names:* Cusparia bark. *French name:* Cusparie. *German name:* Cuspabaum. *Italian name:* Cusparia. *Turkish name:* Kusbaria. *Part used:* Dried bark. *Natural habitat:* Tropical South America. *Constituents:* Angosturin, a colourless crystalline substance soluble in water, alcohol or ether. The bark contains galipene, cusparine, galipidine, cusparadine, and cuspareine, about 1·5 p.c. of volatile oil and a glucoside which yields a fluorescent substance when hydrolysed by heating with dilute sulphuric acid. *Action:* Bitter tonic, febrifuge.

Angostura bark is one of the pleasantest of the bitter tonics, and is therefore largely used commercially in the manufacture of liqueurs and bitters. It has been known medicinally for centuries to the natives of the West Indies and of South America, as a bitter tonic and febrifuge. It is also used in dropsy, and has a reputation as an antispasmodic in tetanus, and as a cure for caries of the long bones. It is prescribed internally and externally for ulcers. It can be taken in alternation with phytolacca.

The introduction of angostura bark into Europe is of comparatively recent date. It was first used in Madrid in 1759, and a few years later was made known in England through Queen Charlotte's apothecary, Brande.

The natives stupefy fish with it as the Peruvians do with cinchona bark.

The shrub grows to about twenty feet in height. It has white flowers which have a peculiar odour, and the leaflets when bruised emit a tobacco-like scent. It grows in great profusion in Columbian Guiana, and thrives best in rich soil.

115

Bitter Herbs

BALMONY

These are rather dull looking and unrefined pentstemons. The pride of the family, however, has passed away into the rich house of pentstemons, and must there be looked for as P. barbatus.

REGINALD FARRER

Botanical name: Chelone glabra (Linn.). *Natural order:* Scrophulariaceae. *Country names:* Turtle head, turtle bloom, shell flower, salt rheum weed, bitter herb, chelone oblique, glatte, white chelone, the hummingbird tree, snake head. *French names:* Chélone, Galane. *German names:* Kahler fünffaden, Schildblume. *Italian name:* Galana spicata. *Turkish name:* Tosbagi çiç. *Part used:* Herb fresh. *Natural habitat:* Eastern United States and Canada.

Balmony is a pretty plant that prefers damp places. The corolla of the flower is shaped like a tortoise hence its botanical name. The flowers grow in terminal spikes of two lipped white, rose, or purple flowers. The lower lip is bearded in the throat, and the anthers are heart shaped.

To gardeners it is better known as Chelone.

It is a favourite tonic of the American Indian. The leaves are antibilious, and have a peculiar action on the liver. Boericke says of it, 'The herb is an enemy to every kind of worm that infests the human body'. It is a remedy for the left lobe of the liver.

There are several species of chelone, but the most attractive as a garden plant is the *Chelone barbatus*, which flowers all through the late summer and autumn. It is rather similar to a pentstemon and is, in fact, now classed as one. The tubular heads are either pink or scarlet and the plant does well in crevices or as I grow it, in the front of an herbaceous border.

BALMONY—CHELONE GLABRA

Bitter Herbs

BARBERRY

Conserve of Barbarie: quincies as such,
With sirops that easeth the sickly so much.

Good Housewife Physicke, 1573.

Next her Orcimelis and achras stood,
Whose offspring is a sharp and rigid brood;
A fruit no season e'en could work upon,
Not to be mellow'd by th' all ripening sun.

ABRAHAM COWLEY

Botanical name: Berberis vulgaris. *Natural order:* Berberidaceae. *Country names:* Barbaryn, barboranne, berber, guild, jaundice berry, maiden barber, pepperidge, piperidge, piperidges, piprage, piperidge tree, rilts, woodsore, woodsour, woodsower. *French names:* Épine-vinette, Vinettier. *German names:* Berberize, Gemeiner Sauerdorn. *Italian names:* Berberi, Berbero, Crespino, Uvetta, Scotanella. *Indian names:* Zirishk, Kashmal, Chachar. *Persian name:* Bedana. *Turkish name:* Diken üzümü. *Arabian name:* Ambar-baris. *Under the dominion of:* Mars. *Symbolical meaning:* Sharpness of temper. *Parts used:* Bark, root bark, berries. *Natural habitat:* Cultivated in European gardens including England but a native of Northern Africa and parts of Asia. *Constituents:* Berberine and a peculiar resinous matter. The fruit contains malic and citric acids and tannin.

All plants containing berberine are of value in medicine.

The common barberry is one of the best of all liver tonics because its bitter principle is more closely allied to human bile than any other substance. It is used in jaundice, gall complaints, and in catarrh, and is a good remedy in diabetes because it allays the thirst that often accompanies that disease.

Two other species are used in English medicine, the *Berberis Aquifolium* and the *Berberis aristata.* In India they also make use of *Berberis asiatica, Berberis coriacea, Berberis lycium* and *Berberis nepalensis.* The Indian medicine known as 'Rasaut' is prepared from *Berberis lycium* which has been identified as the plant known to Pliny.

Many species of barberry are cultivated in the garden because they thrive well in rockeries and shady places, and some of them have very decorative flowers and berries. The common barberry has attractive yellow flowers which are succeeded by purple or yellow berries. The most beautiful species of all is the *Berberis japonica* var. *Hiemalis* which has long racemes of cream-coloured flowers, smelling of lilies-of-the-valley. It comes into bloom in my garden about Christmas and is followed by lovely purple berries.

Another attractive variety not much known is *Berberis repens*, the carpeting barberry which grows about a foot high, spreads quickly and does not get leggy.

BARBERRIES TO PICKLE

Take white wine vinegar; to every quart of vinegar put a half pound of sixpenny sugar, then pick the worst of your barberries and put into this liquor, and the best into glasses; then boil your pickle with the worst of your barberries and skim it very clean. Boil it till it looks of a fine colour then let it stand to be cold before you strain; then strain it through a cloth, wringing it to get all the colour you can from the barberries. Let it stand to cool and settle, then pour it clear into the glasses in a little of the pickle; boil a little fennel, when cold, put a little bit at the top of the pot or glass, and cover it close with a bladder and leather. To every half pound of sugar put a quarter of a pound of white salt.

TO PRESERVE BARBERRIES

Take the ripest and best barberries you can find; take the weight of them in sugar; then pick out the seeds and tops, wet your fingers with the juice of them, and make a syrup: then put in your barberries and when they boil take them off, and shake them, and set them on again, and let them boil, and repeat the same, till they are clean enough to put into glasses.

In Nepal the berries of the *Berberis aristata* are dried and used as raisins, and a good yellow dye is extracted in India from the same plant.

Bitter Herbs

BAYBERRY

And of the spicy myrtles as they blow,
And of the roses amorous of the moon
And of the lilies that do paler grow.

KEATS

Botanical name: Myrica cerifera (Linn.). *Natural order:* Myricaceae.
Country names: Wax myrtle, candle berry, tallow shrub. *French names:*
Arbre à la cire, Cirier. *German names:* Wachsgagel, Wachsmyrte.
Italian names: Albero della cera, Pianta della cera, Mortella cerifera.
Indian name: Kataphala. *Persian names:* Kandula, Darshishaan. *Turkish
name:* Mom ag. *Parts used:* Root bark, seeds. *Natural habitat:* Eastern
North America, Himalaya, Nepal. *Constituents:* The bark contains
tannin, saccharine matter and salts. *Action:* Alterative, astringent,
aromatic, diaphoretic, stimulant.

All the myrtles are remarkable for their aromatic and astringent
properties, and the bayberry is a favourite herbal remedy for liver complaints. The berries contain a green candle wax which burns brightly.

This is probably the species of Myrtle mentioned by Garcia de Orta
in 1562 and referred to as avacani, the root of which smelt of cloves,
and which cured a girl of dysentery when all else failed.

It grows near the Atlantic coast in the sand belt, and on the shores of
Lake Erie.

It is a cleansing and comforting tonic for the liver.

Sweet gale, of which there is an account in my book, *Herbal Delights*,
belongs to the same family, and is a native of Great Britain.

Bitter Herbs

BOGBEAN

Buckee, Buckee, biddy Bene
Is the way now fair and clean?
Is the goose y gone to nest?
And the fox y gone to rest?
Shall I come away?

AN OLD NURSERY RHYME

Botanical name: Menyanthes trifoliata (Linn.). *Natural order:* Gentianaceae. *Country names:* Buckbean, marsh clover, water trefoil, bean trefoil, beckbean, bog-hop, bog nut, brookbean, marsh cleaver, marsh
claver, marsh clover, dondlar, treefold. *French names:* Ménianthe,
Trèfle d'eau. *German names:* Sumpffieberklee, Fieberklee. *Italian names:*
Scarfano, Trefoglio d'acqua. *Turkish name:* Su yoncasi. *Symbolical
meaning:* Calm repose. *Part used:* Herb. *Natural habitat:* Europe including north of England and Scotland. *Action:* Cathartic, deobstruent,
febrifuge, tonic.

The bogbean plant is common in the north of England and in Scotland, though rare in the south of England. It can be successfully cultivated in moist, peaty soils such as azaleas and rhododendrons like. It is
a water plant and likes marshy bogs. Its rose-coloured flowers which
grow in clusters are very decorative and rather like a lily; when the
flowers open they reveal a white silk fringe.

Its botanical name *Menyanthes* denotes that it flowers for a month.

Medicinally the plant is excellent for gouty rheumatism.

The roots can be infused in wine, or added to whey, or an infusion
of the leaves can be drunk. It combines with burdock, wormwood,
centaury and sage.

It has been used successfully, Dr. Fernie says, in the early stages of
amaurotic paralysis of the retina.

In Sweden it is used as a substitute for hops, and the Laplanders boil
the roots and eat them as a vegetable.

It makes such a firm bed in the morasses where it grows in Iceland
that Sir William Hooker remarks on its usefulness to the traveller who
knows that wherever the plant grows he can cross in safety.

Bitter Herbs

BOLDO

An evergreen shrub with large oval aromatic green leaves.

Botanical name: Peumus boldus (Molino). *Natural order:* Monimiaceae.
Country name: Boldo wood tree. *French names:* Boldu, boldo. *German name:* Chilensicher boldobaum. *Italian name:* Boldo. *Turkish name:* Boldu ag. *Parts used:* leaves, bark. *Natural habitat:* Chile. *Constituents:* Boldine or Boldoin—a glucoside obtained from the leaves 1·5 p.c., and a volatile oil 2 p.c. *Action:* Antiseptic, stimulant, tonic and slightly narcotic.

In small doses Boldo is a good tonic in chronic hepatic diseases. In Chile the bark is preferred to the leaves. It is a good remedy for gall complaints, and loss of appetite. It stimulates the gastric juices, and has a popular sale in the French herb shops for liver complaints.

It grows in Chile in the fields of the Andes, and has greenish-yellow fruit which is edible. The bark is used for tanning.

CALUMBA

One of the few bitter tonics that does not contain tannic or gallic acids.

Botanical names: Jateorhiza plamata, Jateorhiza calumba (Miers.).
Natural order: Menispermaceae. *Country name:* Cocculus palmatus.
Arabian name: Sakel hamam. *Indian names:* Kalamb-kachri, Kalamb-ki-jer. *Persian name:* Bikle. *Part used:* Dried root sliced transversely.
Natural habitat: Forests of Eastern Africa, abundant in the forests of Mozambique. *Constituents:* Calumbin, a white bitter crystalline principle, berberine, the alkaloid, identical with the alkaloid of *Berberis vulgaris*, calumbic acid, no tannin.

In many ways the calumba plant resembles yellow parilla. It is an herbaceous vine, climbing over trees in the forests of Mozambique. The flowers are borne in pendulous axillary panicles—the female flowers have six sepals, six abortive stamens and three pistils—the male have

121

six perfect stamens but are otherwise the same. The roots are rather like parsnips but are much larger, more cylindrical, and grow in clusters.

Calumba resembles golden seal as a gastric tonic, but it is not such a positive tonic to the nervous system. It is an excellent restorative, improves general nutrition, increases the flow of saliva and of the gastric juices, improves appetite, and strengthens the digestion generally.

It prevents sea-sickness, and does not constipate or produce nausea or headaches. It is an intestinal disinfectant and an anthelmintic, but it should not be taken in large doses, or over an extended period.

CAMOMILE

The anthemis a small but glorious flower
Scarce rears his head, yet has a giant's tower:
Forces the lurking fever to retreat,
(Ensconc'd like Caeus in his smoky seat)
Recruits the feeble joints, and gives them ease
He makes the burning inundation cease;
And when his force against the stone is sent,
He breaks the rock and gives the waters vent.

ABRAHAM COWLEY

Botanical name: Roman: Anthemis nobilis, *German:* Chamomilla officinalis. *Natural order:* Compositae. *French names: Roman:* Anthemis noble, Chamomille romaine, *German:* Camomille. *German names: Roman:* Romisch Kamille, *German:* Hundskamille. *Italian names: Roman:* Camomilla odorosa, *German:* Camomilla. *Turkish names: Roman:* Papatye cic, *German:* Papatya. *Spanish name: Roman:* Manzanilla. *Under the dominion of:* The Sun. *Symbolizes:* Energy in adversity. *Part used:* Herb. *Natural habitat:* Europe. *Constituents:* The active principles are a volatile oil, of a pale blue colour (becoming yellow by keeping) a little anthemic acid (the bitter principle) tannic acid and a glucoside. *Action:* Anodyne, antispasmodic, stomachic, tonic.

The Roman camomile is the species with which gardeners are most familiar. It befriends all other plants, especially the sickly ones, by its presence, because it contributes to the health of the soil and keeps away obnoxious pests. Hence its old name—plants' physician. What it does for the plants it also does for human beings, relieving their pain and removing weariness from every part of the body. This is why it is used in baths.

The medicinal value of the plant is chiefly concentrated in the yellow centres of the flowers, and the double variety of flowers is most prized.

This double-flowered camomile was introduced into Germany from Spain during the Middle Ages, and had a well-established healing reputation in the sixteenth century.

Camomile tea is a simple and excellent remedy for soothing the nerves and assisting digestion, but it should not be used to excess. Locally it makes a good poultice to relieve toothache and other pains.

The wild camomile, which is generally known as German camomile, is chiefly used to cure children's nightmare. Externally it can be used to subdue pain in the same way as the Belgian or Roman camomile.

CENTAURY

Wormwood and centaury, their bitter juice
To aid digestion's sickly powers, refine.

DODSLEY

Botanical name: Erythraea centaurium (Pers.). *Natural order:* Gentianaceae. *Country names:* Banwort, bitter herb, bloodwort, century, Christ's ladder, earth gall, feltrike, feverfew, gall of the earth, hurdreve, sanctuary. *French names:* Petite centaurée, herbe à la fièvre. *German names:* Tausendgüldenkraut. *Italian names:* Centaurea minore, Biondella. *Turkish name:* Kücük kantaryon. *Under the dominion of:* The sun. *Symbolical meaning:* Delicacy. *Part used:* Herb and leaves. *Natural habitat:* All parts of Europe and North Africa. *Constituents:* Erythro-centaurin.

Centaury is one of the safest of all the bitter tonic herbs, and has been used in England for centuries, either alone or combined with gentian. It was called by the ancients sal terrae, or salt of the earth. It is difficult to cultivate, but it grows wild in barren fields, on heaths, and sometimes in woods, and on chalky cliffs near the sea; its red star-like flowers are a familiar object to country people who use it for fevers—feverwort being one of its old names. Actually the white flowered variety is considered the most useful medicinally. The flowers never open after noon, and only open in fine weather.

For all weaknesses of the stomach, jaundice, agues and gout, there is no better or safer remedy. Its name is derived from two Greek words meaning 'red'; and Chiron the Centaur, who was skilled in its use. The Greeks named it gall of the earth.

CHIRETTA

Though toke she Feldwodde and Verveyne,
of herbes ben not better tweyne.

GOWER

Botanical name: Swertia chirata (Buck-Ham). *Natural order:* Gentiana-ceae. *Country names:* Indian gentian, Indian balmony. *French name:* Swertie. *German name:* Driesenenzian. *Italian name:* Swertia. *Arabian name:* Kasab-ud-daura. *Indian names:* Chirata, Kalapnath, Kalamegh. *Persian name:* Dowa-i-pechish. *Part used:* Herb. *Natural habitat:* Northern India, Nepal, the Transvaal. *Constituents:* Ophelic acid, an amorphous bitter principle; chiratin, a yellow bitter glucoside; resin, gum, carbonates and phosphates of potash, lime and magnesia; ash 4-6 p.c.; no tannin. *Action:* Anthelmintic, alterative, febrifuge, tonic.

Chiretta is an Indian bitter plant which grows in great abundance in the temperate Himalayas, and was used extensively by the Mohamme-dan doctors in the past. Hindu doctors to-day find it an excellent sub-stitute for gentian, and experiments made in the schools of tropical medicine pronounce most favourably on its therapeutic value as a stomachic, febrifuge and anthelmintic. It is closely allied to an English plant called felwort, which at one time had a great vogue among herbal-ists. Felwort is occasionally found on limestone hills in England. It has a very erect habit, square stems often tinted with purple, and purple flowers.

Chiretta is an important ingredient in a well-known Indian fever powder called Sadurashana-Churana, which is sold in the bazaars.

It is a good remedy in hyperacidity, removes biliousness, increases digestion, and cures gout.

It is cultivated in England, and it grows in the Transvaal where it is used as a bitter tonic. It contains two intensely bitter substances, chiratin and ophelic acid, the former being an alkaloid.

DANDELION

Shockheaded dandelion,
That drank the fire of the sun:
Hawkweed and marigold,
Cornflower and campion.

ROBERT BRIDGES

Botanical name: Taraxacum officinale (Weber). *Natural order:* Compositae. *Country names:* Swine snout, puff ball, lion's tooth, white wild endive, priest's crown. *French names:* Dent de lion, pissenlit, chicorée sauvage. *German names:* Kuhblume, Löwenzahn. *Italian names:* Dente di lieone, Radicchiallar, Tarassaco, Soffione. *Turkish name:* Kara hindiba otu, Yabani aci marul. *Indian name:* Dudhal, Baran, Kinphul. *Persian name:* Tarkhash kun. *Under the dominion of:* Jupiter. *Symbolical meaning:* Rustic oracle, depart. *Part used:* Fresh and dried root, herb. *Natural habitat:* Europe, Himalaya, N.W. provinces, N. America. *Constituents:* The milky juice contains a bitter amorphous principle—taraxacin, a crystalline principle, taraxacerin, also potassium and calcium salts, resinoid and glutinous bodies. The root contains inulin 25 p.c.; pectin, sugar, lavulin, ash 5–7 p.c. *Action:* Aperient, diuretic, tonic, an hepatic stimulant given in large doses.

Dandelion is largely used in liver and kidney complaints. The roots are cooked as a vegetable in France, and put into broth, and in Germany are sliced and added to salads. Roasted they make a good substitute for coffee. The country people in England make the leaves and flowers into wine.

The word Taraxacum refers to the many disorders for which the plant is a cure.

As a medicine, dandelion has been recognized as an important alterative and cholagogue since the time of Avicenna. It stimulates the flow of bile into the duodenum, and strengthens the power of the liver to eliminate and so relieve congestion It has a good effect on many skin complaints and is a simple, safe and often effective remedy in most forms of rheumatism.

Dandelion is derived from 'dent de lion' because the leaf is shaped like the teeth of a lion. This grooving of the leaves is nature's ingenious way of supplying the plant with water, by conducting it straight to the root through the rosette of leaves.

FRINGE TREE

It will quickly overcome the jaundice of childhood.

ELLINGWOOD

Botanical name: Chionanthus virginica (Linn.). *Natural order:* Oleaceae. *Country names:* Snowdrop tree, poison ash, snow flower. *French names:* Chionanthe, Arbre de neige. *German name:* Schneeflockenbaum. *Italian names:* Chionanto, Albero di neve mandrap, Fior di neve. *Turkish name:* Karag, Kar çiç. *Part used:* Root bark. *Natural habitat:* U.S.A. from Pennsylvania to Tennessee. *Constituents:* Chionanthin, saponin; solvents —alcohol, water. *Action:* Alterative, aperient, cholagogue, acra narcotic, diuretic, febrifuge, tonic.

This species of Chionanthus is indigenous to the United States of America, ranging from the southern portion of Pennsylvania southwards to Florida and Texas. It is found in rich woods along the edges of streams. The shrub grows from eight to twenty-five feet high and has magnolia-like leaves and flowers resembling snowdrops, which grow in panicles and appear in late spring or early summer.

The root has a specific influence on the liver. It liquefies the bile, and is an excellent remedy in malarial conditions, but though it prevents the formation of stones and helps to expel those already formed Ellingwood considers it is not the remedy for jaundice due to permanent occlusion of the gall duct. It is very helpful in curing the jaundice of childhood and it has been claimed that the root, made into a cataplasm, will heal wounds without causing suppuration.

Another species, *Chionanthus fragrans* is known to most gardeners because of its sweet scent and its habit of flowering in the middle of winter.

FRINGE TREE—CHIONANTHUS VIRGINICA

Bitter Herbs

GENTIAN

'See how the giant spires of yellow bloom
of the sun loving Gentian, in the heat
are shining on those naked slopes like flame.'

Should Maro ask me in what region springs
The race of flow'rs inscrib'd with names of kings
I answer, that, of flow'rs deservedly crown'd
With royal titles, many may be found,
In royal loosestrife royal gentian grace
Our gardens, proud of such a princely race.

COWLEY

Botanical name: Gentiana lutea (Linn.). *Natural order:* Gentianaceae. *Country names:* Yellow gentian, fillwort, bitterwort, baldmoney. *French names:* Gentiane jaune, Grande gentiane. *German name:* Gelberenzian. *Italian names:* Genziana gialla, Genzian maggiore. *Turkish name:* Güsad. *Indian name:* Pakhanbhed. *Arabian name:* Jintiyania. *Persian name:* Gintiyana. *Under the dominion of:* Mars. *Symbolical meaning:* I love you best when you are sad. *Part used:* Root. *Natural habitat:* Swiss mountains, also found in the Pyrenees, the Apennines, the Black Forest, Corsica, Sardinia and in the Balkans. *Constituents:* Gentopierin, gentisic acid, gentianose 14 p.c., pectin, gum, sugar, a trace of volatile oil 6 p.c., ash 8 p.c., no tannin.

The gentian plant is called after Gentius, a king of Illyria. There is a legend that it was revealed as a cure for plague to King Ladislaus of Hungary, when he prayed that his people might be saved from the pestilence that was ravaging the country.

Several species of gentian are used in medicine, but the yellow gentian, which is common in the Swiss mountains, is considered the best variety. It contains no tannin or astringent properties, and is valuable as a tonic in dyspepsia and other illnesses, because it does not constipate. It increases the appetite, and is used in low fevers, and as a tonic in anaemia. Gentian wine was a popular aperitif in the eighteenth century, and a liqueur is still made from it in Switzerland.

The English marsh gentian is of great benefit in cases of enlarged spleen and torpid liver. It has a special influence on the portal veins.

Bitter Herbs

Take of Gentian root, half an ounce.
Cinchona bark, one ounce.
Seville orange peel dried, 2 drachms.
Canella alba, one drachm.
Diluted alcohol, four ounces.
Spanish white wine, two pounds and a half.

First pour the diluted alcohol on the root and barks, sliced and bruised, and, after twenty-four hours, add the wine; then macerate for seven days and strain.

Wines of this kind are sometimes introduced at the table of epicures in Italy, to assist the stomach in digestion. The quantity given is from two to three drachms, in water, three or four times a day, or an hour before dinner, to create an appetite and assist digestion.

One variety of gentian (*Sabbatia campestre*) has rose-coloured flowers and is an arresting sight in midsummer in the prairies of America. The gentian, amarella, with small lavender flowers also grows in America; and the blue gentians fringed and shaded from the daylight blue to the palest sky blue are to be found from Quebec to Manitoba in bloom in the autumn. New Zealand produces a group of gentians with bronze coloured foliage and white flowers, of which the easiest to grow is *G. saxosa*. Of the European gentians *G. acaulis* is the most popular because of its dazzling blue trumpet flowers, but it does well in few gardens. I have found *Gentian asclepiadea*, the willow gentian, much the easiest. In my garden it is planted in a badly drained border where the soil is sticky and moist, and it does remarkably well, flowering in late July and early August. The loveliest of all gentians is the magnificent hybrid, *G. macaulyi*, which flowers in August and September and has large trumpet flowers of a celestial blue.

CYCLOPOEDIA OF BOTANY

Excellent Stomachic.

Thinly slice two ounces of gentian root, chop small one ounce of dried seville orange peel, add half an ounce of cardaman seeds bruised and husked and infuse the whole in a quart of brandy for twelve days, shaking it once a day, except the last day. Filter it through blotting-paper and take a dessertspoonful two hours before meals.

Bitter Herbs

GOLD THREAD

Parasitical orchids cover the trunks
Of oak, while Thalictrum and Geranium
Grow under their shade.
            Hooker's Himalayan Journal

Botanical name: Coptis trifolia. *Natural order:* Ranunculaceae. *Other names:* Helleborus trilobus, mouthroot, vegetable gold, chrusa borealis, Anemone greenlandica, coptide, Helleborus pumilus. *French names:* Savoyarde, Rue des Près. *German name:* Falscher Rhabarber. *Italian names:* Cottide, Ruta dei prati. *Turkish name:* Altun ipligi. *Arabian name:* Uruk. *Assam name:* Tita. *Indian name:* Mishonitita, mamira, mahmira. *Chinese names:* Nuang lien, Soulene, Chynlen. *Part used:* Dried rhizome, with roots, stems and leaves. *Natural habitat:* North America, Asia, Greenland, Iceland and the mountainous regions bordering on Upper Assam. *Constituents:* Berberine $8\frac{1}{2}$ p.c., a colourless alkaloid coptine and resin. *Action:* Alterative, anti-periodic, stomachic, tonic, stimulant.

The gold thread plant is a small trifoliate perennial—a native of Canada and Siberia. It is used by the natives to dye skins and wool. As a medicine it is sold in large quantities in the dried herb shops of Boston. It contains berberine. Medicinally it restores appetite, improves digestion, reduces inflammation of the liver and spleen, influences the gall bladder and stimulates the mucous membranes. It is a useful tonic to assist in the curing of dipsomania.

Locally it makes a good gargle.

In India it has a good reputation in the treatment of eyes.

An allied species *Thalictrum folliolosum,* with similar properties, is also called gold thread and the root is often mistaken and substituted deliberately for *Coptis trifolia.* It is a good febrifuge and is sometimes used as a substitute for rhubarb. The French call it Rue de près, the Germans, Falscher rhabarber and the Italians, Ruta dei prati.

The thalictrums grow easily from seed and are very often planted at the back of herbaceous borders because they grow to a height of about six feet, and have mauve flowers and pretty maiden-hair foliage.

LIVERWORT

The noble liverwort does next appear,
Without a speck, like the unclouded air;
A plant of noble use and endless fame,
The liver's great preserver, hence its name.

ABRAHAM COWLEY

Botanical names: Peltigera canina (Hoffm.), Lichen cinereus terrestris. *Natural order:* Lichenes. *Country names:* Ground liverwort, lichen caninus, land lung. *Under the dominion of:* Jupiter. *Symbolical meaning:* Confidence. *Part used:* Lichen. *Natural habitat:* Britain, on molehills and mud walls. *Action:* Tonic, demulcent.

English liverwort is a lichen found on molehills and on mud walls throughout Britain.

It is in no way related to the American liverwort, a member of the buttercup family, or to the water liverwort, the white liverwort, or the wood liverwort.

It was formerly greatly valued as a remedy for hydrophobia, and is now recommended by herbalists as a mild, safe, and effective tonic for the liver—hence its name.

Iceland moss and the Indian remedy, stone flowers, are also lichens, and are prescribed for their tonic and demulcent properties. There are no poisonous plants belonging to this family.

The distinctive character of liverwort is its rounded lobes and greyish colour. It is downy above but whitish underneath and has white rootlets.

OAK

Lord of the wood, the long surviving oak.

COWPER

Botanical name: Quercus robur. *Natural order:* Cupuliferae. *Country names:* Aac, acherne, achorn, ackern, ackeron, acorntree, aik, aik tree, akcorn, ake, akers, akehorn, akernel, akeron, akher, akhern, akran, akyr, archarde, atckern, atchorn, cups and ladles, cups and saucers, eike tree, frying-pans, hatch horn, Jove's nuts, knappers, mace, mast, oak atchern, ovest, pipes, rump, trail, woke, wuk, yackrans, yak, yapper, yeaker, yek, yik. *French names:* Bouvre, chêne pédonculé, chêne à grappes. *German names:* Stieleiche, Rotheiche, Roteiche. *Italian names:* Rovere, Quercia peduncolata, Eschio farnia, Querciola, Querce maschia, Querce rovere. *Turkish name:* Pelud mesesi. *Under the dominion of:* Jupiter. *Symbolical meaning:* Hospitality. *Constituents:* Quercitannic acid 10 p.c., oak red, quercin, resin, and pectin. Queri-citannic acid is a yellowish or reddish brown, amorphous mass. Virtues extracted by water or alcohol. *Action:* Astringent, febrifuge, tonic.

The English oak is an indigenous tree and is deeply rooted in the history of Great Britain. The Druids protected the oak tree; and later national sentiment turned it into a symbol of our strength because our English grown oaks built our ships. Until the age of steam and steel our navy was built of oak, and until our coal resources were exploited our iron ore was smelted by oak wood fires. The famous hammer ponds of Sussex are surrounded by oak trees curiously shaped because their branches were lopped off to feed the fires.

Oaks also provide the material for tanning hides and leather, and in the Middle Ages acorns gave fodder for the herds of pigs which provided the medieval Englishman with his principal meat supply.

The gospel meetings of the time of Herrick were held under oak trees which became known as gospel oaks, and these oak trees were famous for a hundred years or more. The oak tree was so much a symbol of England that, until the crown replaced it, an oak tree appeared on every English coin.

The strength of the tree can be imparted through an infusion of the bark, and medicinally it is regarded as one of the most powerful tonics. Like Peruvian bark it quells fevers and renews tissue.

131

Every part of the tree, from the bark to the acorns and the galls that grow on it, are used in medicine.

Acorns were used in ancient times to cure drunkenness. Galls are still valued for their astringent properties.

QUASSIA

Called after a Negro called Quassy, who first made the bark of the tree known as a remedy for malignant fever.

Botanical names: Picraena excelsa (Lindl.), Simaruba amara. *Natural order:* Simarubeae. *Country names:* Bitter ash, quassia amara, bitter wood, Jamaica quassia, bitter damson. *French name:* Simaroube officinale. *German name:* Simarubabaum. *Italian names:* Simaruba, Corteccia di simaruba. *Turkish name:* Simaruba ag. *Indian names:* Kashshing, Bharangi. *Parts used:* Wood of trunks, branches. *Natural habitat:* Surissam, Jamaica, Guiana, West Indian Islands. *Constituents:* A bitter principle, picrasmin or quassin, an alkaloid, resin, mucilage, pectin, calcium, sodium, nitrate of potash and other salts, no tannin.

Quassia is one of the best of the stomach bitters. It is indicated in extreme inactivity of the digestive organs. It aids assimilation of food and has pronounced tonic effects after prostrating illnesses. It has a marked action on the eyes, is a good febrifuge, and has anthelmintic properties. Quassia is often used to keep away insects and is sprayed when diluted with water on roses and fruit trees to cure blight.

In appearance the tree is rather similar to the ash. It has bright red flowers and the wood is light and very white. All parts of the tree contain a bitter principle which has much the same effect as Peruvian bark in restoring vigour to the debilitated.

It is used by brewers to add bitterness to beer, and by cooks to increase the bitterness of orange marmalade.

QUASSIA—PICRÆNA EXCELSA

RAUWOLFIA

Used in India to antidote the stings of scorpions.

Botanical names: Rauwolfia serpentina, Ophioxylum serpentina. *Natural order:* Apocynaceae. *Indian names:* Chandra, Harkal, Chota-Chand. *Cingalese name:* Avulpori jovana. *Malayan name:* Chivan avelpori. *Sanskrit names:* Sarpagandha, Chandraka. *Part used:* Root. *Natural habitat:* India, Ceylon. *Constituents:* Alkaloid Ophioxylin, an orange-coloured crystalline principle, resin, starch and wax. The ash contains iron and manganese.

Rauwolfia is a climbing plant which grows wild in Java, the Malay States, in the tropical Himalayas and in the plains from Morahabad to Sikkim. It is also found in the Deccan Peninsula and in Assam and other places.

It has been used from the earliest times to antidote the stings of poisonous reptiles.

Medicinally the plant possesses powerful sedative properties and is much prescribed in the treatment of mental disorders, to lower blood pressure, and as a remedy for insomnia and fevers.

It has been used largely by the natives as a narcotic to send excitable children to sleep, and to quieten the insane for whom it is said to be a specific in restoring the mind to a normal condition.

This scarlet-flowered ophioxylum flowers in May in the East Indies and is the only species known.

Bitter Herbs

SIMARUBA

A tree allied to the quassia.

Botanical names: Simaruba amara (D.C.), Simaruba officinalis. *Natural order:* Simarubaceae. *Country names:* Bitter damson, dysentery bark, mountain damson, quassia simaruba, slave wood, stavewood, sumaruppa, maruba. *Part used:* Dried root bark. *Natural habitat:* French Guiana. the islands of Barbados, Dominica, Martinque, St. Lucia and St. Vincent.

The Simaruba tree was imported into France in the early eighteenth century when it was used with greater success than other remedies, in an epidemic of dysentery that broke out in France. The tree grows to a good height and the bark of young trees is grey, smooth and marked with yellow spots. The bark of old trees is black and furrowed. The flowers are yellow and grow in long panicles.

The bitter principle resides in the root bark. It gives its virtues better to cold water than to hot and is particularly recommended for people who have lived a long time in the tropics.

The root bark, which is the part used in medicine, is extremely bitter, but it restores tone to the intestines, helps digestion, promotes proper secretions, and produces sleep.

This tree, which is closely allied to quassia, is a native of tropical America, India and Africa, but is also found in Nepal. The Brazilians steep the bark in brandy which they drink as a tonic. The bark is also used in the making of beer as quassia is.

Bitter Herbs

TULIP TREE

Whose candles light the tulip tree?
What is this subtle alchemy
That builds an altar in one night
And touches the green boughs with light?
Look at the shaped leaves below
And see the scissor marks they show,
As if a tailor had cut fine
The marking of their every line.

SACHEVERELL SITWELL

Botanical name: Liriodendron tulipifera. *Natural order:* Magnoliaceae.
English names: Lyre tree, saddle tree. *French names:* Tulipier, Tulipier
de Virginia. *German name:* Tulpenbaum. *Italian name:* Tulipifero.
Turkish name: Amerika lale otu. *Part used:* Bark. *Natural habitat:*
United States of America, China. *Constituents:* Volatile oil, resin,
liriodendrin, tulipiferine, tannin. *Action:* Bitter tonic, febrifuge.

——— ——————————

The tulip tree is given medicinally as a bitter restorative tonic to improve appetite and as a febrifuge in intermittent fevers. It cures some
forms of rheumatism.

The tulip tree of Brazil, *Physocalymma floribunda*, has a wood of a
very beautiful striped rose colour and is much valued in cabinet making.
The wood of the liriodendron is only esteemed in the same trade because
it takes such a high polish. It is not otherwise of value.

The tulip tree often grows as high as a hundred feet and is one of the
handsomest trees of North America. The scent and brilliance of its
flowers which are large, tulip-like in form, and variegated in colour,
would in themselves make the tree conspicuous, but the leaves have a
peculiar formation which is not found in any other tree. They are three-
lobed. The fruit forms a cone two or three inches long.

The bark is bitter and aromatic.

A fine specimen of the tree can be seen at Longleat.

Bitter Herbs

WORMWOOD

The stomach Eas'd, its office does repeat,
And with new living Fire concocts the meat,
The purple tincture soon it does devour
Nor does the chyle the hungry veins o'erpower.
The visage by degrees fresh roses stain,
And the perfumed breath grows sweet again.
The good I do Venus herself will own.
She, though all sweets, yet loves not sweets alone.

ABRAHAM COWLEY

Botanical names: Common: Artemisia absinthium (Linn.), *Roman:* Artemisia pontica, *Sea:* Artemisia maritima. *Natural order:* Compositae. *French names: Common:* Absinthe Alvine, Herbe aux vers, *Roman:* Petite absinthe, Armoise pontique, *Sea:* Armoise maritime. *German names: Common:* Wermut, Absinth, *Roman:* Römischer Beifuss, *Sea:* Strandbeifuss Seewermut. *Italian names: Common:* Assenzio, A. domestico, *Roman:* Assenzio pontico, Piccolo assenzio, *Sea:* Assenzio marino, Assenziola. *Turkish names: Common:* Absent, *Roman:* Yavsan otu, *Sea:* Deniz Pelini. *Arabian names:* Afsantin-e-hindi, Kashus-Rumi. *Indian names:* Mastaru, Nagdoni, Machiparna, gundmar mastaru, Duna murwa. *Persian names:* Barunga-sif-i-kohi, Artemassaya. *Sanskrit name:* Indhana. *Under the dominion of:* Mars. *Symbolizes:* Absence. *Part used:* Herb. *Natural habitat:* Europe, Siberia, U.S.A. *Constituents:* Volatile oil, a bitter extractive matter (absinthin), tannin, resin, succinic acid, malates and nitrates of potassium and ash 7 p.c., stimulant, narcotic, bitter tonic.

'As bitter as wormwood', is a very ancient saying and all the wormwoods are distinguished by their bitter tonic properties. For this reason wormwood was used by brewers at one time instead of hops.

In the days when herbs were used as disinfectants it was one of the principal strewing herbs.

An old writer says:

> *It is a comfort for hart and the braine,*
> *And therefore to have it is not in vaine.*

The French make absinthe from it and both the French and Italians use it as an ingredient in the vermouth for which both countries are

136

famous. It creates an appetite, stimulates the brain, has febrifuge and tonic properties, and is a useful herb if not used to excess.

It is a good remedy for a weak digestion and according to Dr. John Hill the flowers infused in brandy prevent the formation of gravel, and are helpful in relieving the pain of gout.

Wormwood was dedicated to the goddess Diana, and was greatly esteemed by Hippocrates who claimed that it had such an effect on the brain, that it could restore any disorder there.

The Greeks infused it in their wine to make it less intoxicating.

Mugwort, southernwood, and tarragon, belong to the same family and are closely related.

YELLOW-WORT

Both foliage and stems are thickly covered with that pale sea green bloom, which like the grey powder on the plum, may be rubbed off by the finger.

ANNE PRATT

Botanical name: Chlora perfoliata. *Natural order:* Gentianaceae. *Country names:* Yellow gentian, blackstonie, perfoliate centaury, yellow sanctuary, yellow wort, great centaury, more centaury, yellow centaury, perfoliate yellow wort. *French name:* Clore. *German name:* Biberkraut. *Part used:* Herb. *Natural habitat:* Britain.

The yellow-wort is found on chalky soils in the south of England and in Ireland. It is never a common weed but Anne Pratt says 'on the cliffs of Dover one might see on any summer day a hundred plants during a morning walk, the yellow flowers reminding us, both in form and hue, of some of the garden jessamines. But the yellow-wort is an herbaceous and not a shrubby plant; and its pale sea green stem, a foot or a foot and a half high, runs through the leaves, and like them, is thickly covered with sea green blooms'.

The yellow-wort's yellow flowers only open to the sun. The centre flower unfolds first and closes at noon and the lateral flowers then open and remain open until the sun goes down. The seeds yield a yellow dye as does the whole plant. In medicine the herb is a good bitter tonic, the best English equivalent of the yellow gentian.

137

CHAPTER THREE
TONIC HERBS

Acacia; Anemone; Box; Burr-Marigold; Celery; Cherry; Cle-
rodendron; Combretum; Dodder; Everlasting flower; Heather;
Herb-patience; Hollyhock; Hornbeam; Horsetail; Hydran-
gea; Jacob's Ladder; Jasmine; Labrador Tea; Lady's
Tresses; Love-in-a-mist; Lupins; Magnolia; Maidenhair;
Mango; Marjoram; Marshwort; Masterwort; Papaw;
Peach; Platycodon; Poplar; Pothos; Rhubarb; Rose;
Rose of Jericho; Rue; Saff-Flower; St. John's wort;
Scurvy Grass; Spindle; Squaw vine; Sweet Cicely;
Sweet Sultan; Tansy; Teasels; Thistles; Wafer
Ash; Wallflower; Wild Cinchona; Willows;
Yellow Parilla

It is not generally realized that a tonic can be either a stimulant or a sedative.

Herbalists, like homeopaths, do not use tonics in the accepted familiar sense of the word; they prescribe for whatever is wrong. A relaxed system, or organ, requires toning up or stimulating; an over-stimulated body or brain, or a hyper-active organ, needs soothing and relaxing; and in the vegetable kingdom there are tonics for every condition of the nervous, muscular, or circulatory system, as well as for every organ of the body.

Different herbs have stimulating or quietening and soothing effects on specific organs. There are herbs to nourish the brain, herbs that calm it, herbs that strengthen or stimulate or increase the activity of the lungs, the spleen, the liver, the kidneys, the nerves, the glands, the muscles, the tissues, the bones, the sinews; and there are also herbs that correct and check any tendency to abnormality or hyper-activity in these organs.

In fact, for every herbal stimulant there is a corresponding herbal sedative, and in the case of an overwrought or overstrung nervous or mental condition, a sedative is as much a tonic as is a stimulant in the case of a lethargic or sluggish state of the circulation or glands; like a string in a musical instrument, an organ out of tone can be either sharp or flat, and a tonic is that which retunes.

Some herbal tonics have astringent properties, others are stomachic bitters.

Flabby muscles can be given renewed elasticity by such tonic astringents as the garden wallflower, and tired muscles soothed by black cohosh or other herbs with similar properties. Bones that are decaying require herbs containing calcium, such as barberry. Inflammation of the joints indicates a lack of phosphate of iron, and herbs containing iron are the best medium for administering such mineral salts. Scarred tissue requires herbs that heal; relaxed tissues must be stimulated. Aching bones can be relieved by anodynes and obstructed circulation revitalized by discutient herbs.

Tonics for the blood are called alteratives because they catalyze the mineral salts in the blood and change its chemistry. The best blood tonics are the various sarsaparillas belonging to the Smilax family, most of which contain saponin.

Some herbs, if combined, increase each others' powers, so that when a general nerve tonic is needed it is often more effective to prescribe a blend of herbs. Valerian is one of these, and instead of combining it with bromides which produce an after effect of depression, its tonic or sedative virtues can be increased with skullcap, mistletoe, vervain or black willow.

There are herbs that influence the ductless glands and their secretions, and such herbs have a naturally rejuvenating effect upon the human body.

In fact, every part of the body, from the skull to the toes, can be directly strengthened or soothed by its own appropriate herb.

Tonic Herbs

ACACIA

And over all his rough and writhing boughs and tiniest twigs
Will spread a pale green mist of feathery leaf,
More delicate, more touching than all the verdure
Of the younger, slenderer, gracefuller plants around.
And then when the leaves have grown
Till the boughs can scarcely be seen through their crowded plumes,
There will softly glimmer, scattered upon him blooms,
Ivory white in the green, weightlessly hanging.

J. C. SQUIRE

Botanical name: Acacia senegal (Willd.), Acacia nilotica (Linn.)
Natural order: Leguminosae. *French names:* Acacie à gomme arabique,
Gommier blanc. *German names:* Weissliche akazie, Verekbaum.
Italian name: Acacia del Senegal. *Turkish name:* Beyaz zamk ağ. *Symbolical meaning:* Friendship. *Parts used:* Gum which exudes from the
stem, bark. *Natural habitat:* Sudan, Arabia, India, Morocco. *Constituents:* Gum acacia consists chiefly of Arabin, a compound of arabic
acid with calcium, varying amounts of the magnesium and potassium
salts of the same. The pods contain saponin, malic acid, resin, glucose,
gum and colouring matter. *Action:* Demulcent, nutritious, acid being
also present.

The acacia is a small shrub which grows in dry desert land. It produces
a gum which is nutritious and which is used to relieve coughs either alone
or mixed with marshmallow root or liquorice. It is also used to make
emulsions. The bark of the *Acacia decurrens* or the *A. arabica* is used as
a substitute for Peruvian bark.

In India the native women wash their hair with another species, the
soap acacia of India and Burma, *A. concinna.*

The acacia farnesiane was introduced into Southern Europe from
San Domingo by John Tradescant in 1656, though it was cultivated in
Rome before this date. It has globose heads of highly scented yellow
flowers and is found wild and cultivated in Italy and the south of France.
It grows in great abundance in the valley of the Dead Sea where it is
covered with a parasite with brilliant scarlet flowers so in the distance
the trees look as if they were on fire.

Tonic Herbs

ANEMONE

"When streams his blood then blushing springs a rose,
And when a tear has dropped, a wind flower blows."

Botanical name: Anemone pulsatilla (Linn.). *Natural order:* Ranunculaceae. *Country names:* Easter flower, blue money, Coventry bells, Dane's blood, pasque flower, wind flower, flaw flower, Dane's flower. *French names:* L'herbe au vent, Pulsatille, Fleur de Pâque. *German names:* Kuhschelle, Küchenschelle. *Italian names:* Fiore di vento, Pulsatilla coronaria. Fior de dame. *Turkish name:* Rüzigyar çiç. *Persian name:* Shakaykel-naaman. *Under the dominion of:* Mars. *Symbolical meaning:* Sickness, expectation. *Part used:* Herb. *Natural habitat:* England, Central and Southern Europe and Siberia. Limestone pastures in Berkshire, Oxford and Suffolk and Yorkshire. *Constituents:* An acrid yellow oil, anemonal, which is converted in the presence of water into anemonin or pulsatilla camphor; the chief active principle anemonic acid; an acrid anemone camphor, anemonin, anemoninum or pulsatilla camphor is obtained from various species of anemone. *Action:* Antispasmodic, diuretic, expectorant, emmenagogue, galactagogue, mydriatic, sedative, stimulant.

Pulsatilla is not the species of anemone we are accustomed to see in the woods through England in the spring. The whole plant is covered with silky hairs, and the sepals of the flowers are dark purple in colour and very silky on the underside. The juice of the sepals is often used to dye Easter eggs green. It grows wild in Switzerland and can be grown in England from seed. I have from one packet of seed produced several clumps of this attractive perennial rock plant.

There is another variety with sulphur yellow flowers, *Anemone multifida*, which should be in a rock garden—the *Anemone narcissiflora*, which is akin to the woodland variety, needs protection from a very hot sun.

Pulsatilla is called by homeopaths the weathercock of remedies because it suits best those of a changeable nature, and patients with constantly changing symptoms. The root can be mixed with milk and given as a medicine, or it can be used in the form of an extract or a tincture. It is used in painful affections of the pelvic organs, in nervous headaches, and rheumatism of the joints of the hands and feet. When chewed it increases the secretion of saliva and influences the heart rather like

141

cactus, increasing its power and improving the strength and rate of the pulse; it slows down the rapid pulse of nervous prostration, has a direct influence upon the brain and spinal cord, and gives tone to it and the whole sympathetic system.

Pulsatilla is used by homeopaths in measles and is also given for bronchial asthma.

The roots and flowers are used in Chinese medicine.

The wood anemone, *A. nemorosa*, is also used in medicine as a nerve tonic, and so is *Anemone hepatica* which under the name of American liverwort is an innocent and effective remedy whenever a healing agent is required. It has demulcent and vulnerary properties which are useful in the early stages of consumption, and as a liver tonic it has considerable value.

It makes a pleasant tisane. This anemone is indigenous to the cooler latitude of the north temperate zone. To-day it has been introduced into so many English gardens where its delicate blue flowers soon follow the golden aconites:

> *Blue as the heaven it gazes at*
> *Startling the boisterous in the naked grass*
> *With unexpected beauty, for the time*
> *Of blossoms and green leaves is yet afar.*

BOX

> *I will set in the Desert*
> *The Fir tree, the Pine and the Box.*
>
> Isaiah

Botanical name: Buxus sempervirens (Linn.). *Natural order:* Buxaceae. *Country names:* Dudgeon, bush tree. *French names:* Buis, Buis toujours vert. *German names:* Buchs, Buxbaum. *Italian names:* Bosso, Busso, Auscio, Bossolo, Martello. *Dutch name:* Palm. *Spanish name:* Box. *Turkish name:* Şimşir ağ. *Symbolical meaning:* Stoicism. *Parts used:* Wood, bark, leaves. *Natural habitat:* Western and Southern Europe, Southern and Central England, Himalayas and Japan. *Action:* Alterative, cathartic, diuretic, febrifuge, sudorific, vermifuge.

The box is one of the trees that are traditionally clipped into hedges and edgings. A friend of Julius Caesar is said to have been the originator of the clipped, ornamental box hedge, and Martial speaks of the clipped box trees in the garden of Bassus. The Greeks dedicated the tree to Pluto and firmly believed, Francis Bacon says, that it produced honey and of such a poisonous kind that men were driven mad by it.

The ancients valued box wood because it made the best musical instruments. If left to grow naturally the tree will reach a height of fifteen feet. It grows wild in most parts of Europe. Many villages in England are called after this tree—Box Hill, Boxgrove, Boxmoor and others.

Medicinally the box tree was at one time a celebrated cure for intermittent fevers and it has the tonic properties that are common to herbs with febrifuge properties.

It has narcotic and sedative properties in full doses, and can be used as a vermifuge. To dream of box portends long life, prosperity and a happy marriage.

BURR-MARIGOLD

It strengthens the lungs exceedingly.

NICHOLAS CULPEPER

Botanical name: Bidens tripartita (Linn.). *Natural order:* Compositae. *Country names:* Water agrimony, hepatorium, Spanish needles, nodding marigold, double tooth. *French names:* Chanvre aquatique, Cornuet. *German names:* Sumpfzweizahn, Wasser hanf. *Italian names:* Canapa acquatica, Eupatoria acquatica. *Turkish name:* Su keneviri. *Under the dominion of:* Jupiter in the sign Cancer. *Symbolical meaning:* Prediction. *Part used:* Herb. *Natural habitat:* Damp places in England and Europe, Siberia and the Caucasus. *Constituents:* Iron, sodium, phosphorus and tannic acid. *Action:* Antiseptic, aperient, astringent, diaphoretic, diuretic, febrifuge, narcotic, sedative, styptic.

Burr-Marigold is largely used by herbalists for its mild narcotic and sedative properties. It is a useful remedy in fevers, ruptured blood vessels, and in haemorrhages of all kinds, internal and external. As a styptic it can hardly be equalled.

The plant is found in damp places in England—in ditches, ponds and beside rivers and occasionally on dry land. It has brown drooping flowers and each flower has an extension of prickly bracts which stick to anything they come in contact with. It blooms in July, August and September. The plant is an annual. The root is spotted rather in the same way as spotted hemlock. Its old name is water agrimony.

CELERY

Culture corrects the strong, grateful, small and warm bitterish taste, and renders the plant mild and esculent.

Botanical name: Apium graveolens (Linn.). *Natural order:* Umbelliferae. *Country names:* Ach, ache, apyum, smallage, marsh parsley, salary, small ache. *French names:* Céleri, Achte, Achte des marias. *German names:* Sellerie, Cellerie. *Italian names:* Sedano, Seleno, Appio, Accio. *Turkish name:* Kereviz. *Parts used:* Herb, root, seeds. *Natural habitat:* Levant, Southern Europe, cultivated in Great Britain. *Constituents:* The seeds contain apiin and glucoside, a jelly-like substance which when boiled with dilute sulphuric acid splits up into apigenin and glucose. Apiin is slightly soluble in cold water, easily soluble in hot water, more easily in hot alcohol and insoluble in ether. Also volatile oil, apiol or apiolum. *Action:* The fruit is aromatic, carminative, stimulant, tonic, deobstruent, and resolvent.

Wild celery is prescribed in rheumatism, bronchitis, and intermittent fevers; and is used as a poultice to swollen glands, combined with lin- seed. The roots and seeds were at one time given for diseases of the liver and spleen. The cultivated celery which is derived from the wild plant is stimulating and diuretic and its active properties reside in the blanched stems which are the part eaten. A very attractive form of celery can now be grown, which blanches itself and has a more solid heart.

In England wild celery is found chiefly in marshland, particularly near the sea. The stem grows about two feet high and the clusters of white flowers are seen from June to September.

BURR MARIGOLD—BIDENS TRIPARTITA

Tonic Herbs

CHERRY

Pris'ner of war from Cerasus he came;
(From native Cerasus he took his name)
From thence transplanted to th' Italian soil
Lucullus triumph brought no richer spoil;
Loud paens to your noble gen'ral sing,
Italian plants, that such a prize did bring
The conqu'rous laurels, as in triumph wear
The blushing fruit, and captive cherries bear
Yet grieve thou not to leave thy native home,
E're long thou shalt a denizen become,
Amongst the plants of world-commanding Rome.

ABRAHAM COWLEY

Botanical names: Prunus cerasus, Prunus serotina (Ehrl.). *Natural order:* Rosaceae. *Country names:* Black cherry, Virginian prune. *French names:* Cerisier, Griottier. *German names:* Kirsche. *Italian names:* Ciliegio agerotto, Ciriegio. *Turkish name:* Kiraz ağ. *Under the dominion of:* Venus. *Symbolical meaning:* (tree) Good education, (blossom) Insincerity. *Parts used:* The bark, fresh leaves, stalks. *Natural habitat:* North America and Canada but cultivated in Europe. *Constituents:* The bark contains amygdalin, emulsin, a bitter principle, a volatile oil, hydrocyanic acid, tannin, gallic acid, resin, starch—in the presence of water it yields hydrocyanic acid. The root bark contains a glucoside phloridzin which is also found in the root bark of the apple, pear and plum tree. *Action:* Astringent, pectoral, sedative, tonic.

The cherry tree is a useful remedy in fevers, bronchial coughs, and asthma. It increases the appetite and promotes metabolism. William Cole says of the fruit: 'They strengthen and stir up appetite to meat. A tisane of the stalks has astringent and pectoral properties and makes a pleasant beverage.'

Culpeper says: 'The gum of the cherry tree dissolved in wine is good for colds, coughs and hoarseness of the throat; mends the colour of the face, sharpens the eye sight and provokes appetite, and dissolved, the water thereof is of much use to break the stone and to expel gravel and wind.'

On the authority of Pliny the cherry tree was introduced into Italy from Pontus and was brought to Britain by the Romans. 'Cherries on the ryse' was a London street cry as early as the fifteenth century.

The wild cherry grows in England about the height of an apple tree. Its pure white flowers, either single or double, are a familiar sight in the English countryside. In the country of its origin it grows to about sixty feet in height.

At Hamburg they commemorate the relief of their town from the Hussites in 1432, by a Feast of Cherries, because they sent their children dressed in black to plead with the enemy who promised to spare the city and sent the children back with their arms full of cherries.

TO MAKE BLACK CHERRY WATER

Take six pounds of black cherries, and bruise them well; then put to them the tops of rosemary, sweet marjoram, spearmint, angelica, baum, marygold flowers, of each a handful, dried violets one ounce, anise seeds and sweet fennel seeds, of each half an ounce bruised; cut the herbs small, mix all together and distil them off in a cold still.

Tonic Herbs

CLERODENDRON

After leaving the wooded Terai at Siligoree, trees became scarce, and clumps of bamboos were the prevalent features. . . . A powerfully scented Clerodendron and an Osbeckia gay with blossoms like dog roses, were abundant; the former especially under trees, where the seeds are dropped by birds.

Hooker's Himalayan Journal

Botanical names: Clerodendron phlomoides, Clerodendron inerme, Clerodendron serratum, Valkameria inermis. *Natural order:* Verbenaceae. *English name:* Garden quinine. *French name:* Clérodendron fortuné. *German name:* Losbaum. *Italian name:* Clerodendron. *Arabian name:* Kahwa. *Turkish name:* Kismet ağ. *Indian names:* Coffi, Kapi, Banjuen, Dariai jai, Vanjai. *Sanskrit names:* Bhàndira, Kundali, Aquimantha. *Malayan names:* Nirnotajil, Jarutika, Peragu. *Persian name:* Cahwa. *Part used:* Juice, leaves. *Natural habitat:* Ceylon, Indian near the sea coast. *Constituents:* A bitter principle like that found in Chiretta, a fragrant stearopten to which its apple-like odour is due, resin, gum, a brown colouring matter and ash containing a large amount of sodium chloride. *Action:* Alterative, febrifuge, tonic.

The leaves of the clerodendrons are prescribed in fevers, and scrofulous skin diseases. They are pounded with coarse lime and applied to discoloured skin. The natives make fomentations, embrocations and liniments of the plant for rheumatism. The leaves are used as a tonic in Malaya, and are made into a lotion in which to bathe sufferers from fevers.

The *Clerodendron infortunatum* is a common shrub throughout India and Ceylon, where its pink flowers are to be seen on waste land. The juice which is extracted from the leaves is a well-proved remedy for periodic malaria, and a decoction of the leaves is used as a vermifuge.

The *Clerodendron inerme* has fragrant white flowers with long purple stamens and grows well near the sea.

Most of the clerodendrons are sweet scented and those that grow in South Africa have pale blue, deep violet, white and sometimes light green flowers. The flowers often look like butterflies. Those that are most noticeable are the *Clerodendron triphyllum*, which has very deep blue flowers, and the *Clerodendron myricoides*, and *Clerodendron glabrum*.

Tonic Herbs

COMBRETUM

Or plant in jewelled swagger, twin with use,
Myrobolans, prolific cherry-plum,
Topaz and ruby, where the bees may hum
In early blossom, and, with summer come,
Children and wasps dispute the wealth of juice.

V. SACKVILLE-WEST

Botanical name: Combretum sundaicum. Myrobalans. *Natural order:* Combretaceae. *English name:* Jungle weed. *Indian names:* Bhoree loth, Thoonia loth. *Parts used:* Roasted leaves, stalks. *Natural habitat:* China.

Combretum is used medicinally in China in the form of a decoction to cure those addicted to morphia. A fluid ounce is taken every four hours. It is a powerful tonic.

In India *Combretum pilosum* is prescribed in the same way as an anthelmintic.

The plants of the Myrobalan family are noticeable for their astringent properties. The crane tree, the gum of which is used as a substitute for gum arabic, belongs to the same family, so does the Chinese honeysuckle, and the *Terminalia chebula* which yields the fruit known as Myrobalans. These gall-like excrescences are produced by the puncture of an insect. They are sold in India at various stages of maturity, and very large fruits are sold at fancy prices. It is said to have an aperient effect if merely held in the hands. Great medicinal properties are attributed to it, and it bears such names as Life Giver, Physician's Favourite, Nectar.

The flowers of the Myrobolan family are unisexual, red, white, or green in colour and very decorative.

Lady Rockley says, 'On the African veld as also through the tropics there are various species of combretum with appropriate local names; some are quite small bushes, others grow into fair-sized trees; they all have characteristic fruit with wings. In some they are very bright red or rich brown, with four wings over an inch long and half an inch wide, standing out from the four sides of the one seed at even distances. The most common on the veld north of the Orange River and in Natal are known as bush willows, *Combretum kansii*—and *salicifolium*. The hiccup nut of Natal and Rhodesia, *C. braceatum*, has no wings to the fruit. This is considered edible, but eating it has the unfortunate result of causing violent hiccough.'

Tonic Herbs

DODDER

The liver and the spleen most faithfully
Of all oppressions she does ease and free.
Where has so small a plant such strength and store
Of virtues . . . ?

ABRAHAM COWLEY

Botanical name: Cuscuta europaea. *Natural order:* Convolvulaceae.
Country names: Beggarweed, devil's guts, hellweed, scaldweed, strangle
tare, bind, hailweed, hairweed, hale, hell, hairy-bind, scaldweed, scald.
French name: Cuscute. *German name:* Seide. *Italian names:* Cuscuta,
Barba di Monaco. *Turkish names:* Kusuta, Aftimon. *Under the do-
minion of:* Saturn. *Symbolical meaning:* Dodder (of thyme), baseness.
Part used: Herb. *Natural habitat:* Europe including Britain.

Both the parasitical dodders, the greater and lesser, are useful in
medicine. The lesser dodder, *Cuscuta epithymum*, prefers to grow on
thyme which gives it, as Culpeper says, 'a hotter nature than the other
though all of them come under the cold planet Saturn'. They have
creeping stems like threads and flowers with globular wax-like heads
but no leaves. Their special value in medicine is as a tonic for the spleen.
They are the remedy for the spleen when affected by grief.

Helvetius in his collected knowledge of the Doctrine of Signatures
places the dodders under the intestines, but most of the herbs that
influence the spleen also act on the intestines.

Tonic Herbs

EVERLASTING FLOWER

Trim Montmartre! the faint
Murmur of Paris outside;
Crisp everlasting flowers
Yellow and black on the graves.

MATTHEW ARNOLD

Botanical names: Gnaphalium arenarium, Gnaphalium dioicum, Gnaphalium uliginosum, Gnaphalium stoeches, Antennaria dioica, Helichrysum ˈstoeches. *Natural order:* Compositae. *Country names:* Catsfoot, eternal flowers, chaffweed, life everlasting, mountain everlasting, cotton weed, cud weed, dwarf cotton, petty cotton. *French names:* Gnaphale, Pied de chat, Hispidule antennaire, Fleur immortelle. *German names:* Ruhrpflanze, Katzenpfötchen. *Italian names:* Gnafolio, Piede di gatto, Occhio di cane. *Dutch name:* Droogbloeme. *Turkish name:* Kedia ayaǧi. *Under the dominion of:* Venus. *Symbolical meaning:* Never ceasing remembrance. *Part used:* Whole herb. *Natural habitat:* Europe, America. *Action:* Astringent, discutient, pectoral

---

The everlasting plants are of great use in medicine. The homeopaths prescribe gnaphalium with success in sciatica, when there is a condition of pain alternating with numbness.

Culpeper recommended the juice of everlasting flower to be taken in wine or milk, or a decoction of the root or the powdered root in haemorrhages of all kinds, for bruises and wounds inwards or outwards, and for quinsies. The cudweeds were known to Pliny, who says they were called chamaezelon, and were prescribed for quinsies and mumps.

The Indians are said to use one of the cudweeds to cure themselves in public, of rattlesnake poisoning, and in India two species, *G. multiceps* and *G. polycephalum*, are regarded as anti-malarial and anti-febrile.

The Chinese prescribe G. multiceps for malaria; and G. polycephalum to drive away moths and insects of all kinds.

HEATHER

*"Beyond the moorland has its wealth
Of pink and purple, blue and gold;
Heather and gorse, whose breath gives health,
And ling, a hive of bees that hold."*

Botanical names: Erica vulgaris, Calluna vulgaris. *Natural order:* Ericaceae. *Country name:* Ling. *French names:* Bruyère, brande. *German names:* Heidekraut, Heide. *Italian names:* Brendolo, Scopa carnicina, scopiccio, sorcelli, Erica. *Turkish names:* Supurge otu, Funda. *Swedish name:* Liung. *Spanish name:* Breyo. *Russian name:* Weresk. *Symbolical meaning:* Solitude. *Part used:* Herb. *Natural habitat:* Europe including England, temperate parts of Russia.

The seeds of the heather provide food for the famous red grouse; the stem is used for thatch and for fuel, the flowers give us some of the best honey produced in the world, and flavour the mutton that comes from the Welsh hills. The shoots are used for tanning leather and the flowers yield several brilliant orange and yellow dyes, which in the Hebrides have been in use for centuries. In these islands they also make a beer from heather, using two parts of the young tops to one part of malt. The ancient Picts were said by Boethius to have made a similar beer from the flowers of the heather.

*Though unobtrusive all thy beauties shine,
Yet boast thou rival of the purple vine
For once thy mantling juice was seen to laugh
In pearly cups, which Monarchs loved to quaff:
And frequent wake'd the wild inspired lay,
On Teviot's hills beneath the Pictish sway.*

LEYDEN

The secret of heather beer is said to have died with the Picts. There is a tradition that two survivors, father and son, preferred to die than to yield the secret to a victorious enemy.

Formerly the young flowering tops were made into ale, a liquor much esteemed by the Picts.

A water distilled from the flowers cures inflamed eyes and an oil made from the flowers has the reputation of curing shingles and other cutaneous eruptions.

Tonic Herbs

HERB-PATIENCE

Herb Patience does not grow in every man's garden.
                                               An old proverb.

Botanical names: Rumex alpinus (Linn.), Rumex patienta. *Natural order:* Polygonaceae. *Country names:* Spinach dock, monk's rhubarb, passions, patience. *French names:* Patience, Parelle, Oseille épinard. *German name:* Winterspinat. *Italian names:* Lapazio, Pazienza, Romices. *Turkish name:* Yabani ashun otu. *Under the dominion of:* Mars. *Symbolical meaning:* Patience. *Part used:* Herb. *Natural habitat:* Alps of Europe. *Virtues:* Antiseptic, carminative, laxative.

Herb-patience has the reputation of making meat tender if it is cooked with it. In this respect it is the English equivalent of the Papaw melon tree of India. It was cultivated in the old physic gardens as a liver medicine and was used in the same way as Turkey rhubarb.

It has the tonic properties of the docks to which family it belongs. They all contain rumicin or chrysophanic acid, which is valuable in the treatment of the skin. It purifies the blood, is mildly laxative, and well adapted to those who suffer from dysentery. It is a very wholesome and safe herb.

It is not indigenous to Great Britain, but is found in various parts of the country in the vicinity of ancient monasteries, where it is an escape from the herb gardens. Monk's Rhubarb is one of its old names.

Tonic Herbs

HOLLYHOCK

The Holihock disdains the common size
Of Herbs, and like a tree do's proudly rise;
Proud she appears, but try her, and you'll find
No plant more mild, or friendly to mankind.
She gently all obstructions do's unbind.

ABRAHAM COWLEY

Botanical name: Althaea rosea (Linn.). *Natural order:* Malvaceae. *Country names:* Bysmalow, hock, hock-holler, hollek, hollinhocke, holy hoke. *French names:* Passe-rose, Rose trémière. *German name:* Stockrosen. *Italian names:* Alcea vossa, Malva rosa, Rosa di mare. *Turkish name:* Gülhatem çiç. *Symbolical meaning:* Ambition, fecundity. *Part used:* Flowers. *Natural habitat:* China. *Action:* Demulcent, diuretic, emollient.

The hollyhock was introduced into England as a pot-herb, but it soon became a garden favourite because of its decorative beauty and the variety of its colour. Gardeners through all the ages have claimed it as an indespensable ornament of the walled garden. John Lawrence says:

'Proper places against walls or the corners of gardens should be assigned to Hollyhocks where they can explain their beauty to the distant views.'

Medicinally the plant has a most soothing effect on all parts of the body and is so safe that it can be used without fear for an indefinite period.

In China, which is its natural home, it is called K'ui and used as a pot-herb for its mucilage. It is cooked in the seventh month.

The flowers of the Hollyhock are useful medicinally in chest complaints, and combine well with marshmallow.

Tonic Herbs

HORNBEAM

*'Here hornbeam hedges regularly grow
Here hawthorn whitens and wild roses blow.'*

Botanical name: Carpinus betulus (Linn.). *Natural order:* Betulaceae.
Country names: Horse beech, horn elm, harber, hard beam, yoke elm,
husbeech. *French names:* Charme, Charmille. *German names:* Hain-
buche, Weissbuche, Hornbaum. *Italian names:* Carpino bianco,
Carpine, Carpano. *Turkish name:* Gürgen ağ. *Symbolical meaning:*
Ornament. *Part used:* Leaves. *Natural habitat:* Europe.

The hornbeam is very like the elm, but the leaves are smoother and
are folded into plaits before they open. Its chief distinguishing feature
is its catkins which are lax and scaly, pale yellow green in colour and two
or three inches long. These are succeeded by nuts which form inside a
cup. The French make a feature of Charmilles hedges because they do
not lose their leaves in the winter and will grow in poor soil.

Hornbeam makes excellent charcoal and is burnt because of the length
of time that it gives a bright flame.

The wood which is very hard is suitable for agricultural implements
and was at one time sought after for beams and yokes for horned oxen,
hence its name. The Romans made the same use of it. The leaves make
good fodder for cattle and the bark yields a yellow dye, used in Sweden.

In parts of France, near Valenciennes, branches of hornbeam are
hung outside the doors of men's sweethearts as a symbol of their de-
votion.

Medicinally, the leaves can be made into an infusion and drunk as a
tonic and blood purifier.

They have much the same effect as birch leaves.

Tonic Herbs

HORSETAIL

It cures ruptures in children.

NICHOLAS CULPEPER

Botanical names: Equisetum arvense, Equisetum sylvaticum, Equisetum maximum, Equisetum hyemale. *Natural order:* Equisetaceae. *Country names:* Joint weed, bull pipes, snake pipes, tad broom, tidy pipe, toad pipe, frog pipes, dishwashings, shaveweed. *French names:* Equisette, Queue de cheval. *German name:* Ackerschachtelhalm. *Italian names:* Rasperella, Equiseto dei boschi. *Turkish name:* At Ruyrǔgi. *Under the dominion of:* Saturn. *Part used:* Herb. *Natural habitat:* Temperate Northern regions. *Constituents:* Silica, resin, wax, sugar, starch, salts, fixed oil. Solvents—alcohol and water.

The horsetails are unrelated to other plants and are a relic of the carboniferous age. They are more closely allied to ferns than to other plants and seven of them are indigenous to England.

They contain so much silica that they are often used by country people to clean their saucepans.

In medicine horsetail is of great value as a strengthening medicine for the lungs, the heart and the kidneys. It is a good wound herb, and it gives strength to the weak in the same way that silica does in a flower border when plants become limp and unable to hold up their heads.

HYDRANGEA

The name is derived from a Greek compound signifying water-vessel.

Botanical name: Hydrangea arborescens (Linn.). *Natural order:* Saxifragaceae. *Country name:* Seven barks. *Symbolical meaning:* A boaster. *Parts used:* Dried rhizome, root. *Natural habitat:* U.S.A. *Constituents:* Gum, albumen, starch, resin, ferrous salts, sulphuric and phosphoric acids. *Action:* Alterative, diuretic, sialagogue, stomachic, tonic.

The name hydrangea is derived from a Greek word for water vessel because it is a marsh plant. This is why it needs so much water and begins to wilt without it, but it wants sun as well.

The plant is a valuable tonic for the bladder and kidneys. It has a mild but permanent tonic effect on the mucous structures of these organs, dissolves calculus, removes pain, and subdues inflammation. It can be safely be used in all complaints connected with these organs. The garden hydrangea, *H. hortensis*, and the oak-leaved hydrangea, *H. quercifolia*, are cultivated for their beauty.

Two other varieties, *Hydrangea vetchii* with flat turquoise-coloured heads surrounded by white, and *H. riverain* with brick-red flowers, are of striking beauty.

JACOB'S LADDER

'The plant not strange to Scottish skies,
Whose leaflets, ladder-like arise,
Pointing to azure vaults above—
The Patriarch's Dream—in southern grove
Infrequent.'

Botanical name: Polemonium caeruleum (Linn.). *Natural order:* Polemoniaceae. *Country names:* Charity, Greek valerian, blue jacket, Joseph's walking-stick, ladder to Heaven, poverty. *French names:* Valériane greque, Polémonie bleue. *German names:* Sperrkraut, Himmelsleiter. *Italian names:* Polemonio, Scala di Giacobbe, Valeriana azzurra, Valeriana greca. *Dutch name:* Spierkruid. *Turkish name:* Yunan kedi otu. *Under the dominion of:* Mercury. *Symbolical meaning:* Come down. *Part used:* Herb. *Natural habitat:* Britain from Stafford and Derby to the Cheviots. *Action:* Astringent, diaphoretic, expectorant, nervine.

Jacob's ladder has delicate white or blue flowers which grow in bunches very close to each other. The leaves are pinnacled as the botanical name denotes. It was named Chilodynamia by the Greeks because of its valuable astringent properties. It is an old cure for the vapours and was given as a tonic in hysterical complaints. It had a reputation for curing epilepsy and can be used in the same way as valerian.

JACOB'S LADDER—POLEMONIUM CÆRULEUM

Tonic Herbs

JASMINE

'The night has made a nosegay of the stars
Bound with a straying fragrance from the south
Of wax white jasmine, and of that dark rose
That sombre rose—to whom the fountains sung.'

Botanical names: Jasminum officinale (Linn.), Jasminum grandiflora. *Natural order:* Oleaceae, Jasminaceae. *Country names:* Jeshamy, Jesse. *French names:* Jasmin cummun, Jasmin blanc. *German names:* Echter jasmin, Weisser Jasmin. *Italian name:* Gelsomino bianco. *Turkish name:* Yasemin çiç. *Chinese names:* So-hsing, Yeh-hsi-ming. *Indian names:* Chambeli, Jati. *Malayan names:* Mĕlor, Pĕkan. *Natural habitat:* Northern India, Persia. *Constituents:* Resin, salicylic acid, an alkaloid named jasminine, and an astringent principle. *Action:* Astringent, bitter, tonic, pectoral, sedative, anaesthetic, vulnerary.

The flowers of the jasmine abound in a volatile oil. The Spanish jasmine, *J. grandiflora*, is very similar to the *J. officinalis*. Medicinally the leaves and flowers are used as a nerve sedative, and the fresh juice of the leaves applied to corns removes them. The Malays prescribe seven jasmine flowers as a remedy for puerperal septicaemia and they give a decoction of the leaves and root in fevers.

In India twelve species of jasmine are used medicinally, the *J. arborescens* is regarded as a useful bitter tonic, the *J. auriculatum* is given in the treatment of consumption and the *J. officinale* as a nerve sedative.

In China the root of the *Jasmine sambac*, though used medicinally as a powerful sedative, is said to be poisonous. 'One inch of the root extracted with wine will provide unconsciousness for one day, two inches for two days, three inches for three days and so on.' The bruised flowers are prescribed in the treatment of abscesses. One of the most popular Chinese songs is in praise of jasmine flowers which are cultivated in China for scenting tea. Their fragrance and beauty make a great appeal to the Chinese.

A syrup made from the ordinary white jasmine cures hoarseness and coughs. The syrup is made by placing in a jar alternate layers of sugar and jasmine flowers. It is well covered with wet cloths and left in a cool place for 24 hours when the sugar will have absorbed the essence of the flowers and can then be eaten.

Tonic Herbs

Steep a quarter of a pound of white jessamine flowers in two quarts of spirit for two days and two nights. Then strain off the spirit and mix it with one and a half pints of cold clarified syrup. Filter till clear and bottle carefully.

JULES GOUFFÉ, 1871

Jessamine flowers were made into unguents by the Greeks and Romans, who perfumed their bodies with them after bathing. Cowley's words refer, of course, to the Presbyterians who disapproved of such self-indulgence.

> *Thy ointment Jessamine without abuse*
> *Is gain'd, yet grave old Scots condemn the use*
> *Tho' Jove himself, when he is most enrag'd*
> *With thy ambrosial odours is assuag'd.*

LABRADOR TEA

Affects especially the rheumatic diathesis, going through all the changes from functional pain to altered secretions and deposits of solid, earthy matter in the tissues.

BOERICKE

Botanical names: Ledum latifolium (Jacp.), Ledum greenlandicum. *Natural order:* Ericaceae. *Country names:* St. James's tea, marsh rosemary, crystal tea. *French names:* Lédon palustre, Romarin sauvage. *German names:* Sumpfporst, Wilder rosmarin. *Italian names:* Ledone, Ledo a foglie strette, Ramerino di padule. *Turkish name:* Laden ağ. *Part used:* Leaves and young tops. *Natural habitat:* Labrador, Greenland, Nova Scotia, Hudson Bay.

The Ledum plant is found in woods and bogs. It has large decorative cream flowers which grow in flat terminal clusters. The leaves have a spicy aromatic taste and smell, and are used as a substitute for tea. They have tonic and pectoral properties and are a useful medicine in rheumatism especially when the pains start in the feet and travel upwards. They also cure some forms of eruptions. The tisane can be drunk in the same way as maté tea.

LADY'S TRESSES

The flower of sweetest smell is shy and lowly.
WORDSWORTH

Botanical names: Neottia spiralis, Spiranthes autumnalis. *Natural order:* Orchidaceae—Spiranthedeae. *Country names:* Autumnal lady's tresses, sweet ballocks, lady's traces. *French name:* Spiranthe. *German name:* Herbstdrehling. *Italian name:* Spiranthes. *Turkish name:* Tere. *Part used:* Herb. *Natural habitat:* Europe including Britain.

This sweet-scented orchid grows wild on the Sussex Downs where, as a child, I have often picked it. It somewhat resembles the lily-of-the-valley in scent and appearance, except that the leaves are greyish-green in colour and hairy, and the flowers are not so white.

The plant has aphrodisiac properties and is a good eye tonic.

There are three varieties of this plant, the other two being, N. aestivatis, and N. cernua, the summer's lady's tresses and the drooping lady's tresses, the latter is the rarest of all European orchids. Anne Pratt says, 'it was not known to be a British plant until the year 1810 when it was discovered by Mr. Drummond at Castletown, Berehaven, County Cork, in Ireland. This is the only European locality for the plant, though it is also found in Kamtschatka.'

Tonic Herbs

LOVE-IN-A-MIST

Their names were nymphs, and they were nymphs indeed
A whole mythology from pinch of seed,
Nemesia and Viscaria, and that
Blue as the butterfly, Phacelia;
Love in mist Nigella whose shining brat
Appears unwanted like a very weed.

V. SACKVILLE-WEST

Botanical names: Nigella damascena (Linn.), Nigella sativa. *Natural order:* Ranunculaceae. *Country names:* Bishopswort, chase the devil, devil-in-a-bush, Jack in prison, Katherine's flower, Kiss-me-twice-before-I-rise, love entangle, love-in-a-puzzle, old man's beard, blackcumin. *French names:* Faux cumin, Quatre épices, Nigelle, Toute épice. *German name:* Schwarzkummel. *Italian names:* Nigella, Gittaione, Cuminella, Melanzio domestico. *Turkish names:* Coreg otu, Karamuk. *Indian names:* Kal-Zira, Kelanji, Kalajira. *Persian name:* Siyah-berang. *Malayan name:* Karum-Chirakum. *Egyptian name:* Habes-souda. *Arabian names:* Kamune-asvad, Hubba tussouda. *Sanskrit names:* Krishna-jeralka, Karavi. *Symbolical meaning:* Perplexity. *Parts used:* Seeds, herb. *Natural habitat:* Syria, cultivated in Southern Europe. *Constituents:* The seeds contain a fixed oil 3·75 and volatile oil 1·5, albumen 8·25, mucilage 2, albumen 1·8, organic acids 0·9, metarabin 1·4, melanthin resembling helleborin 1·4, ash 4·5, moisture 7·4, sugar glucose 2·5 and arabic acid 3·2. *Action:* Anthelmintic, carminative, diaphoretic, emmenagogue, stimulant, tonic.

Love-in-a-mist has finely divided leaves like fennel and is sometimes called fennel flower. It is used in the East to flavour curries and bread, and to scent drawers to keep away insects.

Medicinally it is combined with plumbago root for digestive complaints and intermittent fevers. It is a favourite medicine in India to give after childbirth, and is probably the black cumin seeds of the Bible.

The species of love-in-a-mist that we grow in our gardens is the *Nigella damascena.* The fennel flower, *N. sativa,* which is a closely allied species, is used in medicine for dropsy and kidney complaints, and its properties were well known to Abraham Cowley:

Tonic Herbs

The fennel flower dost next our song invite,
Dreadful at once, and lovely to the sight;
His beard all bristly, all unkemb'd his hair,
Ev'n his wreathed horns the same rough aspect bear;
His visage too a watrish blue adorns,
Like Achelous, o'er his head wore horns,
Nor without reason (prudent nature's care
Gives plants a form that might their use declare).
Dropsies it cures, and makes moist bodies dry,
It bids the waters pass, the frightened waters fly
Do's through the bodies secret channels run;
A water goddess in the little world of man.

The fennel flower is a native of Syria. The Romans used it as a flavouring herb and the French use the seeds as a substitute for pepper and call them quatre épices or toute épice. They have a spicy, pungent taste and an agreeable odour of nutmeg. In the East they are used to flavour curries and are sprinkled over bread and cakes before they are baked.

In India they are put among linen to keep away insects.

Tonic Herbs

LUPINS

Lupine unsteep'd, to harshness doth incline,
And like old Cato, is of temper rough
But drench the pulse in water, Him in wine,
They'll lose their sourness and grow mild enough.

ABRAHAM COWLEY

Botanical names: Lupinus albus, Lupin lutens, Lupinus angustifolius (Linn.), Wild lupin. *Natural order:* Leguminosae. *Country names:* White lupin, yellow lupin. *French name:* Lupin. *German name:* Lupinen. *Italian name:* Lupino. *Turkish name:* Yabani turmus. *Indian names:* Turmus, Zurmish. *Persian name:* Tira misha. *Symbolical meaning:* Voraciousness. *Parts used:* Seeds, herb. *Natural habitat:* Egypt, Italy, Sicily and Mediterranean countries. *Constituents:* Malic, oxalic and citric acids; a golden yellow oil 5 p.c. and wax containing a little phosphorus, no starch, no inulin but a peculiar substance related to dextrine (a white hygroscopic powder soluble in water and insoluble in ether), galactane, a hydrocarbon, a principle similar to galactine obtained from lucerne; also a hydrocarbon paragalastina, which is soluble in water; and when boiled with acid is converted into galactose. The albuminous portion of the seeds consists of conglutin, legumin, and vegetable albumen, also three alkaloids—viz., luzinine, luzanine, and lupulidinol. Germinated seeds contain asparagin, phenyl amido-propionic acid, amido-valerianic acid, leucine, tyrosin, xanthine, hypoxanthine, lecithine, peptone, arginine, and chlorin, also vanillin. *Action:* Carminative, nutritious.

Lupin seeds have the nutritive properties that such crops as clover, fenugreek and lucerne provide. They improve appetite, overcome nausea and subdue irritable skin diseases. The plant was grown by the Romans for fodder, and their women made the seeds into cosmetics.

Lupins have an ancient reputation for increasing courage, and sharpening vision. A celebrated painter of Rhodes called Protogenes lived on a diet of lupins for several years, while he was painting the famous hunting piece of Ialysus, the founder of Rhodes.

Pliny believed that a diet of dry lupin seeds made the mind more active, and increased imagination—that they affected personal appearance and gave a cheerful expression, and a fresh complexion. Many of the old secret recipes for increasing beauty include lupins, though they

162

are usually recommended to be made into a paste and used as a face mask for several hours.

The wild lupin flower is usually white, but in Suffolk, where it grows to perfection in the light sandy soil, the flowers are blue. The plant assimilates nitrogen from the air, and is extremely valuable for enriching the soil.

MAGNOLIA

He told of the magnolia spread
High as a cloud, high overhead;
The cypress and her spire:
Of flowers that with one scarlet gleam
Cover a hundred leagues and seem
To set the hills on fire.

WILLIAM WORDSWORTH

Botanical names: Magnolia acuminata, Magnolia glauca, Magnolia virginiana (Linn.). *Natural order:* Magnoliaceae. *Country names:* Cucumber tree, blue magnolia, swamp sassafras. *French names:* Magnolier acuminé, Arbre à concombre. *German name:* Tulpenbaum. *Italian name:* Magnolia acuminata. *Turkish name:* Hiar ag. *Symbolical meaning:* Magnificence. *Parts used:* Bark of stem and root. *Natural habitat:* Carolina. *Constituents:* Volatile oil, resin, tannin, and a crystalline principle magnolin which is insoluble in water, but soluble in ether and alcohol.

Plants belonging to the order of magnolias are remarkable for their bitter, tonic, astringent, and aromatic properties. Magnolias take their name from Pierre Magnol, a famous botanist who lived at Montpellier in the beginning of the eighteenth century.

The magnificent blossoms of the magnolia and their shiny green leaves are too well known to need a description.

The bark is said to cure the tobacco habit if chewed. It is used in medicine for rheumatism with stiffness and soreness, especially when the heart is affected and there is oppression of the lungs.

It is given in fevers, catarrh, malaria, gout and chronic rheumatism. It arrests the paroxysms in fever and has a stimulating and tonic effect.

The tulip tree belongs to the same family and the bark of the tulip tree is also given in intermittent fever and chronic rheumatism.

163

Tonic Herbs

MAIDENHAIR

But I ev'n dead, on Humans operate,
Such force my ashes have beyond my fate.
I through the liver, spleen and veins the foe
Pursue, whilst they with speed before me flow.

ABRAHAM COWLEY

Botanical name: Adiantum capillus-veneris. *Natural order:* Filices. *Country names:* Hair of Venus, black maidenhair, dudder grass, lady's hair. *French names:* Cheveux de Vénus, Capillaire commun, Adianthe, Capillaire de Montpelier. *German names:* Kapillarkraut, Venushaar. *Italian names:* Adianto, Capel-venere, Capovenere. *Turkish name:* Balderikara. *Arabian names:* Kuzburat-el-bir, Shuir-el-jin. *Indian names:* Galmarium, Hansrago, Mubarakha. *Indian bazaar name:* Râjahansa, Hansorga, Mubârkh. *Persian name:* Parosi-ava-shana, Hansa padi. *Part used:* The fern. *Under the dominion of:* Mercury. *Symbolical meaning:* Fascination, magic. *Natural habitat:* Afghanistan, Himalaya, Persia. *Action:* Demulcent, stimulant, tonic.

———————

Maidenhair is given medicinally in asthma and other pulmonary complaints. It is also good for the liver, and made into a lotion strengthens the hair and is said to make it curl. The Latin name is derived from the Greek Adiantos—unmoistened, in reference to its property of repelling water, a fact commented on by Theophrastus and Pliny. This peculiarity was attributed to the hair of Venus when she rose from the sea.

The ashes mixed with olive oil and vinegar are a local application for alopecia.

It grows off the coast of Galway where it is used as a substitute for tea. The plant does not grow in Scotland. The Persian name, Hansa padi, refers to the resemblance between the segment of the leaves of the fern and the foot of a goose.

CAPILLAIRE
(a recipe which comes from Montpellier)

Boil an ounce of Maidenhair in a bottle of water; lower the fire and leave it simmering for two or three hours; strain it into a syrup prepared in the following way: Put a pound of loaf sugar into a preserving pan with a gill of water; skim it as it boils up, throwing in a little water to make it rise, continue boiling to candy height; pour in the decoction; mix it with the syrup, without boiling; pour it into an earthen vessel that can be closely covered; leave it three days in hot ashes. It is ready when it threads between the fingers. Bottle when perfectly cold; cork and cover it with bladders.

MANGO

Boy, cut these mangoes, and prepare them in slices, because in that way they have a better taste, and the chief thing is to soak them in sweet smelling wine, like nectarines.

GARCIA DA ORTA
in The Simples and Drugs of India.

Botanical name: Mangifera indica. *Natural order:* Anacardiaceae.
French names: Manguier, Arbre de mango. *German name:* Mangobaum.
Italian names: Mango, Mangifera commune. *Turkish name:* Mangu aǧ.
Part used: Fruit. *Natural habitat:* India.

Garcia da Orta tells us that mangoes were eaten in India in the fifteenth century either in conserve of sugar, conserve of vinegar, in oil and salt; stuffed inside with green ginger and garlic; salted, or boiled. He says, 'They are at first pricking and styptic, afterwards acid, at last sweet and the nearer to the stem the more acid, whence it appears that they are cold and damp.'

The mango tree is regarded by homeopaths as one of the best remedies for passive haemorrhages. It is a cure for the swelling of the lobes of the ear.

The stones roasted were said to be good for the flux and the stone, and the kernel when green kills worms if taken internally.

Mythologically the mango tree derives its existence from the ashes of the Daughter of the Sun God. For Indian poets the tree has a peculiar significance. Its flowers are of great beauty and the fruit is much esteemed.

MARJORAM

Not all the ointments brought from Delos isle,
Nor that of quinces, nor of Marjoram,
That even from the isle of Coos came.
Nor these, nor any else, though ne'er so rare,
Could with this place for sweetest smells compare.
Britannia's Pastorals.

Botanical name: Origanum marjorana. *Natural order:* Labiatae. *Country name:* Knotted marjoram. *French names:* Marjolaine, Amarcus, Marjolaine à coquille. *German name:* Marjoram. *Italian names:* Maggiorana, Magorana, Amaraco. *Persian name:* Sansuco. *Turkish name:* Mercankosk. *Under the dominion of:* Mercury. *Symbolical meaning:* Blushes. *Part used:* Herb. *Natural habitat:* Europe.

The Greeks and Romans crowned young married couples with wreaths of marjoram because the plant is said to have been raised by the goddess Venus, to which the following quotation is a reference:

And the sweet Marjoram with your garden paint
With no gay colours, yet preserve the plant,
Whose fragrance will invite your kind regard,
When her known virtues have her worth declared!
On Simor's shore fair Venus raised the plant,
Which from the Goddess' touch derived her scent.
RENÉ RAPIN

In Shakespeare's time three varieties of marjoram were grown in England, the common marjoram, *O. vulgare*, which is a British plant, the sweet or knotted marjoram, *O. marjorana*, which abounds in Southern Europe and the winter marjoram, *O. heracleoticum*, which is a native of Greece but hardy enough to thrive in England in a dry soil.

The sweet marjoram is chiefly known as a culinary spice. It gives a good flavour to soups and stews.

In medicine, however, it is a most useful sexual nerve sedative and can be prescribed in soup, milk or chocolate. When effective, it usually produces rapid results.

The discovery of this medicinal virtue in the plant is attributed to a clergyman who had an asylum for orphans.

MARSHWORT

'I love to go forth ere the dawn to inhale
The health breathing freshness that floats in the gale.'

Botanical name: Helossciadium nodiflorum (Linn.). *Natural order:* Umbelliferae. *Country names:* Fool's watercress, bilders, billers, brooklime, cow cress, sion. *French name:* Berle. *German name:* Wassermerk. *Italian name:* Sio. *Dutch name:* Watereppe. *Part used:* Herb. *Natural habitat:* Britain.

Marshwort is a perennial British plant, sometimes mistaken for watercress, which it resembles. It is not nearly so wholesome as watercress, but boiled in milk, it is a good tonic for the blood.

The leaves differ from watercress by being pointed and serrated and the flowers grow in umbels and are altogether different.

MASTERWORT

And Masterwort, whose name Dominion wears,
With her, who angelick Title bears.

ABRAHAM COWLEY

Botanical names: Imperatoria ostruthium (Linn.), Peucedanoum Ostruthium (Koch.). *Natural order:* Umbelliferae. *Country names:* Fellon grass, fellon wood, fellon wort, false pellitory of Spain. *French names:* Impératoire des montagnes. Benzoin Français. *German names:* Meisterwurz, Falsches Spanischer Glaskraut. *Italian names:* Imperatoria, Imperatoria della montagne. *Turkish names:* Imperator otu, Istrican. *Under the dominion of:* Mercury. *Part used:* Root. *Natural habitat:* Central Europe, introduced into Britain. *Action:* Antispasmodic, carminative.

This member of the umbelliferous family which Culpeper describes as 'hotter than pepper' has leaves somewhat like angelica.

The masterwort grows on very long foot stalks which are divided into three, and often subdivided again in the same way. The flowers grow in large umbels and the fruit is broad winged. The garden masterworts have the botanical name of *Astrantia* and are useful because they like lime and will grow in part shade, though they are intolerant of drought. Two attractive alpine varieties are *Astrantia minor* and *Astrantia carniolica*, the latter with pale rose flowers. All masterworts have beautiful foliage.

In medicine *Imperatoria* is used as an antispasmodic and stimulant with carminative properties. It was a popular pot herb at one time, and it was regarded medicinally as a general panacea. It has febrifuge properties and has been recommended for dropsy.

PAPAW

The papaw is abundantly cultivated, and its great gourd-like fruit is eaten called ('Papita' or 'Chinaman'). The flavour is that of a bad melon, and a white juice exudes from the rind.

Hooker's Journal.

Botanical names: Carica papaya, Carica vulgaris. *Natural order:* Papayaceae. *French names:* Papayer, Arbre de melon. *German names:* Papayabaum, Melonenbaum. *Italian names:* Papago, Fico del Isole, Papaia. *Turkish name:* Kavun aǧ. *Arabian name:* Anabahe-hindi. *Indian names:* Popoyiah, Arand-Kharbuza, Papeya. *Chinese name:* Mukua-wan-shou-kuo. *Persian name:* Anobahe-hindi. *Malayan names:* Papâya-papa, Bate, Kĕtela, Bĕtek. *Parts used:* Milky juice, seeds, pulp. *Natural habitat:* Native of America, cultivated throughout India. *Constituents:* The juice contains an albuminoid or milk curdling ferment—papain. The fresh fruit contains a caoutchouc-like substance; a soft yellow resin, fat albuminoids, sugar, pectin, citric, tartaric and malic acids, dextrine. The dried fruit contains a large amount of ash 8·4 p.c., which contains soda, potash and phosphoric acid. The leaves contain an alkaloid called carpaine, the seeds contain an oil. *Action:* Solvent, stomachic, hepatic, emmenagogue, anthelmintic.

The papaw melon tree is a native of tropical America but is cultivated in China and other parts of the Tropics. The fruit before it is ripe secretes

MASTERWORT—IMPERATORIA OSTRUTHIUM

a milky juice which has the singular power of causing muscular fibre and other nitrogenous substances to decay.

It acts in the same way as pepsin and is a solvent in alkaline, acid, or neutral solutions. It is a powerful digestive of meat albumen and forms true peptones.

It removes the false membrane in diphtheria, reduces enlarged glands, corns and hard skin and is used for eczema, ulcers and hepatic and splenic enlargements. The juice is recommended for ringworm and psoriasis, and the milky juice and the seeds mixed with honey, are anthelmintic.

Seven grains of papayotin can digest a pint of milk.

The tree was introduced into Malaya from South America and is used in Ceylon and the West Indies as an anthelmintic for the intestines.

It is not safe to take the juice unless under medical supervision.

One of the Chinese names for it is 'long-lived fruit'.

It renders meat tender if cooked with it.

PEACH

Then came the glory of the Persian field,
And to Armenia's Pride disclaim'd to yield.
The Peach with silken vest and pulpy juice,
Of meat and drink at once supplies the use
But take him when he's ripe, he'll soon decay:
For next day's banquet he disdains to stay.

ABRAHAM COWLEY

Botanical name: Prunus persica (Stokes). *Natural order:* Rosaceae. *Other names:* Amygdalus persica (Linn.), Persica vulgaris (Mill.). *French name:* Pécher. *German name:* Pfirsich. *Italian name:* Pesco, Persico. *Turkish name:* Seftali ağ. *Chinese name:* Too. *Under the dominion of:* Venus. *Symbolical meaning:* (Tree) Your qualities like your charms are unequalled, (blossom) I am your captive. *Parts used:* Bark, leaves, kernels. *Natural habitat:* Persia, China. *Action:* Demulcent, sedative, diuretic, expectorant.

The peach tree was known to Confucius in the fifth century and is indigenous to China as well as to Persia. It was introduced into Egypt by the Persians who, as recorded by Columella, intended to poison the Egyptians with the fruit.

> *'And apples, which most barbarous Persia sent,*
> *With native poison arm'd (as fame relates):*
> *And now they've lost their power to kill and yield*
> *Ambrosian juice, and have forgot to hurt;*
> *And of that Country still retain the name.'*

The peach has never, like the apricot, been considered poisonous and the Chinese attribute to the flowers the power of driving away evil spirits, so it seems more likely that the trees the Persians sent to Egypt were apricots.

The peach was brought to Rome from Persia in the reign of the Emperor Claudius, but was not introduced into England till the sixteenth century. In America it is so largely cultivated that pigs are fed on peaches, to give a special flavour to ham. The fruit improves the complexion and is good for the lungs.

In medicine the leaves, flowers, kernels and bark are used but not the fruit. The kernels of the fruit have the almond flavour that is common to all the *Prunus* family. Eaten moderately Dioscorides recommended them for their stomachic properties, and Galen advised that they should be eaten before meals to provoke an appetite.

The milk of the kernels and also the oil applied to the forehead induces sleep and cures migraine, and the kernels boiled in vinegar till the liquid becomes thick, is a good external application to make the hair grow, and to cure baldness. The flowers or the bark, steeped all night in a little wine and then strained in the morning and drunk fasting, acts as a gentle purgative.

Culpeper says, 'Venus owns the tree and by it opposes the ill effects of Mars. Nothing is better to purge choler and the jaundice in children and young people, than the leaves of this tree made into a syrup or conserve, of which two spoonfuls at a time may safely be taken.'

The demulcent properties of all parts of the tree make it useful in diseases of the mucous membranes. It is excellent for bronchitis, whooping cough and ordinary coughs.

A syrup of peach flowers is made by pouring a pint of boiling water over a pound of the flowers and leaving them for a day and a half. Then they should be strained but not pressed and two pounds of loaf sugar should be dissolved in the liquid over the fire to make the syrup.

The distilled water of peach kernels is prepared as follows:

Take fifty kernels of peach stones and a hundred of the kernels of cherry stones, a handful of elder flowers, fresh or dried, and three pints of muscatel. Set them in a close pot into a bed of horse dung for ten days, after which distil it in a glass with a gentle fire and keep it for use. The dose is 3 to 4 ounces daily.

The nectarine is a variety of the same tree but the fruit has a smooth skin, is generally smaller in size and has, many people think, a more delicious flavour.

PLATYCODON

'The young plant is eaten as a pot herb and is considered to have vermicidal properties.'

DR. G. A. STUART

Botanical name: Platycodon grandiflora. *Natural order:* Campanulaceae. *English name:* Chinese bell flower. *Chinese name:* Chich-Kêng. *Parts used:* Stem, leaves, root. *Action:* Astringent, sedative, stomachic, tonic, vermifuge.

This decorative Chinese campanula is found in most rock gardens to-day. It has very attractive large dark blue flowers which before they actually come into flower look like grey balloons. The leaves are smooth and strong and the stems are red. As it comes into flower about the middle of July it is a great acquisition in an August garden when so many other flowers have disappeared and it grows very compactly to a height of about two feet.

In China it is used medicinally in many different ways, but particularly in mucous complaints.

It is a popular pot herb in China and like other campanulas is very wholesome.

Its roots are used to falsify ginseng.

171

Tonic Herbs

POPLAR

O'er all the giant poplars, which maintain
Equality with clouds halfway up Heaven,
Which whisper with the winds none else can see,
And bow to angels as they wind by them.

BAILEY

Botanical name: (white) Populus alba (Linn.), (black) Populus nigra. *Natural order:* Salicaceae or Amentaceae. *Country names:* Abbey, abbey tree, abel, abele, arbeal, arbell, white asp, great aspen, arobel, Dutch beech, Dutch arbel, white bark. *French names:* Blanc de Hollande, Peuplier blanc, Peuplier grisard, Bouillard. *German names:* Weisse pappel, Silberpappel, Abele. *Italian names:* Popolo bianco, Pioppo bianco, Galtero, Gattice. *Chinese name:* Pai yang. *Turkish name:* Ak kavak. *Under the dominion of:* Saturn. *Symbolical meaning:* Time. *Part used:* Bark. *Natural habitat:* North America. *Action:* Febrifuge, tonic.

The poplar on account of its spreading growth is usually planted in gardens as a screen to neighbouring houses.

Its silver-lined leaves quiver and rustle even when the air is still and in the spring the tree is particularly attractive because the leaf buds give it the appearance of being in blossom.

These buds have a pleasant aromatic scent and when crushed yield a fragrant substance which burns like wax and which was much used at one time in herbal ointments to reduce inflammations. Galen recommended them for this purpose.

The bark of the tree is the part chiefly used to-day in herbal medicine. It has tonic and febrifuge properties which make it a useful substitute for Peruvian bark, because it can be tolerated when the latter cannot.

The black poplar has much the same properties. The bark is a remedy for sciatica, the juice of the leaves eases the pain of earache and cures ulcers in the ear; and the young buds, bruised in fresh butter and put in the sun were used by women to give an added lustre to the hair. The dried bark of both trees is made into bread in Norway.

The white poplar was dedicated to Hercules and the black poplar to Proserpine. In mythology the Seven Sisters of Phaethon, the Heliades, were transformed into black poplars while sleeping after a mournful watch of four days and nights by the River Po where their brother Phaethon was buried.

The Greeks regarded the poplar as a funereal tree and there is a tradition that the Cross of Christ was made of poplar wood and that the shivering and trembling of the tree has a mystical connection with the original tree from which the Cross was taken, and which became accursed.

POTHOS

The beauty of the drapery of the Pothos leaves is pre-eminent, whether for the graceful folds the foliage assumes, or for the liveliness of its colour.
Hooker's Himalayan Journal.

Botanical names: Pothos officinalis, Saindapsus officinalis. *Natural order:* Araceae. *Indian names:* Gaga-Pipal, Kafee-pipali, Kotu-ralli, Shreyasi. *Malayan names:* Juloh-guloh, Sĕ Genting. *Part used:* Fruit. *Natural habitat:* Bengal. *Constituents:* An alkaloid, gum and ash. The pulp of the fruit contains crystals of oxalate of lime. *Action:* Aromatic, carminative, stimulant.

The pothos plant is a parasite on vines and members of that group. It has stimulant and carminative properties and combines with other herbs of an astringent and alterative character, in the treatment of pectoral complaints, asthma and fevers. The Malays prescribe it for smallpox and asthma, and a lotion made by macerating the leaves in cold water, is used to bathe the bodies of epileptics.

The natives cure the bites of snakes with this plant.

The skunk cabbage, *Pothos foetidus*, another variety, is much used in herbal medicine as an antispasmodic in asthma and hysteria.

It grows in moist ground in the northern and middle United States of America. Every part of it has a strong and rather unpleasant scent.

It contains tonic salts such as iron, silica and manganese.

Tonic Herbs

RHUBARB

Docks and white wine, if you should costive prove,
With shell fish cheap, obstructions will remove.

HORACE

Botanical names: Chinese rhubarb : Rheum palmatum, Turkish rhubarb :
Rheum rhaponticum, English rhubarb : Rheum rhaponticum. *Natural
order:* Polygonaceae. *Indian name:* Revan-chini. *Indian bazaar name:*
Rewand-chini, Lakri. *Persian names:* Chukri, Rewash. *Chinese name:*
Huang-hâng. *Burmese name:* Ta-rak-tsha. *Under the dominion of:* Mars.
Symbolical meaning: Advice. *Part used:* Root. *Natural habitat:* South-
Eastern Thibet, Canton China, Turkey, Himalaya. *Constituents:* Resins
as phoeoretin, aporetin and erythoretin; chrysophan 0·14 p.c., chrysophanic acid 5 p.c.; emodin 2 p.c.; rheumic acid; rheotannic acid,
mucilage, malic acid, fat, sugar, starch, albuminoids, calcium oxalate
and ash 12 p.c. *Action:* Aperient, mildly astringent, tonic, stomachic.

Rhubarb is one of the best aperients for those addicted to dysentery
or colitis. It acts on the duodenum, stimulates the muscles of the bowels
and the intestinal glands, and promotes the action of the liver without
any catharsis. It also purifies the blood, and is one of the most wholesome medicines we have. There has been a prejudice against it because
when taken it so often causes rheumatism, but this is because it stirs up
any poison there may be in the system in order to eliminate it and if
persevered with these symptoms soon disappear with the poison.

The Turkish rhubarb is considered the best and supplies of it reach us
from Northern China and Thibet, where it has been known since the
time of the Five Rulers—3000 B.C. In the Péntsao it is classified as a
poison, probably for the same reason that deters Europeans from
taking it.

Rhubarb is one of the most decorative of plants, but it requires room,
and is not often seen in our kitchen gardens. The finest variety of all from
this point of view is *Rheum nobile,* a Himalayan species, but it is difficult
to grow.

Tonic Herbs

ROSE

No mortal ever knows
How to surrender to a rose;
But simply says 'Suppose
This flower should teach me how to die,
Where would I find eternity?'

ELIZABETH BIBESCO

Botanical names: Rosa gallica, Rosa centifolia, Rosa damascena. *Natural order:* Rosaceae. *English names:* French rose, cabbage rose, damask rose. *French names:* Rosier de France, Rose à cent feuilles, Rose de Damals. *German names:* Gallische Rose, Zentifolien Rose, Damaszener Rose. *Italian names:* Rosa Domestico, Rose centofoglie, Rose di Damasco. *Turkish names:* Kirmizi frenk Gutee, Van qu tu, Murr Gutee. *Parts used:* Petals, leaves, hips. *Natural habitat:* Persian Gulf. *Virtues:* Refrigerant, astringent. *Constituents:* A glucoside guercetrine and quercetin, red colouring matter, volatile oil, sugar, gum, fat.

The importance of rose hip syrup as a tonic for children, for the anaemic, and for those threatened with consumption, as revealed by the last war, has altered the orthodox medical attitude towards roses, as it has towards many plants. Rose hip syrup is made from the pulp of the hips beaten up with sugar, and it provides not only an excellent substitute for sugar but a thirst-quenching, digestive, and healing agent.

Persia is probably the home of the rose, but it is found in temperate regions throughout the two hemispheres, and is cultivated in the mountains of Bulgaria round the town of Kozanlik, for its oil, which is unrivalled by that of any other country.

France has made an otto of rose on a small scale for the last hundred and fifty years, and much of the distilled rose water comes from France.

The Bulgarians use only the damask rose and the moss rose, but medicinally the *Rosa gallica* is officially used in the countries of Europe. In China the *Ragusa* rose is regarded as a very important medicine for the liver, the spleen, and the circulation generally. The leaves of the *Rosa laevigata*, which is found all over China, forms one of the ingredients of a famous Chinese vulnerary called Cühn-Chung-i-nien-chin, which translated means 'a pinch of gold in the army'.

The *Rosa indica* has anodyne properties and is also a wound healer

175

among the Chinese; and in India the *Rosa damascena* is recommended, as it is in Europe, as a heart tonic.

The first rose water was made by Avicenna in the tenth century, but the oil of rose as we know it to-day only dates back to the Great Moguls, when in an entirely accidental way the process of separating the water from the essential oil occurred at a midday feast of one of the Emperors. For the occasion a canal had been dug circling the gardens and it was filled with rose water. The heat of the sun brought about a natural distillation, and the oil was skimmed off the surface and found to be a lasting perfume. The Persian oil, which is probably the oldest, is never exported. Otto of rose is an ingredient of nearly all perfumes, for it improves all other oils and blends with everything.

Though there are more varieties of roses in the world to-day than almost any other flower, one can't help regretting that on the whole scent has been sacrificed to form, and that the tea rose, derived from the *Rosa indica*, is on the whole preferred.

As I write I have before me Sweet's *famous Florist's Guide*, of 1827 to 1832, with its coloured plates, of the favourite roses of the early 'nineties.

Brown's superb rose with its great close petalled pink head is derived from the *Rosa centifolia* (the old cabbage rose) and the Bonaparte rose from the *Rosa gallica*, while the Duke of Wellington, with its cluster of smaller heads and deeper colour, is a sport from the damask rose; in every case the parents remain the sweetest roses in the world.

Roses are so wholesome that they have always been used in food and drink. The Romans put roses in their wine and wreathed themselves with roses while they drank it. Cleopatra carpeted her rooms to a depth of several feet with roses, and rose petals were used for strewing generally, because of their exquisite scent and their health-giving properties.

Roses have been made into electuaries and juleps since the time of Arabian pharmacy, and in the days of English country house still rooms, rose water, conserve of roses, and rose butter, were made regularly through the summer months; and rose petals were dried for the yearly pot-pourri and sweet jars, each family priding itself on its own recipe.

ROSE PETAL SANDWICHES

Line a dish with red rose petals, then place in it some butter wrapped in its own paper. Cover the whole with more rose petals, pressing them closely together until the dish is full. Put in a cool larder overnight. Then cut thin slices of bread and spread them with the butter, make into sandwiches, and place fresh rose petals on the top of the butter so that the edges of the petals show outside the sandwich.

ROSE HIP SYRUP

Gather the hips before they grow soft, cut off the heads and stalks. Slit them in halves, take out all the seeds and whites, then put them into an earthen pan and stir them every day to prevent them going mouldy. Let them stand till they are soft enough to put through a hair sieve. It will be difficult to get them pressed through. Then add their weight in sugar, mix well, add enough water to make a syrup and bring slowly to the boil. Then bottle and seal carefully.

Roses are a simple and very safe tonic for the heart.
They increase the retentive faculty and have a soothing effect on the whole body.

ROSE OF JERICHO

It is said to have first blossomed on Christmas Eve to greet our Saviour; to have remained expanded all through Easter because of the Resurrection.

Botanical names: Rosa hieracontea, Anastatica hierochuntia. *Natural order:* Cruciferae. *Country name:* Mary's flower. *Arabian name:* Kaphe-Miryana, Kaphe-Ayesha. *Indian name:* Garbha phula. *Persian name:* Panga-i-mariam. *Malayan name:* Makkah. *Part used:* The dried herb. *Natural habitat:* Coasts of Red Sea and sandy parts of Palestine and Cairo.

The rose of Jericho is brought from Mecca as a flower from Eve's grave.

There are various legends relating to this curious plant which comes to life every time it is placed in water and retains this property for many years. The water in which the flower expands is used as a medicine by the Malays.

The Arabs call it *Garbba phula*, the first word meaning 'a womb' and the second 'a flower' because it is used to help the labour of a confinement.

In confinements the herb is given in the form of a cold infusion in doses varying from two to six drachms.

It has tonic and strengthening properties.

Tonic Herbs

RUE

—and Rue which cures old age.

GERVASE MARKHAM

Botanical name: Ruta graveolens. *Natural order:* Rutaceae. *Country names:* Herb of Grace, Herb of Repentance. *French name:* Rue des Jardins. *German name:* Garten Raute. *Italian name:* Ruta. *Turkish names:* Sedef otu, Sazabotu. *Chinese name:* Yun-hsiang-ts'au. *Parts used:* Herb—tops of shoots. *Natural habitat:* Southern Europe. *Virtues:* Antispasmodic, stimulant.

Rue was introduced into England by the Romans for its medicinal value.

The Greeks venerated the plant and thought it had magical powers because it antidoted the indigestion that they suffered from when they had to eat before strangers.

It is said to bestow second sight, and it certainly preserves ordinary sight, by strengthening the ocular muscles. It acts upon the periosteum and cartilages, and removes deposits that through age are liable to form in the tendons and joints—particularly the joints of the wrist. It cures the lameness due to sprains, aching tendons, particularly flexor tendons, and pain in the bones of the feet and ankles.

The plant will grow very easily in almost any position, but it does best in a partly sheltered dry situation. It is a hardy evergreen with greenish yellow flowers which bloom from June to September. The leaves have a powerful and rather disagreeable scent. Country people in England make the leaves into a conserve with treacle, and give the leaves to cattle to cure croup and other diseases.

The word rue is derived from its earlier English name, Ruth, which meant incant, sorrow and repentance, and the plant, from being called the herb of repentance, became later the herb of grace—the name for it that is used by Shakespeare. There is an old tradition that rue grows best when it has been 'stolen' from another garden.

They sayen the stolen sede is butt the bestte.

Palladins on Husbandry (*c.*1420).

Pliny is the earliest reference to this theory.

Tonic Herbs

SAFF-FLOWER

The leaves have the property to curdle milk.

Botanical name: Carthamus tinctorius (Linn.), Crocus indicus. *Natural order:* Compositae. *English names:* Bastard saffron, saffron thistle, African saffron, parrot seed. *French names:* Carthame, Safran bâtard. *German names:* Färbersafflor, Bastard Safran. *Italian names:* Croco bastardo, Zafferano falso, Cartamo officinale, Zafferano bastardo, Grogo. *Turkish names:* Kartam, Aspur, Yalan safran. *Arabian names:* Zurtum, Usfar, Bazr-el-ahris. *Indian names:* Kagireh, Kasumba. *Persian names:* Khasaka dânâh, Kâzirah. *Sanskrit name:* Kamalottara. *Malayan name:* Kĕsumba. *Parts used:* Herb, flowers, seeds. *Natural habitat:* India, China. *Constituents:* The flowers contain a red colouring principle carthamin, a yellow colouring matter, cellulose, extractive matters, albumen, silica, manganese, iron. The seeds contain a fixed oil. *Action:* Anodyne, diaphoretic, laxative, tonic.

The seeds of the saff-flower are used instead of rennet to make cheese. They are also used to dye tape a red colour. Medicinally the flowers are given in the form of a hot infusion in jaundice and muscular rheumatism, and the oil is applied externally to painful joints.

Herbalists use the herb as a tonic in measles, and give it in the form of a cold infusion.

The Malays prescribe it for demoniacal possession.

Carthamus tinctorius is an annual plant which grows to a height of nearly three feet, 'the flowers grow single at the end of each branch, the large heads are enclosed in a scaly calyx, the lower part of the calyx spreads open, but the scales above closely embrace the florets, which stand out an inch above the calyx and are of a fine saffron colour'. The Spaniards grow the plant to colour their soups and other dishes. Of this herb Thomas Green says large quantities are imported into England from the Levant for dyeing and painting. The seed doesn't often come to perfection in England.

ST. JOHN'S-WORT

Hypericum all bloom, so thick a swarm of flowers, like flies, clothing its slender rods that scarce a leaf appears.

COWPER

Botanical name: Hypericum perforatum (Linn.). *Natural order:* Hypericaceae. *Country names:* Amber, balm of warrior's wounds, cammock, the devil's scourge, herb John, penny John, the Grace of God, the Lord God's wonder plant, rosin rose, touch and heal, perfoliate St. John's-wort, hundred holes, terrestrial sun, witches' herb. *French names:* Mille pertins, chasse-diable, herbe aux piqûres, herbe de Saint Jean. *German names:* Tüpfelharthen, Johanneskraut. *Italian names:* Pilatro, Iperico commune, cacciadiavoli, Erba di San Giovanni, Perforata. *Spanish name:* Corazoncillo. *Turkish names:* Mayasil otu, Yara out. *Under the dominion of:* Sun in the sign Leo. *Symbolical meaning:* Animosity, superstition. *Parts used:* Herb, flowers, oil. *Natural habitat:* Europe including Britain, Asia. *Constituents:* A volatile oil, hypericum red—a blood-red resin, having the odour of camomile. *Action:* Aromatic, astringent, expectorant, nervine, resolvent.

Since the time of Dioscorides, St. John's-wort has had a great reputation as a wound herb. It was referred to by Paul of Aegina and also by Galen. The leaves contain much oil and the plant has been called the arnica of the nervous system. It relieves excessive pain, removes the effects of shock, and has a tonic effect on the mind and the body. It is a valuable remedy to cure pain following an operation. The flowers are made into lotions and gargles.

The herb used to be hung up over the doors of cottages on the Eve of St. John to drive away evil spirits, and there are many legends associated with it. In the Isle of Man there is a saying that whoever treads on it at night will be carried about on a fairy horse and not allowed to rest till sunrise.

The plant is extremely decorative with its large yellow flowers and tassel-like centre, and it is most accommodating because it will grow under trees and in shady positions that the sun never reaches. The flowers when rubbed together give a red juice which was believed to be the blood of St. John the Baptist and the flowers were gathered on the Eve of St. John's Day—the 24th June. The leaves are marked with red spots the colour of dried blood and both flowers and leaves are made by country people in all countries into a salve for healing purposes.

180

Tonic Herbs

SCURVY GRASS

That wild disease which such disturbance gave
Is led before my Chariot like a slave.

ABRAHAM COWLEY

Botanical name: Cochlearia officinalis (Linn.). *Natural order:* Cruciferae.
Country name: Spoonwort. *French names:* Cranson officinal, Herbe
aux Cuillers, Cochléaire. *German name:* Loffelkraut. *Italian names:*
Coclearia, Erbe a cucchiaìno. *Turkish name:* Kasik otu. *Under the do-*
minion of: Jupiter. *Part used:* Herb. *Natural habitat:* Europe including
England, Scotland and Ireland. *Constituents:* The leaves abound in a
pungent oil containing sulphur, of the butylic series. *Action:* Antiscorbutic, aperient, diuretic, stimulating.

Scurvy grass is a common herb which is abundant on the shores of
Scotland, and in Culpeper's time grew all along the Thames side. It is
one of the most effective remedies for scrofulous diseases if taken internally in the form of an infusion made from two ounces of the fresh or
dried herb to a pint of boiling water—a wineglassful is drunk every two
or three hours.

Scurvy grass ale was at one time a popular drink.

The infusions were drunk regularly on sea voyages before lemon juice
became so easily obtainable, and through Captain Cook's voyages it
became known to the public.

The plant has succulent stems and leaves of a very bright green, and
contains an oil obtainable by distillation. The flowers are pure white.
They appear from May to July and are followed by nearly globular seed
vessels, which distinguish the plant from others of the cruciferous order.

In the Doctrine of Signatures it has been pointed out that when a
plant springs up in profusion in any place it is needed for the health of
the people who live there. Referring to scurvy grass John Ray, writing
at the end of the seventeenth century, says, 'In Denmark, Friesland,
and Holland, where the scurvy usually reigns, the proper remedy
thereof, scurvy grass, doth plentifully grow.'

181

SPINDLE

Thus trees of nature, and each common bush,
Uncultivated thrive, and with red berries blush.

DRYDEN

Botanical names: Euonymus atropurpureus, Euonymus europaeus
(Jacq.), Euonymus alatus. *Natural order:* Celastraceae. *Country names:*
Ananbeam, butcher's prick tree, catrash, cat tree, catty tree, catwood,
death alder, dog tooth berry, dog tree, foul rush, gadrise, gaiter tree,
gaten tree, gatheridge, louseberry, pincushion, pincushion shrub, prick-
timber, prickwood, shewer wood, skiver wood, spindle tree, spoke wood,
witch wood, skiver timber, witch wood. *French names:* Fusain, Bois à
Lardoire, Bonnet de prêtre. *German name:* Spindelbaume. *Italian names:*
Fusano, Fusaggino, Berretta da prete, Bonetero. *Turkish name:* Ly ag.
Indian names: Barphali, Kunku Kesari, Chopra. *Chinese names:* Wei-
mao, Knei-chien. *Symbolical meaning:* Your charms are engraven on my
heart. *Part used:* Root, berries. *Natural habitat:* U.S.A. *Constituents*:
The bark contains tannin, sugar, but no alkaloid, an amorphous bitter
principle, enonymin, atropurpurin identical with dulcite, resins, asparagin, euonic acid, fixed oil, albumen, wax, starch and ash 14 p.c. Euony-
min is soluble in water, alcohol and ether. *Action:* Tonic, alterative,
cholagogue, hepatic, stimulant, diuretic, antiperiodic, antiparasitic, and
laxative.

Medicinally the spindle tree is in action rather similar to podophyllin.
It increases the flow of bile and promotes other secretions. It is a useful
remedy for a torpid liver, for dropsy, and for pulmonary complaints.

One species (*Catha edulis*), the Kat of the Arabs, is eaten by them to
obtain watchfulness. Another species, *Euonymus alatus*, grows in the
Peking mountains. The flowers are infused and used as a substitute for
tea which is called in China, Ch'a-yeh-shu-tealeaf tree. Medicinally it is
used to cure pernicious malaria.

The European spindle tree is admired for its three-cornered, rose-
coloured berries which are a great attraction in the garden in the
autumn.

The wood was used to make spindles, hence its name; and from the
young shoots is made a very good charcoal which is popular with artists
because of its smoothness, and the ease with which it can be rubbed out.

Tonic Herbs

SQUAW VINE

The flowers are followed in Mitchella by scarlet berries; but the plant then considers it has done enough for man, and the fruits though possibly dear to the partridge are savourless to human beings.

REGINALD FARRER

Botanical name: Mitchella repens (Linn.). *Natural order:* Rubiaceae. *Country names:* Checkerberry, deerberry, winter clover, one berry, partridge berry. *Part used:* Herb. *Natural habitat:* U.S.A. *Constituents:* Saponin like body, resin, wax, dextrine, mucilage.

———————

Squaw vine is a useful tonic because it influences the whole nervous system and has a most soothing effect on the organs of reproduction, particularly the female. It is used in the same way as raspberry leaves with which it is sometimes combined, to produce easy labour in confinements.

For this purpose it should be administered three times daily in the last month of pregnancy and in larger doses as the confinement approaches, and until it is over.

It keeps up the strength of the patient.

The squaw vine is an American plant with attractive white waxy fragrant flowers.

In that delightful book, *Nature's Garden,* Mrs. Blanchan says, 'A carpet of these dark, shining, little evergreen leaves, spread at the foot of forest trees, whether sprinkled over in June with pairs of waxy, cream white, pink-tipped, velvety, lilac-scented flowers that suggest attenuated arbutus blossoms or with coral red "berries" in autumn and winter is surely one of the loveliest sights in the woods. Transplanted to the home garden in generous clumps, with plenty of leaf mould, they soon spread into thick mats in the rockery.'

SWEET CICELY

Tansy, Thyme, Sweet Cicely,
Saffron, balm, and rosemary,
That since the virgin through her cloak,
Across it—so say cottage folk—
Has changed its flowers from white to blue.

V. SACKVILLE-WEST

Botanical names: Anthriscus cerefolium, Myrrhis odorata. *Natural order:* Umbelliferae. *Country names:* Chervil, sweet bracken, sweet ciss, sweet fern, sweet hemlock, the Roman plant, sweets. *French name:* Cerfeuil musqué. *German name:* Gartenkerbel. *Italian names:* Felce muschiata, Finocchiella, Mirride. *Turkish names:* Kokulu frenk, Magdanosi, Mur ag. *Indian names:* Rigi-el-Ghurab, Riglel-tair. *Indian bazaar name:* Atrilah. *Part used:* Fruit, seeds, herb. *Natural habitat:* Europe. *Action:* Chervil has aromatic, diuretic, stomachic, deobstruent and tonic properties. It yields its properties to water and alcohol.

Sweet Cicely is an invigorating tonic to the body after it is exhausted. In India the seeds are used to cure white leprosy—the seeds are applied externally and given internally with honey and pyrethrum. The patient sits in the sun till the affected skin blisters when the new skin underneath is found to be a natural colour.

Sweet Cicely is better known to cooks as sweet chervil and is used more in France than in England to flavour salads and soups; but it is recommended strongly as a tonic for young girls as well as for old people. It is so safe that it can be used continuously. The root is antiseptic, and an essence of it was said to be aphrodisiac by the ancient herbalists, who recommended it to increase strength.

The American Sweet Cicely, *Oynorrhiza longistylis*, has the same properties.

Sweet Sicely is a perennial herb and the feathery leaves are excellent in salads if their aniseed-like flavour is not objected to.

The French use it in most of their dishes combined with tarragon.

SWEET CICELY—MYRRHIS ODORATA

SWEET SULTAN

*As a kinde of these corn flowers I must needes adjoyne another stranger
of much beautie and but lately obtained from Constantinople when because
(as it is said) the Great Turks (Suliman the magnificent) as we call him,
saw it abroad, liked it and wore it himself, all his vassals have had it in
great regard and hath been obtained from them by some that have sent it
into these parts.*

PARKINSON

Botanical name: Amberboa moschata, Centaurea moschata. *Natural
order:* Compositae. *French name:* Ambrette jaune. *Italian names:*
Ambretta gialla, Amberboa. *Turkish name:* Amberbuz. *Symbolical
meaning:* Felicity. *Natural habitat:* Constantinople. *Action:* Tonic,
stomachic, diuretic.

The sweet sultan plant is allied to the corn flowers and is in action
rather similar to the thistles and the centaurys. It stimulates the circulation of the blood and is a good tonic. There are three varieties of this
annual plant, the purple *C. moschata*, the white *C. alba* and the yellow
C. slava.

There is also a perennial sweet sultan.

William Lewis, in his *Experimental History of the Materia Medica*,
writes soon after the introduction of this variety of the cornflower :
'Another species of oriental origin, commonly called Sultan flower, or
Sweet Sultan, promises by its musky fragrance to have a good claim
to the cordial and antispasmodic virtues, which some have groundlessly
attributed to our indigenous cyanus'.

Parkinson says : 'It surpasses the best civet that ever is.'

Tonic Herbs

TANSY

On Easter Sunday be the pudding seen
To which the Tansy lends her sober green.

The Oxford Sausage

Botanical name: Tanacetum vulgare (Linn.). *Natural order:* Compositae. *Country names:* Bachelor's buttons, bitter buttons, English cost, parsley fern, scented fern, ginger, ginger plant, Joynson's remedy, cheese. *French names:* Tanaisie, Herbe amère, Barbotine. *German names:* Rainfarn, Wurmkraut, Reinfahren. *Italian names:* Tanasia, Tanacato commune, Aniceto, Daneta, Frangia, Tanacetro. *Turkish name:* Soğlucan otu. *Under the dominion of:* Venus. *Symbolical meaning:* I declare war against you. *Part used:* Herb. *Natural habitat:* Europe including Great Britain.

Action: Anthelmintic, diaphoretic, emmenagogue, stimulant, tonic.

The tansy is dedicated to St. Athanasius. It is particularly associated with the Easter festival, and was an ingredient of the Easter pudding and Easter cakes which took their name from the plant. A tansy took many forms, sometimes it was a custard flavoured with tansy. Izaak Walton's minnow tansy was a dish of minnows fried with the yolks of eggs to which were added cowslips, primroses and the juice of the tansy. A tansy cake was given to the winner at stoolball, a game that was played at Easter time.

William Coles says that the origin of eating tansy at Easter was because it was a wholesome antidote to the salt fish that was consumed during Lent.

Tansy has many valuable medicinal properties, and tansy wine is an old country remedy for stomachic troubles. In Scotland the plant is used for gout; and in Sussex it was worn in the shoe to cure and prevent ague.

The herb is valuable in hysteria, in kidney complaints, and in dysentery. It is said to antidote the bad effects of the poison ivy. It is indicated in ear troubles when there is singing and roaring in the ears, and when the hearing seems suddenly to be blocked by air.

The tansy has flat, round yellow heads of flowers and feathery leaves and the cultivated variety is very decorative in gardens because these heads are often very large. It will thrive in almost any soil. The word 'tansy' is said to be derived from the Greek Athanaton, meaning 'immortal' because the plant lasts so long in flower. Its aromatic scent made it one of the strewing herbs.

Tonic Herbs

TEASELS

Then up hung on rugged tenters to the fervid sun,
Its level surface reeking, it expands,
And brightening in each rigid discipline,
And gathering worth, as human life, in pains,
Conflicts and troubles. Soon the clothiers shears
And burler's thistle skims the surface sheen.

DYER

Botanical names: Dipsacus fullonum (Linn.), Dipsacus sylvestris (Mill.).
Natural order: Dipsacaceae. *Country names:* Fuller's teasel: Clothier's
brush, draper's teasel, Venus bath, Venus basin. Wild teasel: Adam's
flannel, barber's brushes, sweeps' brushes, card teasel, card thistle,
church brooms, gipsy's combs, prickly back, tazzel, Venus' bath, Venus'
basin. *French names:* Fuller's teasel: Chardon à Foulon, Chardon à
bonnetier. Wild teasel: Cabaret des oiseaux, Cardère sauvage. *German
names:* Fuller's teasel: Kardendistel, Weberkarde. Wild teasel: Schutt-
karde. *Italian names:* Fuller's teasel: Dissaco, Fontana degli uecelli.
Wild teasel: Erba mesella, Dissaco salvatico, Scardaccione, Cardo di
venere, Verga da pastore. *Spanish name:* Fuller's teasel: Cardencha.
Dutch name: Fuller's teasel: Vollers kaarden. *Turkish names:* Fuller's
teasel: Coban daragi. Wild teasel: Yabani deve dikeni. *Under the dominion of:* Mars. *Symbolical meaning:* Misanthropy. *Part used:* Root.
Natural habitat: Europe.

Teasels are not thistles though some of the old names for them suggest
it. It is generally accepted that the Fuller's teasel is the plant originally
used by the famous Roman fullers. It was probably introduced by the
Romans and was first planted in Gloucestershire. To this day Gloucestershire teasels are considered the best.

The Fuller's teasel is still grown on a large scale in Gloucestershire
and also in Somersetshire, Wiltshire and Essex, and the heads are still
used for carding wool. In Essex they grow caraways with teasels.

The wild teasel, *D. sylvestris*, is indigenous to England, and so is
another variety, *D. pilosus*. The water found in the leaf basins of the
teasels is considered to have valuable cosmetic properties and it is
sometimes used as an eye wash. An infusion of the root is used as a liver
tonic and appetizer, and as a cure for jaundice.

In China teasels are much used as tonics. Both the great and little teasel, Taki and Siao ki, are gathered in the fifth months and both leaves and root are given.

The great ki grows in the mountains and is collected to cure ulcers and abscesses and the little ki is found in marshland and is used to clear the blood. It has the reputation of not accelerating the bursting of abscesses. The young leaves and roots are eaten as food. The greenish purple flower heads which grow from the heart of the plant are called thousand needles by the Northern Chinese. The stems and leaves are gathered in the fourth month and the root in the ninth, and they are dried in the shade.

THISTLES

'Cut your thistles before St. John,
Or you'll have two instead of one.'

Botanical names: Carbenia benedicta (Berul.), Carduus benedictus, Cnicus benedictus. *Natural order:* Compositae. *Country names:* Blessed thistle, Our Lady's thistle. *French name:* Chardon béni. *German name:* Benedikten Distel. *Italian names:* Cardo beneditto, Cardo santo, Erba turca, Scarline. *Turkish names:* Mubarek dikeni, Sevket otu. *Under the dominion of:* Mars and Aries. *Symbolical meaning:* Austerity, independence. *Part used:* Herb. *Natural habitat:* Europe. *Action:* Diaphoretic, emmenagogue, emetic, stimulant, tonic.

Annoying as thistles are to the farmer, they are extremely useful in medicine in purifying the blood and assisting its circulation. They are good for jaundice and all liver complaints, they strengthen the brain, the heart, and the stomach.

The holy thistle is the species generally used by herbalists, but the milk thistle, *Silybum Marianum*, often called the marian thistle, the Scotch thistle, *Onopordon Acanthiam*, the dwarf thistle, *Carduus acaulis* and the common star thistle, *Centaurea calcitrapa*, are all used for the same purposes, so is the common carline thistle, *Carlina vulgaris*. The carline thistle is distinguished from other thistles by its yellow flower head—actually the florets are purple as in other thistles but the sur-rounding rays of yellow give it the appearance of being entirely yellow. This thistle was called after Charles II because it was taken by him as

Tonic Herbs

an antidote to the plague. It has been used both as medicine and as food; and at one time a popular sweetmeat was made from it with sugar. It is an excellent weather barometer because it always closes before rain. The French, Italian and Spanish name for it is Carlina; but the Germans call it Eberwurz and the Russians Kolintschka.

The leaves of the marian thistle are good in salads, and the young peeled stalks can be baked in pies.

Thistles were said to be sacred to Thor and to be a protection against lightning and thunder. They have a very ancient reputation in medicine. Dioscorides recommended the seeds of the milk thistle to draw babies' sinews together, and the root to expel melancholy.

Culpeper advised it for vertigo on the grounds that it was ruled by Mars in the house of Aries and, for the same reason, suggested it as a herb with which to treat the gall bladder. It strengthens the memory because of its effect on the circulation.

Matthiolus was a great believer in the efficacy of the holy thistle. He recommended it as a blood cleanser, to be used internally and externally. It is also useful in the treatment of wounds. It has a beneficial action on the heart and it has been questioned whether the effect of the herb in improving appetite may not be due to the increased cardiac activity that it gives, which brings about an increased circulation of blood in the abdominal region.

The Devonshire name for thistle is dazzel or dashel flower.

Tonic Herbs

WAFER ASH

It has a soothing influence upon the mucous membranes and promotes appetite, being tolerated when other tonics cannot be retained.

Botanical name: Ptelea trifoliata. *Natural order:* Rutaceae. *Country names:* Hop tree, swamp dogwood, shrubby trefoil, wingseed. *French names:* Ptélée, Orme à trois feuilles. *German names:* Amerikanischer Hopfenstranch, Lederblume. *Italian names:* Ptelea, Olmo a trefoglie. *Turkish names:* Amerika kara ag, Odi Samaria. *Parts used:* Root, bark. *Natural habitat:* U.S.A. *Constituents:* Oleoresin, starch, albumen, yellow colouring matter, berberin, volatile oil, salt of lime, potash and iron. *Action:* Astringent, antiperiodic, febrifuge, tonic.

———————

Wafer ash is a useful remedy in prolapsed organs, and exercises a direct tonic influence upon the digestive organs, soothing the mucous membranes. It can be used in fevers.

The tree was introduced into England in the reign of George I.

It is a shrub, growing in the United States of America, on the edges of woods and in shady places, generally among rocks. It seldom attains more than eight feet in height. The flowers are greenish white and grow in terminal spreading panicles. The fruit is aromatic and bitter and is considered a good substitute for hops in the making of beer. The young green shoots are anthelmintic.

WALLFLOWER

Yon gilly flowers who sit among the ruined walls
And cover with light the grieving stones.

MAETERLINCK

Botanical names: Cheiranthus cheiri (Linn.), Helianthus annuus (Linn.).
Natural order: Cruciferae. *Country names:* Beeflower, bleeding heart,
blood wall, bloody wallier, bloody warrior, chare, cherisaunce, gera-
flour, gilliflower, Jacks, jerroffleris, jilliver, keyry. *French names:* Giro-
flée, giroflier, bâton d'or, mûrailler, ravenelle, ramoneur, carafée.
German names: Goldlack, Levkoje. *Italian names:* Violacciocco giallo,
bastone d'oro, Fiore del muro. *Indian names:* Tedrisurkh, Lahore subu.
Turkish names: Sari, Sebboy. *Under the dominion of:* Moon. *Symbolical
meaning:* Fidelity in adversity. *Part used:* Flowers, stem, seeds. *Natural
habitat:* Northern India. *Constituents:* The seeds contain myrosine and
an oil similar to that found in Raphanus sativus. *Action:* Deobstruent,
emmenagogue, tonic.

The wallflower has a specific action on sinews and muscles. It is used
to purify the blood, for enlarged glands, for uterine and liver disorders
and by homeopaths, for the deafness caused by the cutting of wisdom
teeth.

Nicholas Culpeper says the yellow wallflower work more powerfully
than any of the other kinds and are therefore of more used in physic.

The legend of the wallflower is that it first appeared on the wall of a
tower from which a Scottish maiden who was eloping with her lover,
fell and was killed.

In the Middle Ages this flower was carried in the hand at festivals for
its scent and its cordial properties and it obtained the name of cherisaunce.

Tonic Herbs

WILD CINCHONA

The flowers are night-scented.

Botanical names: Anthocephalus cademba, Anthocephalus indicus. *Natural order:* Rubiaceae. *Indian name:* Kadamb. *Sanskrit names:* Kadamba, Haliprya, Sisupâla. *Malayan name:* Kĕlampi. *Parts used:* Fruit, bark. *Natural habitat:* Himalaya, Ceylon, Darjeeling. *Action:* Febrifuge, refrigerant and cooling, tonic.

The wild cinchona plant has flowers of a pale lemon which grow in large globular heads and only give out their scent at night. The fruit which is the size of an orange is given to children in the form of the juice, to which is added cumin and sugar. It acts as a tonic and allays gastric irritability. One of the Indian names for the plant sisupâla means 'protecting children'. The fruit is very useful in fevers because it cools and quenches thirst.

The leaves are given in the form of an infusion in intermittent fevers and the Malayans heat the leaves in coco-nut oil and apply them hot as an abdominal poultice in malaria.

They also use them for purposes of prognosis. If the leaves are intact in the morning the patient will die, but if they are broken or cracked he will recover.

The Indians antidote snake bites with the bark, which contains a principle similar to cinchotannic acid.

The Indian name for this plant is Kadamb, and it belongs to the same family as the Gardenia.

Tonic Herbs

WILLOWS

Stoop to the stream
That you may share the wisdom of my peace—
For talking water travels undismayed
The luminous willows lean to it with tales
Of the young earth; and swallows dip their wings
When showering hawthorn strews the lanes of light.

SIEGFRIED SASSOON

Botanical names: Black: Salix nigra (March), *White:* Salix alba (Linn.). *Natural order:* Salicaceae. *French names: White:* Saule blanc, Osier blanc. *German name: White:* Silberweide. *Italian names: White:* Salcio bianco, Salicastro. *Turkish name: White:* Ak Soynd ag. *Chinese name:* Liu. *Under the dominion of:* The Moon. *Symbolical meaning:* Freedom, bravery. *Parts used:* Bark, berries. *Natural habitat: Black:* Southern States of America. *White:* Europe. *Constituents:* Salicin, a glucoside, tannin, wax, gum.

The black willow is used in herbal medicine as a nerve sedative in the same way that potassium bromide is used, but it does not act as a depressant. It relieves ovarian congestion and irritation, and overcomes nervous excitement. It produces quiet sleep and combines with other nerve tonics, increasing their good effect.

It is an excellent remedy for all forms of eroticism, especially if the cause is due to local irritation.

The white willow has tonic and astringent properties and is used in debility of the digestive organs. It also has antiperiodic properties and can be used in fevers.

The Chinese willow, the *Salyx babylonica* of the classics, is common all over China and the leaves, root, bark and gum which exudes from the tree are all used in medicine. The Chinese name for willow, Liu, refers particularly to this species.

193

YELLOW PARILLA

Called Moonseed because of the lunate shape of its seeds.

Botanical name: Menispermum canadense (Linn.). *Natural order:* Menispermaceae. *Country names:* Canadian moonseed, vine maple. *Part used:* Root. *Natural habitat:* Canada and United States, cultivated in England as an ornamental shrub. *Constituents:* Berberine, menispine, starch, resin and tannin. Menispine is a white powder, soluble in alcohol and ether. *Action:* Alterative, bitter tonic, diuretic, stomachic.

———————

The yellow parilla is, in common with other plants in the moonseed family, a woody, climbing plant. It is used in the same way as calumba, as a bitter tonic. It stimulates the intestinal glands, but not the liver, and is a good substitute for sarsaparilla in scrofulous conditions. It is one of the few bitter tonics that does not contain tannic or gallic acid.

It is often added to beer in this country.

Cocculus indicus, Pareira brava, and calumba, are closely related, also *Cocculus cordifolius* from which the Indians make a jaundice wreath to hang round the neck of any patient suffering from jaundice. *Cocculus indicus* contains far more narcotic principle in its seeds than any other species of the family.

This plant will grow in English gardens if not placed in too exposed a position. It is easily propagated.

Indexes

GENERAL INDEX

BOTANICAL INDEX

Indexes

COUNTRY NAMES

202

FRENCH INDEX

Indexes

GERMAN INDEX

Indexes

Indexes

ITALIAN INDEX

211

Indexes

Indexes

SPANISH INDEX

MALAYAN INDEX

INDIAN INDEX

Indexes

Indexes

TURKISH INDEX

218

ARABIAN INDEX

CHINESE INDEX

Indexes

SANSCRIT INDEX